"I have to hire a bodyguard,"

Griff said. "I have a daughter who's coming to live with me. If anything happened to her..."

Kelley felt herself softening toward him, though all her internal alarms were screeching. "You want to be sure she's protected, too?"

"If the gunman's out to get me, threatening my daughter would be the best way to do it."

"What does all this have to do with me?" Kelley asked.

"I need to hire a *female* bodyguard, someone I can pass off as my constant companion. I want you."

Dear Reader,

The holiday season is in full swing, and most of us are busy running around buying, wrapping—and hiding—gifts for our families and friends. But it's important not to forget ourselves during this hectic time, and Silhouette Intimate Moments is here with four terrific romances for you to enjoy when you steal a few moments on your own.

First up is Emilie Richards with *Twilight Shadows,* a tie-in to her last book for the line, *Desert Shadows.* Things are never what they seem in the movies anyway, but in this case we're talking about some *real* desperate characters and bad actors. Pick up the book and you'll see what I mean!

After a long—too long!—absence, favorite author Kathleen Eagle returns to Intimate Moments with *Bad Moon Rising.* Kathleen is deservedly celebrated for her portrayals of Native American characters, and this book once again demonstrates why. And for those of you who remember her long-ago Silhouette Christmas story, ''The Twelfth Moon,'' there's an extra treat in store. I guess this book is in the way of being a Christmas present, too!

Mary Anne Wilson's *Nowhere To Run* and Marilyn Cunningham's *Long White Cloud* round out the month. And next year (!) look for more of your favorite authors—Heather Graham Pozzessere, Kathleen Korbel, Dallas Schulze and Kathleen Creighton, to name only a few—coming to you in Silhouette Intimate Moments.

Happy Holiday Reading!

Leslie Wainger
Senior Editor and Editorial Coordinator

EMILIE RICHARDS

Twilight Shadows

SILHOUETTE·INTIMATE·MOMENTS®

Published by Silhouette Books New York

America's Publisher of Contemporary Romance

SILHOUETTE BOOKS
300 East 42nd St., New York, N.Y. 10017

TWILIGHT SHADOWS

ISBN: 0-373-07409-3

First Silhouette Books printing December 1991

EMILIE RICHARDS

believes that opposites attract, and her marriage is vivid proof. "When we met," the author says, "the only thing my husband and I could agree on was that we were very much in love. Fortunately, we haven't changed our minds about that in all the years we've been together."

The couple live in Ohio with their four children, who span from toddler to teenager. Emilie has put her master's degree in family development to good use—raising her own brood, working for Head Start, counseling in a mental-health clinic and serving in VISTA.

Though her first book was written in snatches with an infant on her lap, Emilie now writes five hours a day and "rejoices in the opportunity to create, to grow and to have such a good time."

Chapter 1

"**Y**ou could have eloped." Kelley Samuels jabbed another hairpin into the dark red clump of curls perched demurely—for the moment—on top of her head. "Really, Felice. If you loved Gallagher, you would have climbed out your window some cloudy midnight and driven to Vegas."

"I would have if I'd had any idea what this...this..." Felice flung her arms dramatically, as if she was at a loss for words to describe the event unfolding around her.

"Circus? Fiasco? Spectacle?" Kelley supplied.

"Not *nearly* expressive enough." Felice squinted in the mirror. "I look pale."

"Anyone wearing as much white as you are would look pale."

"I *feel* pale."

"Everyone who's a part of this wedding feels pale."

"Maybe I can cancel."

"The priest is already in his robes. There are guests sitting in the pews."

"Maybe I could tell them...maybe *you* could tell them that I've been struck down with some fatal...temporarily fatal disease."

"Twenty-four-hour bubonic plague?"

"That's the spirit." Felice dropped to a chair, a cloud of white Spanish lace settling around her.

"You're not supposed to sit. It'll ruin the back of the dress."

"You've been listening to my mother. We've *all* been listening to my mother."

Kelley jabbed another pin in her hair, then reached for the floral wreath of white and yellow roses and baby's breath that was supposed to slip over it. "Was this thing—" she held out the wreath with distaste "—this concoction, your mother's idea?"

"No. It's *exactly* what I would have chosen, if I'd been given a choice," Felice said sarcastically. "You know I want you to look like a vestal virgin." She shut her eyes. "Kell, why did I let this go so far?"

"Because you're in love and feeling sentimental." Kelley plopped the wreath on her head and adjusted it. "All I need now is a Maypole."

Felice opened her eyes. "Your hair's coming down."

"I told you it wouldn't stay up."

"It's just a few curls. You look like Shirley Temple."

"I feel like a half-peeled tangerine in this dress."

"You have nice shoulders. And the color's good for you."

Kelley's dress was a deep coral silk that bared her shoulders and had a fitted skirt with an overskirt that draped over one hip and tied in the back. The dress had been a compromise in taste between Felice and her mother, and like most compromises, it left something to be desired. The best thing Kelley could say about the dress was that she could take it off forever in just a few hours.

She finished fastening the wreath and stepped back for one final look. The woman staring back at her was a stranger. Kelley hoped she would continue to stay that way.

She turned to Felice. "Okay, partner. Stand up and let's get your mantilla in place."

"It's not time yet, is it?"

"Sure is."

"I wonder if Josiah's going to be waiting when I get to the altar."

"If he still wants to marry you after he's seen your mother in action, then it's true love."

Felice stood. "Mother's been at her worst since the day we told her we were going to get married." Her voice softened a little. "But the wedding's meant so much to her. That's why I've let things get so out of hand. I was never exactly the kind of daughter she'd had in mind. This seemed like the least I could do...."

Kelley wrapped her arms around her friend for a quick hug. "She's crazy about you. And you've been a brave, brave soldier to go through with this for her."

Felice laughed. "All I ever wanted was a little wedding. You, a few other friends, a case of Dom Pérignon, a little beluga."

The door to the dressing room whipped open. "You're not ready, and it's quarter to five!"

Felice rolled her eyes before she faced her mother. "But I will be, and in plenty of time. Don't you look fabulous?"

Nita Cristy calmed visibly, like a prize hen preening her feathers. She was a shorter, curvier version of her beautiful dark-haired daughter, a woman who had the money to take exquisite care of herself. *Her* dress hadn't been a compromise. Of royal blue silk in a flattering princess style, the dress was one of the few signs Kelley had seen of Nita's famed good taste.

The woman who had entered the room with her looked like a chorus girl in comparison. A bleached blonde with the olive coloring of a brunette, she was dressed in a bubble-gum pink miniskirt that revealed every dimple in her chubby knees. "Felice, dear." The woman held out her hand. "I'm Susan Sanders. I write for the—"

Felice took her hand. "I've read your column. Hello, Miss Sanders. This is my maid of honor, Kelley Samuels."

Susan held out her hand to Kelley. "Call me Suzy."

Kelley restrained her response to a polite murmur, but Suzy was already speaking to Felice again.

"Thank you for inviting me. This is exactly the kind of event I like to cover. Heiress marries top government official. Society guests. Movie star guests. What more could anybody ask for?"

Felice's gaze flicked to her mother's. Nita had the grace to examine her shoes. "I'm glad to have you," Felice said politely, returning her gaze to Suzy's. "And I hope you'll come to the reception?"

"I wouldn't miss it, dear. Will Griff Bryant be there, too?"

Kelley listened to the polite exchange. Griff Bryant was the icing on this, Palm Springs's most elaborate wedding cake. He was a friend of Felice and Gallagher's, and Kelley had not had the opportunity to meet him yet. But, along with a million other moviegoers, she had seen him in living color more than once. He was Hollywood's man of the moment, and had been for several years.

As a breed, Kelley disliked actors with an intensity born of experience. But as fantasy material, she, like almost every woman who had ever seen one of his films, didn't think Griff Bryant could be topped. Apparently Suzy didn't, either.

The conversation ended and the door closed behind Suzy's jiggling tush.

Felice held her mother back when she tried to follow. "Mother! Suzy Slander, for God's sake. Tell me you didn't really invite her."

"I sent the wedding announcement to all the Los Angeles newspapers, and Suzy called and asked me if she could attend. What could I say?" Nita gave a helpless shrug.

"I think I'm going to check on the flower girl . . . or somebody," Kelley said. She ignored Felice's emerald-eyed plea. "Mrs. Cristy, you'll help Felice with the mantilla?"

"I'd like that."

Kelley nodded. "I'll be back in a few minutes."

In the hallway she had to restrain herself from disappearing into the parking lot. She was here because she was Felice's best friend, but where she wanted to be was at home in jeans and a sweatshirt watching the Dodgers play the Giants and screaming her heart out. She wanted a beer and popcorn and the company of her almost-purebred Newfoundland monster, Neuf.

Instead she was going to get French champagne and pâté de foie gras and the company of the who's who of Southern California. And if she was truly unlucky, by the end of the night somebody was bound to tell her who had won the game so that she couldn't even enjoy her videotape.

"You don't look like you're having fun."

Kelley looked up and saw Gallagher coming toward her. He was a big man, and his shoulders seemed to strain his black tux. Kelley had never seen him this dressed up, although his style was always a bit more formal than hers. Almost anybody's was.

"What are you doing here?" she asked, barring the door to Felice's dressing room. "You're not supposed to see Felice before she comes down the aisle."

"I'll bet her mother told you that."

"Good sense tells me that. I mean, she hasn't spent the last two hours getting ready so that you can give her a quick once-over before you ask if she remembered to invite old Uncle Fred to the reception."

Gallagher grinned, and one very masculine dimple signaled relaxed good humor. He, at least, seemed to be enjoying himself. "How's she doing?"

"She keeps threatening to call the whole thing off. You should have eloped."

"She's heard that suggestion from me, too." He touched Kelley's wreath. "Not exactly a Dodger's cap."

"Now, that would have been a unique touch." Kelley propelled Gallagher back the way he had come. "Go away. We'll see you in a little while."

"Then tell Felice that Simon and Tate finally got here. Simon's dressed and ready to go."

Kelley had never met Simon, but she knew he was Gallagher's best man. Before moving to Southern California to head the FBI offices here, Gallagher had worked in Washington in a high-level Justice Department position. Simon Vandergriff had often worked for him, although what he had done was top secret.

Kelley was familiar with top secret. She was familiar with law enforcement all the way from high-tech computer crime down to parking tickets. She had once been a cop. So had Felice. Now she was a private investigator, and so was Felice—when she wasn't too busy getting married.

"You know, a good third of the people sitting in that church right now routinely carry guns," Kelley said.

"Nobody's carrying a gun today."

"You, me, Felice, Simon. All our friends from the LAPD. All your FBI buddies." She smiled. "Even Griff Bryant. He's a regular walking arsenal in his movies."

"Have you met Griff yet?"

"Nope."

"He's nothing like the guy he plays on-screen."

"He's an actor. That's worse."

"Hollywood brat."

"Arrogant Fed," she said cheerfully.

He shot her another grin. "Tell Felice I'm going home for a shot of Scotch."

"I'll do no such thing." She stood on tiptoe and kissed his cheek. Then she shooed him down the hall. She wondered, as she watched him walk away—all supreme male confidence and stalking-lion grace—if somewhere in the world there was a Josiah Gallagher for her.

She hoped so. But if she ever found him, *her* mother wasn't going to run the wedding.

She was whistling "The Chapel of Love" when she went back into the dressing room to rescue Felice.

"You're late."

"The traffic on the freeway wasn't to be believed."

"I asked Cam for one cameraman. I get an entire production company?" Griff Bryant pulled his starched white collar away from his throat. It might be officially fall, but no leaves were turning in Palm Springs. The sun was on its way down, but the temperature was still above eighty. Even the tall palms lining the churchyard looked wilted.

"You said you wanted the best. We're the best. You said you wanted discreet. We're so discreet Superman couldn't find us in the shadows. You know Cam, she overcompensates." The spokesman of the three men hurriedly unloading equipment from the van marked Zephyr Productions shrugged. "You want us or not?"

"I suppose you come as a team."

"You got it."

"I'm not kidding about discreet. I told the bride I'd get somebody to film this so that her mother wouldn't hire one of those guys who parades backward up the aisle two steps in front of her. This is my wedding gift, but Felice won't even want to know you're there."

"As far as she's concerned, we're not."

"Go on in, then, and set up." Griff watched the men finish unloading. Two carried in the equipment while the spokesman got back in the van and moved it to the parking lot.

Though the afternoon was uncomfortably warm, Griff liked the atmosphere here in the shadows by the side door of the church better than that inside. At least here no one was pointing at him, or worse, trying not to show that they'd ever seen his movies. He was used to having a face so familiar that even the sea lions at Knott's Berry Farm seemed to recognize him. He *wasn't* used to the feeling of alienation that went with it. He never would be.

He rarely went to weddings. Marriage in his part of the world often seemed nothing more than the first step toward divorce. True, he knew a few Hollywood marriages that had held together through the ups and downs of screen careers, but he knew many more that hadn't.

His own hadn't, and now he had a hostile ex-wife and an unhappy daughter to show for it. It was no wonder that he didn't usually want to celebrate what had turned out so sadly for him.

He reminded himself that he had come tonight because Felice and Gallagher's relationship seemed to have all the earmarks of success. He was not so jaded that he couldn't see love when confronted by it. He was nothing if not a disciple of possibilities.

Inside the church the wedding prelude began. Griff had been unable to attend the rehearsal, but Felice's mother had made certain he received a schedule of events. He knew that the carefully timed pipe organ prelude would last exactly twelve minutes. Then Felice's attendants would process. That would take four and a half minutes, five if the flower girl forgot to drop her rose petals and went back and started over again. Then

Felice would process on her father's arm. Two minutes flat, and Lord help her if she tripped.

He had been on movie sets that weren't as well structured as this, and he'd worked with directors who couldn't summon half the fear in hearts that Felice's mother did. Nothing was going to go wrong with this wedding, because nobody would have the courage to face Nita Cristy and tell her.

The desert sky was turning a darker blue as the sun edged toward the horizon. Stars would be out for the wedding supper. For the moment Griff was diverted by the music, the prelude to a glorious sunset, the thought of the vows that were about to be exchanged. Life seemed a kinder thing than it had in the recent months. Love seemed real, something to strive for, something that might even be attained.

He laughed a little, embarrassed at his own sentimentality, and he wondered if maybe he should attend weddings more often.

"You look perfect. Exquisite. Dazzling." Kelley redraped one side of Felice's mantilla over her shoulder. It had belonged to Felice's grandmother and perfectly complemented her dress.

"I should have a rose in my teeth."

"You can have one of the ones from my bouquet."

"Not unless you have castanets to go with it."

"Fresh out of them. But I could stand behind you and pop gum in rhythm."

Felice whirled. "I'm leaving."

Kelley held her by the shoulders. "No, you're not, not unless it's to go out there and get married." She glanced at her watch. "Which you're supposed to do in one minute."

"I just have a bad feeling about all this."

"Every bride gets the jitters."

"How would you know?"

"I read. I'm planning to get them myself someday, just as soon as somebody cranks out another Josiah Gallagher."

"The world wouldn't survive it."

"The world would be a better place. Now, come on. Gallagher's having fun. He looks relaxed and confident. You do the same."

There was a knock at the door, and Felice's father poked his head inside. "Prelude just started. Your mother's being seated."

Felice slapped her hand over her heart. "You mean she won't be back in here to tell me what to do?"

"Things are looking up." John Cristy, tall and distinguished, beamed at his daughter. "You're gorgeous."

Kelley started toward the door. "I'd better get in position. Mr. Cristy, don't let her go anywhere except down that aisle."

"You look gorgeous, too, Kelley," he said gallantly.

"Yeah, yeah." Kelley kissed his cheek as she passed. "I'll warm up the crowd for our glamour girl." She turned and threw Felice a kiss, too. Then, without a backward glance she abandoned her.

There were three bridesmaids, distant relatives of Felice's, and Gallagher's fidgety four-year-old niece, who was shredding rose petals faster than her mother could snatch them away. Kelley took her place behind them, whispering her appreciation of how lovely everybody looked.

She was calculating what inning was being played at Dodger Stadium when the music for the flower girl began. The little girl straightened her petticoat and held out her hand for her basket, as confident in her role as any movie queen. Her mother reminded her that just this once it was all right to litter, and the little girl was off. Her mother disappeared, and Kelley was left alone with the bridesmaids. In another minute and a half they were gone, too.

The church was packed with people. Felice had been firm about wanting the wedding in Palm Springs, where she and Kelley had their office. The church here was smaller than the one her parents attended outside of Santa Barbara. Felice had believed that a smaller church, away from her childhood home, would mean a smaller attendance. She had underestimated her mother's influence.

Kelley's introduction sounded. She had what a Hollywood vocal coach had called a tin ear. But even she could recognize

her introduction now. Mrs. Cristy had taped it and urged her
to play it every night for a week so that she wouldn't fail to enter on time. Kelley knew better than to miss a cue.

She started down the aisle. The church, with its ornate statues, its dark wood and gold leaf trim, seemed strange to her.
She was Kelley O'Flynn Samuels, Irish-American hybrid but
also daughter of Dottie and Fletcher Samuels, who had always
thought that Christmas, Easter and funerals were the only ac-
ceptable excuses for darkening a church door. As a child, when
she might have been disciplined and instructed by nuns, she had
run wild on a Hollywood back lot, learning things about the
world and its inhabitants that the sisters probably didn't know.

She walked slowly and serenely and wondered who was up at
bat.

By the time she took her place at the front and turned to
watch Felice come up the aisle, she had put baseball out of her
mind. The woman walking slowly toward the altar didn't look
like the same rookie police officer who years before had walked
through the door of Kelley's division and announced that they
were going to be friends. She didn't look like the woman who
had held Kelley's hand and let her cry when, despite Kelley's
best efforts, a child she had rescued from an automobile accident had died in her arms. She didn't look like the woman who
had gotten her gold shield the same year as Kelley, or who had
gotten fed up with police bureaucracy and convinced Kelley to
be her private-eye partner in Palm Springs.

She looked like Gallagher's bride.

For the first time Kelley realized how different things would
be now that Felice was getting married. She wanted to stop
time. She understood Felice's last-minute panic; she, too, was
seized with the feeling that everyone in the church should leave.
And though she told herself that she was just experiencing a
natural reluctance to change, she realized she was standing as
erect as a soldier, as tense as a tightrope.

Felice's father presented his daughter to Gallagher. The priest
began the ceremony. The words were solemn, important, and
Kelley could not concentrate on them. She let her gaze drift
over the wedding party, then to the front row where Felice's

parents sat. Mrs. Cristy looked weepy; Mr. Cristy looked as if he wished he were allowed to cry.

Behind them sat a man only familiar to her from movie theater screens. Just as she got her first good glimpse of him, he stood and started toward the altar. She had known Griff Bryant was going to do a reading, but she hadn't realized it was so soon in the ceremony.

Kelley knew a lot about film stars. She knew that some photographed superbly and looked ordinary in real life. She knew that some looked ordinary on the screen and were as handsome as the devil if encountered on the street. Rarely had she known anyone with the same presence, the same larger-than-life persona offscreen and on. Griff Bryant was one of those men.

Felice and Gallagher liked Griff. They had met him while investigating the case that had brought them together. Later they had bought a house not far from his, and he had extended the friendly hand of a neighbor to help them with renovations. Because they liked him, Kelley had been prepared to give him a chance. Now she found that hard to do.

She knew in one glance that he *was* the man he played onscreen, or worse, he believed he was. To her knowledge, Griff had never starred in a film where the equivalent of a small city's population didn't expire somewhere between the credits. He had taken more gunfire, had more grenades and bombs launched in his direction, survived more daggers and bayonets than a regiment of soldiers.

She'd rarely seen him in a role that required anything but fatigues, but the perfectly tailored suit he was wearing tonight did nothing to detract from his masculine swagger. He walked like a pirate, a man comfortable with the rolling swell of waves, a man comfortable anywhere. He was gracefully lean, honed to nothing but muscle, bone and sinew by a life of action and drama. His eyes were a peculiar blue, the color of a bleached winter sky, a blue that could freeze the heart of an enemy. His mouth was locked in a cynical smile, his dark hair cut with military precision.

Undoubtedly he thought the world was a better place because he was in it.

She watched as he settled himself in position not six feet away from her. If he was going to do a reading, he had forgotten to bring it with him. His hands were relaxed, dangling at his hips. He surveyed those gathered before him, like a television evangelist benignly calculating souls by the dollar. Then he began to recite.

The congregation of guests was in his pocket before he had uttered six words. His voice was a rich, mellow baritone, his enunciation perfect. He spoke as if to friends, but Kelley knew how much work, how much training and talent had gone into sounding that warm, that natural. Reluctantly she admired him. He was more than a screen sex symbol, more than an image that other men wished they could live up to. He was an actor, a good one. He was giving the gift of his talent to Felice and Gallagher tonight.

She felt the tension in her spine melt away. Sometime during her childhood she had been told that an actor's greatest talent was transportation. If he—or she—couldn't transport his audience to the fantasy universe he inhabited, then he wasn't an actor at all. Knowing that, knowing that Griff was just manipulating words to take her to some mythical place where love existed and happily-ever-afters happened every day, she still felt herself succumb. Tears welled in her eyes. She looked at Felice and Gallagher and silently wished them a long and happy life together.

At that precise moment the first burst of automatic-weapon fire exploded through the room.

Chapter 2

The burst of gunfire was like the triumphant applause at the conclusion of a Mann's Chinese Theater premiere. For just a fraction of a second, Kelley was disoriented, then she was flat on the ground, crawling toward the first pew to protect herself.

The church began to fill with smoke. Immediately she recognized the source. It spread too quickly and rapidly grew too dense to come from a fire. The smell that reached her was chemical and familiar. She was almost certain that the smoke was coming from smoke grenades, like those used in riot control.

The lights went out, leaving the church bathed in the pastel glow shining through the stained-glass windows. For the next seconds, pandemonium reigned. There were screams and crashing noises as pews were overturned by stampeding guests. Through the thickening smoke she could see Gallagher and Simon sheltering the bridesmaids between them and, crouched low, moving toward the nearest door. Felice, the train of her wedding gown trailing ghostlike behind her, had the flower girl in her arms and was following the two men.

Another fusillade began. She saw the wedding party duck lower still, then, when the shooting had stopped again, continue onward, seemingly uninjured. She saw Felice's mother being pulled from the church by her father. She imagined some of the screams she heard were from Mrs. Cristy's throat. Still buffered from fear by the suddenness of the onslaught, she wondered irreverently how anyone had gathered the courage to ruin this wedding and face Nita Cristy's wrath.

She began to cough, and her eyes streamed protective tears. Hidden behind the solid rail in front of the first pew, she knew she could continue crawling safely until she was close enough to make a dash for the door. She wasn't sure why she felt compelled to look over her shoulder, but instead of crawling, she stopped and turned back toward the altar. Perhaps a sixth sense, the same one that had filled her with dread as Felice came down the aisle, warned her that something was wrong behind her.

Through the smoke, through tears and haze, she saw two figures moving toward the altar. She recognized Felice's priest by his robe. She recognized the man following him by his pirate's swagger.

She could have continued toward the door. The others were making slow, careful progress. She had seen Felice look around for her and seen the look of relief on her face when she realized Kelley was following. She could have gone on; no one would have faulted her.

Instead, crouched low, she started back the way she had come, shouting for Griff and the priest to get on the ground. If they heard her over the other screams and the next hail of bullets, they didn't respond. The smoke grew thicker in the front. Something whizzed by her head, and an explosion of smoke just in front of her almost made her turn back. She dived through it, coughing her plea to the two men to get down.

Finally close enough to launch herself at them, she did exactly that. The smoke was so thick that she didn't know who she had contacted until Griff turned and grabbed her shoulders.

"Get down!" she choked out.

"Tell him!" He let go of Kelley and started for the priest.

She shoved him with every ounce of strength she possessed. She knocked him off balance as he stepped forward, and he stumbled. She shoved again and he went down on one knee. "Father, get down. Right now!" she choked out over Griff's head. "You're risking lives!"

Her words seemed to penetrate. The priest, who had been trying to protect the sacrament, got down on the floor and crawled toward cover.

Kelley collapsed on the floor next to Griff. "Stay low and let's get out of here."

"How?" Another round of fire sounded. Griff drew her closer, as if shielding her with his body. He was large enough, strong enough, to offer protection. But the largest, strongest man was no match for automatic-weapon fire, and Kelley hadn't chosen police work and private investigation as careers because she wanted to be taken care of.

"Look, I can take care of me." A coughing spasm interrupted her next words. "You worry about you," she finally got out. She lifted her head and tried to peer through the blinding smoke. She wished she had paid more attention to the layout of the building. In most churches the sacristy, a room where robes and sacred items were kept, was just off the altar with a connecting door. She wanted to be out of firing range, and she wanted it immediately.

The smoke had thickened until she could hardly breathe. Her head was spinning from too little oxygen, and her range of vision was narrowing. She peered through the smoke to the left, but she couldn't see a thing, not even the priest, who had crawled in that direction. The smoke wasn't as dense to the right. She could see what might be a door leading off the altar.

"Right," she managed to tell Griff. He was coughing, too, and she wasn't sure he had heard her, but she started off, hoping he would follow. The fit of her skirt made it difficult to crawl. The overskirt had torn when she'd hit the floor. Now it hung by threads and flopped under her knees. With one jerk she ripped it off and flung it away.

The smoke made it impossible to see very far, but she had gone only a few feet before she knew she was going the right way. There was a door about fifteen feet from her. She choked out the good news to Griff, hopeful that he had taken her advice and followed close behind.

As she stared at her good fortune, the door swung open, less than a foot but enough to alert her that someone was there. She stopped and peered through the smoke, willing her eyelids apart. The crack widened, and light filtered through. She could just make out the figure of a person standing there. She flattened herself on the floor, and her arm brushed something hot. She jerked her arm away at the same time that an acutely acrid smell warned her what it was.

There was little time to consider what to do next. Through the smoke the figure in the doorway lifted something in her direction. She had been in law enforcement long enough to guess what it was. The whine of a bullet passing over her head confirmed her theory. Two more followed closely.

Her fingers rested on silk. Gathering the abandoned overskirt in her hand as protection, she felt for the smoke grenade she had touched. Lifting herself on her knees, she hurled the grenade toward the doorway. As she did, two more bullets passed only inches from her shoulder.

The man wavered, extending his arms as if to block the attack. Something clattered to the floor, along with the grenade that billowed clouds of evil black smoke at his feet. As Kelley watched, the doorway was enveloped.

The man would be a fool to stand there and let the smoke choke him. *She* would be a fool to go after him, but another round of gunfire behind her reminded her she would be a fool to do otherwise. If she tried to crawl back the way she had come, she could die. If she went after him, she could die.

The second possibility seemed safer. And if not safer, a quicker death.

Holding her breath, she threw herself forward and started for the door. She didn't know if Griff was behind her, and she wasn't sure she wanted him to be. She might be making a terrible mistake, and if she was, she didn't want to be responsible for taking him with her.

Only a good sense of direction carried her to the door, which by now was completely obscured. She pushed it open wider and crawled past the smoke bomb and into the doorway.

Her hand passed over something cool, something metallic. She wanted to weep with relief. Her fingers closed on the butt of a gun, a high-caliber, death-dealing revolver.

She stumbled to her feet. Her legs were rubbery, her eyes streaming, her throat raw from coughing. The room was dimly lit and smoky, but compared to the church the air was crystal clear.

There was no one there but her. It took her a moment to be sure, a moment to trust her blurry, streaming eyes. She scanned the racks of vestments again, but finally she was sure she was alone. Another door, leading from the sacristy into the hallway, was cracked, as if the man who had so thoughtfully dropped his gun had hightailed it out of there at his first good whiff of smoke.

Cautiously she started toward the door. There were no lights and no windows. The gunman and his buddies were evidently good at locating switches. For the first time since the initial blast of gunfire, she had seconds to wonder who had made a travesty of Felice's wedding and tried to kill—or perhaps had succeeded in killing—guests or participants. Whoever they were, the attackers were good with lights but not courageous in the face of a little smoke.

There was no more time to theorize. Kicking off her shoes and thrusting the gun in front of her, she reached the door. She kicked it open with her foot and stood in the doorway, checking the hall in each direction. It was silent, empty and as dark as the inside of a tomb.

Her eyes still streamed, and she had to exert every bit of willpower she possessed not to cough. She knew she was not in condition to creep silently down the hall, to peer deeply into shadows, but no one else was there to do it for her. She had a gun, and a would-be assassin could be nearby to provide answers to questions she hadn't even had time to formulate.

Inside the church, events had unfolded so quickly she hadn't been frightened. Now she realized she had skipped fear and moved beyond it to fury, and it was fury that carried her across the threshold and into the hallway.

The hallway was enclosed, flanked by doors along its length and one door at each end. The end door to her left had a sign, and she guessed, although she couldn't make out words, that it was the door to the priest's study or church office and probably locked. The end door to her right had a small dark window, like that leading into a stairway or another corridor.

She started right, swinging her head from side to side as she moved. The darkness was so thick, her eyes so blurry, that she was afraid that if her opponent was still nearby, she might not see him until she was on top of him. She coughed once, a sudden barking noise that split the stillness and infuriated her. She plastered herself against the wall, watching and waiting to see if the noise brought anyone out, but the silence settled around her once again and nothing seemed to change.

Halfway down the hall she noted that one of the doors was ajar. She approached it cautiously, pushing it open with her foot as she aimed the revolver inside. It seemed to be a classroom or workroom, with tables, chairs and shelves lining the walls. No one was in view, and the light switch beside the door didn't work when she flicked it on. She guessed that circuits had been broken or fuses removed. The attackers had done their work well.

The room was softly illuminated by fading light through one window. Across the room were two doors that she guessed were closets. She debated crossing the room to check them. All possibilities occurred to her. The least likely was that the man whose gun she held would have secreted himself in one of them. But if he had, he was hers. If he hadn't, if he had made an immediate rush for the door leading out the hallway and he had been gone for minutes already, then she had little chance of catching him.

She crossed the room as quietly as she could, breathing through her nose to protect herself from coughing again. She held the revolver with her right hand and used her left to open the first door. Neatly stacked boxes were the closet's only occupant.

She moved along the wall to the second and repeated her maneuver. Coats and sweaters hung from hooks. She peered into the deepest recesses and found no one there to wear them.

She backed out of the room, although she didn't think she had missed anyone hiding in there. At the doorway she turned and peered into the darkness at her left. She was turning right when someone grabbed her arm.

The man appeared so suddenly that even though she had believed herself to be prepared, she wasn't. The gun slipped from her hand and clattered to the floor. It bounced at her feet before she could respond, but the moment it landed, her brain and body began to work together again. She shot her foot out and kicked the gun down the hallway and out of immediate reach.

Countless self-defense classes had honed her reflexes, and as the man snapped her wrist backward she turned, thrust her elbow sharply into his abdomen and bent, using the law of gravity to her advantage. The force of her blow doubled him over, and he collapsed on her. She grabbed his arm with her free hand and flung him over her shoulder. He landed in a heap at her feet.

He wasn't a large man, but she was a small woman. He outweighed her by fifty pounds, and she had made him angry. He grabbed her legs and brought her crashing to the floor beside him. She pushed against his shoulders as he tried to pin her to the ground. When that didn't work, she jabbed at his eyes. He leapt back, covering one with a gloved hand. He made a fist with his other and smashed it toward her, but she ducked and twisted so it only grazed her shoulder. She got to her knees and started to her feet, but he grabbed her again and she fell forward.

She could see the gun three yards away. He was larger than her but sluggish and not particularly brave. No matter how well trained she was in self-defense, however, his greater size guaranteed that they were evenly matched. Getting hold of the gun would tip the scales for one of them.

She kicked out at him, but he threw himself on top of her to keep her on the ground. She used her elbow again, in nearly the same place, and he grunted and rolled sideways. She was able to turn just far enough to give him a good kick. She hoped he'd already had all the children he'd planned.

He doubled over, shrieking in pain, and she was free of his weight. She started toward the gun and had it in her hands before he was on her again. He slammed her arm against the ground, and the gun fell from her grasp. It was only inches away, but she had to concentrate on keeping it from him. She twisted beneath him, but he had learned enough to know what she might do if freed. He settled himself over her, pinning her with his greater weight. His arm, longer than hers, shot out and reached for the gun.

A foot appeared in front of Kelley's streaming eyes and kicked it out of the man's reach.

She was free, so suddenly that all she could do was gasp for air. Then she was sitting up, watching shadows dance and bend. The larger shadow straightened and held the gun in front of him with an ease born of familiarity.

"Move, and you're a dead man."

The voice was one that Kelley, until recently, had only heard in theaters. The line could have been a piece of dialogue from his last film. Griff Bryant held the gun on the man with whom she had fought and motioned him toward the wall.

"It's about time," she muttered, gingerly getting to her feet.

"Are you all right?" Griff asked.

"I thought you'd been shot."

"It took me a while to find the door."

"Glad you managed."

Griff jerked his head toward the man against the wall. "You want to take the gun while I search him?"

"You've watched—*been* in too many movies. If he had another gun, he'd have used it by now." She shrugged when Griff didn't reply. "I guess it won't hurt to check, but I'll do it. Just keep him under cover."

She started forward. "Besides, this little sweetie and I—" she swallowed blood and realized she'd bitten her lip "—got to be on real intimate terms. I know parts of him better than his best girlfriend."

At the exact moment when she crossed between Griff and their unwilling captive, the man leapt forward, thrust her toward Griff and bolted down the hall. Kelley dived for him, but she couldn't reach him in time to stop him.

"Stop! Damn it, I'll shoot!" Griff positioned himself to do exactly that, but no bullet exploded in the man's direction.

Kelley didn't think. She launched herself at Griff and grabbed for the gun. It fell to the floor, and her fingers closed around it. Then she did what Griff had not. She squeezed the trigger.

The man yelped in pain, but he continued his escape, dragging a leg. Kelley lifted the gun to fire again, but Griff knocked her arm so that the bullet went wild. The man went through the door as Griff wrenched the gun from her grasp.

There was no time to protest. Suddenly the hall seemed to fill with people coming through the sacristy.

"Are you two all right?"

Kelley recognized Gallagher's voice. She pointed toward the end of the hallway. "There's a man trying to escape. Tall, skinny, in black. He's been shot."

Gallagher started down the hall. Someone, who she thought might be Simon, followed. The world seemed to spin. The combined effects of smoke and her struggle with the gunman caught up with her, and the only thing she could do was slide down the wall to a sitting position, shut her eyes and take deep breaths.

She felt a woman's arms around her and the scratch of lace against her cheek. "Kell? Are you okay? I thought I'd lost you."

She leaned against her friend. "Your mother plans a damned fine wedding, Felice."

Felice made a noise somewhere between a laugh and a sob. "The church is cleared out now. Whoever it was got away."

"Do you know how many people have been hurt?" Kelley couldn't bring herself to ask how many had died.

"I don't know. I don't even know if anybody was shot."

"There were enough rounds of ammunition to fill a barrel!"

"I know."

"What happened here?" a woman's voice demanded.

Kelley opened her eyes just in time to see the lights go on once more. The woman in pink standing in front of her was vaguely familiar, although Kelley was too dazed to place her immediately.

Felice stood. "Miss Sanders, you shouldn't be back inside. We don't know if anyone's still lurking—"

"I want to know what's going on! The press has a right to know!"

Felice narrowed her eyes, and her voice was icy. "You know as much as we do. Somebody sent a hit squad to the wedding. We don't know how, why or who, and that's your story."

Suzy Sanders turned toward Griff, who was leaning against the wall talking to a man who had come in with Gallagher and Simon. "Griff? Griff Bryant? Maybe you can tell me."

Kelley watched Griff shrug. He looked tough and cynical again, nothing like a man who couldn't make himself pull the trigger of a gun that would have stopped a fugitive from fleeing, a gun he still held in his hand. And nothing like a man who would stop a woman from pulling the same trigger.

"Some guy was shooting from the sacristy," Griff said as if dismissing her.

"Well, what happened to him?" Suzy demanded.

"He ran and got shot in the process." He turned back to the man to finish his conversation, pointedly excluding her.

"Shot?" Suzy turned back to Kelley. "Is that what happened?"

Felice answered for her. "Look, there are men chasing the guy down right now. And the whole Palm Springs police force is about to descend on the church. You want a story, you go talk to them. But for God's sake, be careful, or you could be in headlines yourself."

Suzy humphed, then started down the hall.

"What's the plan now?" Kelley realized she was feeling better. With Felice's help, she managed to stand.

Felice stepped back and looked at her, then, shaking her head, she removed Kelley's wreath, which was draped over one ear and handed it to her. "When the police arrive, everyone's going to be questioned."

"Well, good. I mean, there are just a couple of little things we don't know, like who was shooting and who they were shooting at."

"I've got to get back outside and see if anyone needs first aid while the ambulances arrive."

"I'll come, too." Kelley touched Felice's arm. "Does Gallagher have any ideas? Or have you even had a moment to ask him?"

"He thinks it's a mob hit. He thinks he and Simon were probably the targets."

"I wondered."

"He and Simon locked up most of a new organized crime family forming out in the northwest. They've come after Simon before and Gallagher's friend Aaron who's here, too. The way these guys think, they probably figured they could get all three men together, unarmed, and get rid of them in style. Trouble is, nobody thought any of those guys were still around, or we'd have had security."

"It might not have been them they were after. There were other prominent people here who could have been targets."

"I know. There were lots of other law enforcement types here tonight who could have put some creeps away and made them real mad." She stopped. "Including you and me."

"They'd have to be pretty mad and damned well organized."

Kelley felt a large hand rest on her shoulder. She didn't have to turn around to know whose it was. She did turn, though, and stared into the ice blue eyes that made women yearn to get trapped in a terrorist attack with this man.

"Thanks," Griff said.

She shrugged. Felice moved toward the sacristy door. Kelley wanted to follow her, but she knew she'd better finish this first. "I could say the same."

"I could have been killed if you hadn't knocked me down at the altar."

"I'd be black and blue if you hadn't gotten that creep off of me."

"Just black and blue?"

"Maybe worse," she admitted.

"I don't know. I thought you were holding your own."

"I thought you and I were holding our own pretty well together until . . ."

"I didn't shoot?"

"Why didn't you?" Kelley stared back at him. She felt no awe at being face-to-face with the man she had often ogled on-screen. She felt no embarrassment that her dress was slipping down one arm or that she was shoeless and half her hair was cascading over one eye. She brushed her hair back, but only to see him better. "Why the hell didn't you shoot? We'd have a suspect in custody now if you had. And if you couldn't do it, then why didn't you let me?"

"You were mad enough to kill him."

She told herself that Griff didn't know her and that he didn't know her background or profession. She reminded herself that for centuries men had been taught to believe foolish things about women, and women had foolishly allowed it.

"I wouldn't have killed him," she said after a pregnant silence. "But if I had, I'm not sure the world would be a worse place because of it." She realized how angry she was, both at the man who had fled and the one standing before her. She didn't believe in killing anyone; she had become a cop to keep people from killing each other. But she was too angry to take back her words.

"Death lasts a long time," Griff said. "And neither of us was his judge or jury."

"He won't *see* a judge or a jury now. Not unless one of us can identify him in a mug book."

"Did you get a good look at his face?"

"Oh, I saw his face all right."

"It was pitch-black in here. I'm not sure I could make a positive—"

"*I* could."

Griff shook his head. "I don't know how."

"Easy," she said. "I've seen him before. I don't know where, and I don't know when. But I've seen him, and I'll find him." She nodded curtly, then she turned and followed Felice's path.

Chapter 3

"No, none of them on this page." Kelley thumbed through the fourth mug book the police had provided. "Not on this one, either."

"Coffee?"

She shook her head at Detective Sergeant Fred Pollock, the man sitting beside her. He was in his midfifties and in the past hour he had smoked most of a pack of cigarettes and drunk a pot of coffee, all by himself. He looked like he needed a good night's sleep.

She knew she did, too. She hadn't been given a chance to go home and change. She was still wearing her maid-of-honor dress, but somewhere along the way someone, Gallagher or Simon, after an abortive search for the gunman, had draped the jacket of his tux over her bare shoulders. She had located her shoes and removed the remaining pins from her hair, but she still wasn't going to win any beauty prizes.

"You're sure you'd know him?" the sergeant asked.

"I told you, Fred, I've seen this guy before. I just can't remember where or when." She closed the book, finished with it. "That bothers me, too. I was cursed with this crazy memory. My head's like a computer. Feed it data, and it keeps it on file forever. Usually I can access it like that." She snapped her fingers.

"Maybe we should try to figure out why you're having trouble this time." He lit the last cigarette in his pack.

"I've been working on it." Kelley got up and opened a window. She didn't smoke, but she used to—she couldn't imagine why.

"Got any ideas?"

"A couple. Maybe he's changed his appearance somehow, and he's too changed for me to zero in on."

"Possible."

"Maybe I just got a glance at him somewhere, like the cleaners, or the crowd at Dodger Stadium."

"You remember everybody you see?"

"Not really, not unless I make some sort of connection."

"So maybe you saw him on the street somewhere and noticed something, like a crazy tie he was wearing, or the way he kicked a dog...."

"Maybe."

"Any other possibilities?"

She shrugged. "Maybe my computer banks are finally overloaded. Too much data, not enough chips."

Fred stubbed out his half-smoked cigarette. "Let's call it a night. If you think you can do it, tomorrow you can help us put together a composite."

"I wanted to find him. By the time I remember who he is, he might be in Bora Bora."

"Yeah. So? How different's that gonna be? The bad guys are always two steps ahead of us. We only get them when they trip."

"This one *would* have tripped if Griff Bryant had let me fire again."

"You really can't go around shooting at every creep you meet, Kell. You don't carry a badge anymore."

"We'd have a suspect if I'd stopped him. And besides, I was shooting low, just to let him know I meant business."

"I know that. You know that. Some fleabag attorney might have gotten him off, anyway."

"Well, he's off now, but good."

"There were a lot of people at that wedding, lots of them trained professionals. Maybe somebody will know something."

"Yeah. Maybe." She gave a wan smile. "Are they still interviewing guests?"

"Bryant's still here. Some of the others are helping us comb the church."

"Griff's here?"

"Looking at the same books you did."

"Know if he's had any luck?"

"Not that I've heard."

"That's because the guy isn't in those books." Kelley sighed. "I guess you're right. We'd better call it a night."

Fred stood. "You'll let us know when you remember something?"

"I'm not going after the guy alone, if that's what you mean."

"Don't."

"I'm not a glory hound."

"I know. But let us take care of investigating this one. You've done your share. Go home and get some sleep."

"Sleep? I've got a ball game to watch before I open up the paper tomorrow morning." She held up her hand. "And don't you dare tell me who won."

"Not me."

She crossed to the door, one step ahead of him. "You're going to let me know if you find out something, right?"

"I'll let you know everything I can."

In the hallway she started toward the exit. The building was familiar. She knew just about every cop there. She also knew where every file and document was kept and who could be counted on to look through them in a pinch. Her reputation was good; lots of clients had been steered in her direction by people working inside these walls. Unlike some other investigators, she and Felice could be counted on to stay within the limits of the law and to share what they'd found when it was appropriate.

She lifted her hand in farewell to the man at the desk. Cops, all of whom looked as exhausted as Fred Pollock, melted in and out of doorways. No crime this splashy had hit the Coachella

Valley in anyone's memory, and exhausted or not, everyone who could be was there tonight to help.

She was almost to the door when she saw Griff Bryant coming out of one of the interrogation rooms. She watched him say goodbye to a subordinate of Fred's, then she waited as he walked toward her.

"Did you have any luck?" she asked.

He shook his head. His cheeks were shadowed with the beginning of a beard, and his eyes were heavy-lidded with fatigue. He still looked magnificent. "I don't know if I'd have recognized the guy if they'd shown me an eight-by-ten glossy of you wrestling him in the hallway."

She smiled, too tired not to. "Well, he wasn't in the books I saw."

"Are you all right? That guy was trying to work you over good."

She was surprised by the concern in his voice. "I'm okay. My arm will be bruised tomorrow, and my lip will swell. But he'll be in worse shape."

"Have you remembered where you know him from?"

"No, damn it."

"A good night's sleep might help."

"I don't know if anybody who was at the church tonight is going to get a good night's sleep."

"Have you heard a report on how many people were—"

"Hurt? Dead? I know they took some to the hospital while I was out front. One old man with emphysema was overcome by the smoke. Someone else was trampled and may have a broken leg. I heard . . ." She stopped. What she'd heard was so preposterous she wasn't even sure if she should get his hopes up.

"What?"

"Well, after I got here I heard somebody out in the hall say that nobody had been shot. But that can't be right. You were there, you know how many rounds of ammunition were fired."

"Maybe all those rounds were fired over everybody's heads."

"Does that make sense?"

He gave a cynical half smile. "Does anything?"

"It never makes sense to me when people try to kill each other." She turned, and Griff opened the door for her, following close behind.

They started toward the parking lot. Kelley hoped her station wagon would start. It usually waited until moments like these, moments when she was really at her limit, to play dead.

"None of this seems real."

For a moment Kelley wasn't sure Griff had been speaking to her. It was almost as if he had been thinking out loud. "What do you mean?" she asked.

"Well, when I heard gunfire, it seemed perfectly natural. I wasn't afraid. It never really occurred to me that I could be shot."

"That makes sense."

"Does it?"

"Sure. You're shot at all the time, but the bullets are never real. The line between reality and fantasy isn't always clear, anyway. For actors, it rarely is."

"You sound like you know what you're talking about."

"I've thought about it some."

They stopped beside her car, and she wondered what Griff thought of it. By Palm Springs's standards, it was a no-class domestic wagon of the gas-guzzling variety. The last time she'd taken her Cub Scout den on a field trip, they had strewn candy wrappers from seat to seat. It wasn't a car anyone would expect a P.I. to drive—which was part of the reason she did.

Griff leaned against the side of the hood. "You know, you look familiar to me."

"Well, I hope we both have luck searching our memory banks," she said, although she didn't really hope *his* luck would be good. He probably had seen her before, and she would just as soon ignore the where and when.

"Have we met?"

"Nope."

"Maybe I need a good night's sleep." He smiled, and the effect was enough to bowl over a more susceptible woman.

She was still standing firmly on two feet by the time the smile faded. "Yeah," she agreed. "Go home and go to bed. You can read all about this in the morning."

"You're right." He didn't move.

"You don't seem to be leaving."

"I'm waiting for you to get in and start this thing."

She searched his eyes. "How do you know I have trouble starting it?"

"I used to drive one of these babies."

"You were already on your way to being a star when this car was built. Don't tell me you weren't driving a Cadillac or a Rolls ten years ago."

"I was frying hamburgers and busing trays when this thing came off the assembly line. I bought my version used. Every time I really had to be somewhere, it sat like a lump of lead."

She bent over to unlock the door. "It must have gotten you somewhere. You're not busing trays anymore—at least I haven't seen you play any waiters."

"I played a bartender once."

"Yeah, but if I remember right, you were really a CIA plant."

"The pay was better."

She opened the door and slid behind the wheel. The car started without a hitch. She slammed the door and rolled down her window to say goodbye as he moved away. "She must have liked our conversation. But thanks for waiting."

"Lock your doors tonight."

"Why? A burglar would be nothing after what happened at the church."

"You're so sure it wasn't you they were shooting at?"

She frowned. "What does that mean?"

"I was told to be careful for a while since it's not clear who the targets were. Weren't you told the same thing?"

She realized it had never occurred to her that Griff could have been the target of the shooting. "I'm not worried," she said. "My dog would lick an intruder to death." Kelley put the car in gear and backed out of her slot, giving one careless wave before she drove away.

Only when she was home rewinding her videotape, Neuf settled comfortably beside her, did she realize she had never introduced herself to Griff. She knew his name, but she doubted he knew hers. She imagined that happened to him a lot.

She assured herself he would have forgotten her name immediately and put him out of her mind. She had already showered and changed into soft, worn pajamas. Now she had a cold beer can against her throbbing lip, and the remote control for her VCR on the table beside her. It was 2:00 a.m., but the world finally seemed almost sane again. The tape finished rewinding. She pressed Play and waited for the game to begin.

A jungle appeared; a shot rang out; a man in army fatigues fell from a tree. Kelley squinted at her channel selector to be sure the VCR was working.

The man got up and began to run.

She grabbed the remote, ready to fast-forward the tape. The man stopped and looked directly at the camera.

"No!" She stood up and punched the button, hoping against hope that somehow this was just a used tape she had grabbed by mistake, that somehow she hadn't rewound it right to the beginning when she had set the recorder.

There was a moment of silence as she pushed Stop, then Play again, a moment of fierce, I'll-promise-anything hope. Then a voice, an unforgettable baritone, spoke, telling another soldier about his moments of terror.

She threw the remote on the sofa, narrowly missing Neuf. Hope died. In the rush to get out the door and to the church that afternoon, she had set the recorder to tape the pay movie channel by mistake. Fate had presented her with Griff Bryant once again.

"You look like hell."

"Try getting shot at repeatedly, and see if your health spa tan doesn't pale." In the sunshine of his own poolside patio, Griff poured a cup of coffee strong enough to grow hair on the shiniest head. It was late morning, and he needed something to get him going. It had been well after midnight when he had come home from the police station, and surprisingly he had slept the sleep of the dead. He winced at the analogy.

His friend and personal manager, Dwayne Fagan, made a different kind of face. "That stuff's going to give you wrinkles."

Still standing over Fagan, who was sprawled comfortably at the round glass table, Griff toasted him with his coffee cup. "This stuff's going to get me through the day."

"I had yogurt and oat bran for breakfast and a glass of raspberry-carrot juice."

"You know, you can eat yogurt, you can juice vegetables and fruits until you have a compost pile the size of Cincinnati, but all it takes is one bullet, one car an inch or two off course, one airplane with faulty landing gear and wham!" He slapped the glass in front of Fagan. "Dead and gone. And think of all the good stuff you would have missed."

"Funny man," Fagan grumbled. Fagan, forty, tanned and trim, balanced stress against vitamins, minerals and exercise, like St. Peter at the scale of judgment. He had a theory that any Hollywood job was a killer, and that every year spent at his took two off his life. He was a man expecting to die any moment—and sometimes he seemed perturbed that he hadn't.

Griff added cream to his coffee. "Not funny. Philosophical. I can have Mrs. Robbert whip up some scrambled eggs for you, too."

"Poison." Fagan opened the newspaper to the front page. "I'm gonna read you this while you eat."

"First thing when I got up I called the detective I talked to last night. He tells me the word is that nobody was seriously hurt yesterday. That's all I want to know."

"Oh, I think you'll want to hear this."

"You couldn't wait till I'm done?"

"If I'd paid a fortune to get you this kind of publicity, I couldn't have done any better."

Griff put his hand on the paper. "You *didn't* pay a fortune for it, did you, pal?"

"What's that supposed to mean?"

"Just that I've been in this business a long time."

"You think I'd hire assassins to come after you at a wedding just to get you some free newspaper space? You think I'd do that to you?"

Griff didn't reply.

"You're crazy." Fagan grinned. "I couldn't have done it, because I didn't *think* of it."

"Read."

Fagan shook the paper and Griff released it. "I'll skip the stuff you know."

"I was there, remember? I know it all."

"Did you know you're a hero?" When Griff just sipped his coffee, Fagan shrugged. "Well, here's what Susan Sanders is telling the world."

"Suzy Slander? Isn't that a real paper you're reading?"

"She was there, so her story was the one that made the wire services. Listen to this, second paragraph."

He began to read.

"Individual acts of heroism shone brightly in the long moments of terror. Guests risked their own lives to try to protect others younger or weaker than themselves. Among the most memorable was the relentless pursuit of one of the would-be assassins by film star Griff Bryant. Bryant, known for his roles as a law-and-order strongman, faced down a man intent on shooting one of the female guests. Unarmed, Bryant single-handedly disarmed the man, then shot and wounded him as he escaped."

Fagan looked up. "You know, Griff, when they shoot at you in pictures, the bullets aren't real. You could have been killed yesterday playing the good guy. Then where would I be?"

"Damn!"

"Damn?"

"That's not what happened."

"Read it yourself." Fagan offered him the paper.

Griff waved it away. "You say the wire services got hold of this?"

"You don't know Suzy very well, do you? Her thing in life is to be taken 'seriously.' She sees herself as the next major network news anchor. She was probably on the telephone calling her paper with this story before the church was emptied."

"I didn't face down anybody, and I sure didn't disarm this guy. The so-called female guest did that. She's a little thing, too, cute and sassy, but she fights like a trained guerrilla."

"Then you jumped in and rescued her? Got the gun and shot the guy as he ran off?" Fagan asked hopefully.

"*She* shot him. She took the gun out of my hand and shot him. She'd have shot him again, too, if I hadn't stopped her."

Fagan shut his eyes.

Griff tried to picture what he'd been doing when Suzy had arrived in the hallway. "I was holding the gun when Suzy got there," he said. "And the woman—damn it, I never got her name."

"I can see the tabloid headlines now." Fagan opened his eyes and swept his hand in front of them slowly. "Movie Hero A Coward. Life Saved By Ninety-Four-Pound Female."

"A hundred and five, maybe a hundred and ten, but no more." Griff set his cup down hard enough for coffee to slosh over the rim. "Damn it, I've got to find out who she is."

"Why, so the papers can spell her name right when they make a fool out of you?"

Griff sent him a look that had made stronger men cower. "So she'll know I didn't give anybody this version of the story. I don't want her to think I tried to pass myself off as a hero."

"God, no. Let's not take credit for the best publicity, mistake or not, that anybody's ever given you," Fagan said sarcastically.

"I want Suzy's number." Griff held out his hand.

"You think I'm gonna help you cut your own throat?" Fagan slapped his hand protectively over his sports coat pocket, where he kept a bulging address book.

"If you don't give it to me, I'll get it from someone else."

"Talk to Ninja Woman before you talk to Suzy, okay? Just do that much for me. Maybe she doesn't want to be written up as some sort of superhero—heroine. Maybe she won't want anybody to know her name."

Fagan was obviously thinking fast. "Maybe..." He pounded the table in emphasis. "Maybe she won't want to be identified! I mean, she made a fool out of that guy, right? Will she want him to know who she is? He could come after her. She probably saw his face. You could be responsible for putting her in danger if you use her name," he finished triumphantly.

Griff knew exactly why Fagan was trying to put off his call to Suzy, but he also realized that Fagan's fast-on-the-feet logic had some merit. He crooked a finger. "Give me the number."

"Griffin, you're like a brother to me. You think I'm gonna help you look like a fool?" He sighed when Griff's hand remained outstretched. He reached inside for his address book and jotted the number down on the back of a business card. Then he shoved it across the table. "But call Ninja Woman first."

"I'm going to. I don't want her put in danger."

"And that leads to the reason I'm here."

Griff flopped down across from Fagan. He waited until Mrs. Robbert, a large woman who loved her own cooking, had served his breakfast and gone back inside before he took Fagan's bait.

"So why else did you come? You've seen for yourself I'm alive. You've got the whole, sorry story."

"I want to hire a bodyguard for you."

Griff chewed on as if he hadn't heard.

"Look, I've talked to the cops, too," Fagan said. "They tell me they don't know who was being attacked last night."

"So?"

"It could have been you."

"It could have been a hundred people." Griff reached for a basket of toast.

"I don't represent anyone else who was there. I represent you. The cops say you should be careful. The shooting started while you were speaking."

"So? There were others up front with me."

"I'm not saying it *was* you. I'm saying it could have been. And if it was, you could be shot at again."

"The cops warned me last night."

"So what are you going to do?"

Griff shrugged and spread blackberry jam.

"Look," Fagan went on, "I'm not crazy about some big bruiser in a striped suit tailing you everywhere you go. There's no question everybody'll figure out you've got a bodyguard, and it won't look good. But it'll look better than your body splattered all the way to Disneyland.''

"Sure you won't let Mrs. Robbert get you something to eat?"

"I'm not kidding about this, Griff. Zephyr was on my tail first thing this morning. They're gonna foot the bill for somebody to follow you around, Cam Johns's orders. They've got too much invested in your next picture to have you end up in a morgue before the film ends up in the can.''

"Don't you love the movies?"

"The police are gonna do it if we don't! They'll assign someone to tail you. Taxpayers' expense. They've already got somebody driving by your house on the half hour looking for anything suspicious.''

Griff looked up from his plate.

"Think about it," Fagan continued. "How's it gonna look if Palm Springs's finest sat back and let Griff Bryant get murdered in their town? It's not like they haven't been warned. You were shot at last night.''

"So were a church full of other people."

"They don't live here, not a lot of them, anyway. And they weren't standing up front. And they weren't Griff Bryant, a household name who just happened to see the face of one of the crazies who was shooting.''

"There's no reason anybody would want me dead."

"No? There are some pretty famous corpses out there that died with those words on their lips.''

"Tell the police to forget it."

"I don't tell the police anything. I say 'yes sir, officer' and 'no sir, officer,' just like any good American citizen.''

"Then I'll tell them."

Fagan reached for a piece of toast and began crumbling it on his place mat. "And who's gonna tell Tara? Huh? Who's gonna tell your little girl that her father doesn't care enough about himself to be sure he's around to see *her* wedding?"

"Fagan—"

But Fagan was on a roll. "Come to think about it, who's gonna tell her that her father's putting her in danger by not getting protection? She's coming here to live with you, isn't

she? Are you gonna let her get shot at, Griff? What if somebody aims at you and misses?''

Griff stared at him, meal forgotten. He rarely discussed Tara
with anyone, even Fagan. She was eleven, the one person in the
world he loved without reservation. She was also spoiled, confused and unhappy that her mother was sending her to Palm
Springs while she and her third husband toured Europe for a
year. He loved Tara, but he wasn't used to being more than a
weekend father. He hadn't had time to think about her or the
danger she might be in if someone started shooting at him
again.

''You're done?'' he asked.

''Done.''

''Then do me a favor.''

''Anything.''

''Go home.''

Fagan stood. ''You'll think about it?''

He didn't answer.

''How are you gonna make yourself *stop* thinking about it?
Don't think about it, Griff. Don't think about the best idea I've
ever had. Make yourself forget it.'' Fagan grinned. ''I'm giving you a juicer for Christmas and I'm teaching you to use it.''

Griff ignored him and went back to his breakfast, but when
Fagan was gone he pushed the plate away and went inside to get
his car keys.

Chapter 4

More than anything, Neuf resembled a black bear with a perm. He was the ninth puppy in a litter that was never supposed to happen, the mating of a prize Newfoundland bitch with a lowly poodle-Newfoundland mistake. Had the breeder not had a heart, Neuf and his brothers and sisters would have ended up in that great kennel in the sky right after their births. As it was, each puppy had found a home. Neuf, already significantly bigger than a bread box, had ended up at Kelley's house.

The afternoon after Felice's almost-wedding, Kelley regretted the soft spot in her heart that had convinced her she could deed over a part of her little house to a dog. She woke up at one to find Neuf taking up most of the bed. His head was pillowed on his paws, and his eyes were open, willing her in the politest of ways to wake up.

"Coffee," she croaked, then cleared her throat and tried again. "Coffee."

Neuf didn't move.

"Remember?" Kelley sat up and stretched. "I say coffee, you go in the hall and nudge the light switch."

Neuf didn't move.

"Remember?" she prodded. "The Cub Scouts trained you. Kenny gave you a whole box of treats? Jared gave you a pound of hamburger I was defrosting for dinner?"

At the word "treats," Neuf's head came up. His tail wagged at "dinner."

"You want to eat? Earn your keep. Coffee!"

Neuf stretched, and Neuf stretching was a fearsome thing. Kelley ducked. The bed rose inches when he jumped off and started toward the hallway.

She looked at the clock and was ashamed, but not very, that she had slept so long. Getting to sleep hadn't been easy, and she'd awakened more than once to the realistic smell of smoke and the rapid fire of machine guns in her dreams.

Her arm was bruised. She could see what looked like fingerprints against her flesh. It was too bad they weren't the real thing; she knew that when the lab ran the prints from the gun, they would be hers and Griff's. Their assailant had been wearing gloves.

She reached for her bedside phone and dialed the number of Felice's condo. There was no answer, but she wasn't worried. After the wedding trauma, Felice and Gallagher could have gone anywhere to spend the night. Since they were almost finished renovating and moving into their first home together, they could even be there, where no phone yet existed.

She tried the office next, but since everyone there had been given the rest of the week off, she wasn't surprised to find her own voice responding on the office answering machine. She punched the code to listen to messages, but none of them concerned last night.

Since she knew she would get the runaround if she called anyone official, she decided to get up and eat, then dress and head over to see Fred Pollock. In person she would get better information and a better sense of what she should do next. Then, if appropriate, she could head to Felice's new house.

The coffee was brewing by the time she got into the hallway. She was certain that she had the only house in Palm Springs with a coffee maker plugged in the electrical socket by the front door. Her Cub Scouts had rigged it up for her when she'd mentioned, in passing to somebody's mother, that she needed a coffeepot that acted like an alarm clock. She could have bought one that really did, but the five eight-year-old delinquents-in-training didn't know that. Together they had planned strategy and trained Neuf to go along with it. It was the first time they had cooperated on a project and seen it through to a conclusion.

Anybody who tried to move it now would have to answer to her.

The coffee maker sat on an antique walnut pump organ. She had solved the problem of scarring the beautiful old wood with hot coffee by placing the coffee maker on a silver tea tray. The organ had once graced the parlor of a mansion located on a major movie studio's back lot. The mansion had been used in half a dozen horror films. Her father had bought the organ and brought it home when the mansion was demolished to make way for a small Western town. Likewise, the tea tray had once sat on a coffee table between Joan Crawford and Hedy Lamarr while the two women carried on a very private conversation—in front of movie audiences throughout the world. The cups on the tray were relics from a studio commissary.

There were very few things in the house without a Hollywood history. Including her.

Since her Cub Scouts hadn't seen fit to move the rest of her appliances into the hallway, Kelley got the newspaper off her front porch, then went into the kitchen for the rest of her breakfast and Neuf's first meal of the day.

She was at her table with a burrito and a plate of peanut butter toast before she opened the paper. Halfway through the article about Felice's wedding, she slammed the paper to the floor.

She told herself she should have expected something like this. She didn't care that her name hadn't been mentioned anywhere, or even that once again in the media, a woman had been made to look helpless instead of courageous. What she did care about was the way the article had been manipulated, shamefully so, to make Griff Bryant look like the man he played onscreen. Reality had taken back seat to fantasy, something it routinely did in this part of the world.

She would be one of the first to agree that life needed its quota of heroes and heroines, but she vastly preferred the thousands of men and women who performed quiet, courageous acts on police forces or rescue squads, in hospitals or high school classrooms, over a make-believe hero like Griff Bryant.

How had this article found its way into print? Had Griff called his publicist? Had his publicist twisted the facts and presented them in such a way as to make his client look heroic? Or had Griff himself given misinformation to the press? Had he purposely changed yesterday's events to suit himself and his career?

She was mulling this over, angrily wolfing down her burrito when the doorbell rang. Neuf, giving his best imitation of a watchdog, led her to the front door, barking loudly as if he actually cared who was there. Standing on the front porch was the hero himself.

She opened the door and popped the last bite of burrito in her mouth.

"Kelley?" Griff asked.

She nodded.

He examined the five-foot-three, angrily-chewing keg of dynamite in front of him. She was dressed in blue gym shorts and a gray sweatshirt with the sleeves chopped off. Her auburn hair licked at her shoulders like summer wildfire.

"I see you've read the paper," he said, watching as she wiped her fingers on her shorts. His gaze traveled down her legs to her bare feet and enjoyed the journey.

She swallowed, then leaned against the door frame and folded her arms. He was dressed in California casual, an expensive designer shirt with the three requisite buttons unfastened and pleated pants the color of oatmeal. He looked more like a yachtsman today than a pirate.

"Amazing, isn't it?" she said. "I read. Bet you thought I couldn't."

"I'd like to explain."

She considered; it took her a while. "There are some ground rules," she said at last. "You should know them before you come inside. I'm not easily charmed, so it's not worth your time to try, especially not when your time is so valuable. And my business, unlike yours, depends on being able to tell the truth from lies. I get paid well to do it, and I'm damned good at it."

He cut straight to the point. "I didn't tell anybody the facts the way they appeared in the paper. Susan Sanders saw what she wanted to and made up her own story."

She weighed that piece of information, weighed what she knew of Suzy Slander and what she knew of this man. He had a slightly favorable edge. She stepped inside to let him in.

"Does he bite?" he asked, waving his hand toward Neuf.

"Only liars," she lied.

He followed her through the house, trying not to be distracted by the attractive clutter surrounding him. He was distracted, though, by both the clutter and the woman. He liked the way she moved, not with come-hither allure like her friend and partner Felice, but with purpose, with vitality suppressed just enough to keep her from breaking into a run.

"Do you want some coffee?" she asked at the kitchen threshold.

"If you promise not to poison it."

She turned without a word and started back the way they'd come.

He followed. "Are you going to throw me out already?"

"I'm getting your coffee. You did say you wanted some, didn't you?"

He followed, intrigued, and stopped just short of the front door.

She challenged him silently to say something, anything, about the peculiarity of the coffee maker on the organ. He only stretched out his hand when the coffee had been poured and smiled.

She disliked his smile. She had seen him aim it at too many gorgeous women, on-screen women, to trust it. Some of those women had ended up dead for love of this man; some—the betrayers, the terrorists, the assassins—had ended up dead by his hand. Had he killed as many women in real life as he had in his films, he would have gone down in history with Jack the Ripper.

"I like your house," he said, following her back toward the kitchen. "I'm beginning to know the hallway well."

"How'd you find me?"

"I went over to see Felice this morning, after I read the newspaper article. I didn't even know your name. I'm sorry, but yesterday was kind of chaotic."

"Just your usual sort of day."

"Let's get beyond my profession, okay? Acting is what I do for money. Nobody's paying me now, and there was nothing usual about yesterday. For either of us."

She waved him to a seat at the table and flopped down in her own. "If you don't mind, I'll finish my breakfast while you grovel."

He lounged back in his chair. "I'll call Suzy from here, if you want, and insist she run the story the way it really happened, with your name spelled right and mine dragged through the mud." He paused, admiring the contents of her plate. "That looks good."

She put a piece of toast on a napkin and slid it across the table at him. "I've got frozen burritos to go with it if you want to pop one in the microwave." She looked up. "Do you know how to use a microwave?"

"Yeah. A refrigerator, too, and sometimes a stove, though I always have trouble remembering whether I'm supposed to put a pan or a plate over the burner."

"Neuf," she called. She jerked a thumb at Griff. "Eat this man."

Griff picked up his toast. "Suzy came in, saw me holding the gun, saw you on the floor against the wall, heard that a man had been shot and put the facts together the way she wanted them to run. That's how she does her column. Why should real news be any different?"

Despite herself, Kelley knew things could very well have happened that way. "She never interviewed you?"

"And ruin her story?"

"Your manager or publicist didn't get to her and distort the facts?"

"My manager didn't know anything about yesterday until he read it in the paper this morning."

"Bet he was happy."

"He thinks somebody's trying to rob him of his fifteen percent."

Kelley looked up again. "Fifteen's the going rate these days?"

"It keeps him in spare change."

She bet that fifteen percent of Griff Bryant kept Griff's manager in Rolls-Royces and Beverly Hills mansions. She finished, stood and stretched on the way to the sink to wash her dishes.

Griff watched her shorts ride up her legs until the legs looked as long as a chorus girl's. They were wonderful legs, slender ankles, shapely calves, trim, taut thighs. He could tell she believed in exercise, but he doubted she did it in an aerobics class. She wouldn't swim or jog, either, not unless she was swimming or jogging somewhere important. She would play sports competitively. Volleyball and baseball. Touch football. He thought about her struggles with the gunman yesterday. *Contact* football, maybe even Australian rules, with no padding, and no holds barred.

"Have you heard anything today? Did they catch the bad guys while I was sleeping?" She couldn't resist. "Or did *you* catch them single-handedly, maybe? With Suzy watching and taking notes?"

"You're not going to give me a break, are you?"

"You've come up smack-dab against my personal prejudices."

"Let me see. Race, color, creed—*profession?*"

"Actors don't do. Actors are."

"It's everything about me, then?"

"I'm trying to be fair."

"You could have fooled me."

"Of course, I know I'm not *being* fair. I've been discriminated against myself because of what I do." She turned. "Do you know what I do?"

"I didn't yesterday," he admitted.

"Felice and I are partners."

"She told me this morning."

"There are lots of people out there who think I couldn't possibly be any good at investigation. I'm too female, too short." She shrugged. "Too cute."

He laughed at the disgust in that last word. "Cute's a state of mind. There's nothing cute about you."

She faced him, leaning back against the sink. "Anyway, I understand better than almost anybody how stupid prejudices are. But I've got them, just the same."

"Why?"

"Let's just say it's personal experience."

He admired her in a way he hadn't had time or inclination to do yesterday. She wasn't beautiful, at least not by the standards of this decade. There was nothing elegant about her turned-up nose or her small, square chin. Her blue-green eyes were frank, not seductive, and her riotous hair was never going to conform to anybody's notions of style. But there was something beguiling about her, something naturally and powerfully female. Faces with this kind of unaffected beauty had stared back at him from the hills of Ireland and the moors of Scotland. There was character and strength here, the kind of character and strength that had gotten families through famines and wars and depressions.

"Who was he?" he asked.

She smiled. "You're assuming a lot."

The smile went with the face. Wide, generous and genuine. Also familiar. He didn't smile in response. The feeling he'd had yesterday returned. He knew her.

"Nobody hurt me," she said. "At least, nobody stepped on me on their climb up to the silver screen, if that's what you're thinking."

"Where do I know you from?"

"I told you, we haven't met."

He switched the subject, because he knew she wasn't going to give him any clues. He would remember eventually; an actor's memory was almost as good as an investigator's. "Felice tells me that no one from the wedding was hospitalized overnight. There was an old man who needed oxygen and someone who had to have a leg set. They observed some others for a while, then sent them home."

"The gunshots were blanks." Kelley turned back to the sink. "I don't know why it didn't occur to me yesterday, except that during the excitement it just didn't seem like a possibility. They sure as heck sounded real. I realized the truth in the middle of the night."

"You're right. They confirmed it this morning."

"The guy who was shooting at us was shooting the real thing. I wounded him with his own gun. They found blood on the floor where I'd shot him."

"I know."

"Do you know if they checked the videotapes? I know there were people taping the wedding. Maybe somebody got a picture of somebody who wasn't invited."

"I hired the camera crew myself. That was supposed to be my present to Felice and Gallagher. They're some of the best, too, recommended by my producer at Zephyr. The police have already seen what footage they could salvage. Unfortunately they dropped their cameras and ran when the shooting started. If they'd been newsmen, instead of Cam's people, they'd have probably gotten something we could use. As it was, they didn't get anything, and they're threatening to sue somebody for damage to their equipment."

"Great."

"You might say I screwed up all the way around."

She made herself ignore the sincerity in his deep baritone, the startling surge of warmth in his ice blue eyes. "Well, you didn't get yourself killed. We can give you that much."

"Thanks to you."

"So you're going to call Suzy and tell her a woman saved your life? That you didn't shoot and wound the fleeing gunman, that you kept me from shooting him a second time?"

"If you'd like."

"And right about now, don't you expect me to say 'Don't bother. Offering was good enough'?"

Both his voice and eyes cooled. "I don't expect anything, except maybe to be treated like a man who came here to try to set something straight."

Kelley didn't want to give an inch. There was something about Griff that gave new meaning to the old proverb. He might take a mile, and a mile with this man would be one incredible trip. Still, she didn't want to be unfair, either, and she knew she was bordering on it.

"Well, just tell me one thing, then," she said. "Why didn't you call Suzy and set the story straight without asking me if you should? Why come here at all?"

"Because Suzy's mistake might be good fortune for you, and I didn't want to unintentionally put your life in danger."

"My life? What—"

"And because Suzy's mistake might be *my* good fortune, but not for the reasons you think."

She frowned, and he could see he had interested her. He continued. "My manager pointed out that you might not want the man with the gun to know who you are. Of course, there's a chance he does, anyway. But let's say he doesn't and he can't find out. Every minute you're not identified is a minute you're safe. You saw his face and you recognized him, although you're not sure from where. If—"

She shrugged. "If I recognized him, he probably recognized me."

"Not if he's somebody you've just seen casually. He may never have noticed you, or he may not have your kind of memory."

She knew he was right. "So?"

"As soon as your name goes in the newspaper, he can find you."

"I'm not worried. He's out of shape and a lousy shot."

"And probably furious."

"So you're worried about protecting me?"

"That's part of it. Also it occurred to me that in your line of work, you might not want that kind of publicity. I'd think your job depended on keeping a low profile. If they plaster your picture all over the papers, the next time you try to follow somebody, they'll recognize you."

"No one would ever recognize me. *You* wouldn't recognize me."

He smiled a little, but this wasn't the time to tell her she would be hard for any man to ignore. "There's another reason."

Without thinking, she hoisted herself to the edge of the tile counter and waited. If nothing else, his reasons were well thought out, even if they could also be termed "self-serving." She crossed her legs and leaned back on her hands. "Let's hear it."

He stared at her for moments without speaking, then he shook his head. "Well, you were a lot younger the last time I saw you. I guess I can be forgiven for not remembering."

"We haven't met. I—"

"*Strawberry Finn*. There's a scene somewhere in the middle of the film where you hoist yourself up in a tree house and sit just exactly that way. Sammy O'Flynn. I'll be damned."

"Kelley Samuels," she said, enunciating every syllable. "And you *will* be damned if you continue with that."

He stood and crossed the room before she'd finished. His hand shot out and gripped her chin. He turned her head to the left, then the right. Finally she slapped his hand away. "Cut it out."

"You're not going to tell me you and Sammy aren't the same person?"

"I haven't been that person in a long, long time. Not since I was twelve."

"But what's the big deal? You were a wonderful little actress. *Strawberry Finn* is a classic. People all over the world wished you were their kid. Kids all over the world wished you were their best friend."

"But I wasn't. I had my own parents and they were great. And I had friends. I didn't need more. Acting was something I did because I hated to sit quietly in a classroom all day. It was no big deal. It still isn't."

"America's tomboy sweetheart."

"Who grew up, got breasts, hips and her period. And suddenly she also got told to call back tomorrow. Every single day."

"You're bitter?"

"No." She realized she wanted him to understand, although she couldn't have said why. "I'm not bitter. My parents and I talked it over, and we decided that acting was fun when it was easy. But it wasn't fun if I had to struggle and face rejection and feel worthless just because I was growing up. So I quit, with their blessing, and I never went back to it.''

"But you hide your identity."

"No. My identity *is* Kelley O'Flynn Samuels. Sammy O'Flynn never existed. I can't hide someone who never was."

"You hate actors."

"Come on, that's putting more energy into it than it's worth. I don't hate actors. I just don't trust them. I remember how easy it is to believe you're that person everyone thinks you are. You act cute and funny on-screen enough, you think you're cute and funny. You act tough and cynical on-screen, you think you're tough and cynical. I just know how it is. I was there."

Up close he liked her face even better than he had from far away. Her skin was luscious, peach tinted, freckle splotched and perfect. Her eyelashes were shades darker than her hair, a remarkable contrast to her aquamarine eyes. He had the absurd urge to bury his hands in the wealth of her hair and test the softness of her lips against the harshness of her words.

It was an absurd urge. He took a step back. "You were a kid when you acted. Some of us aren't kids. We're adults, with adult perceptions. I no more believe I'm the guy I play on-screen than I believe *you're* incapable of forgiving. Or of being wrong about someone."

She stared at him. Her cheeks grew warm as he stared back. "You said you had another reason," she said at last. "What was it?"

"I have to hire a bodyguard. If I don't, the police are going to start following me around. In fact they followed me here."

She hadn't given the matter any thought, but she knew immediately why the police weren't going to take chances with Griff Bryant. She nodded. "Go on."

"I have a daughter. She's coming to stay with me. If anything happened to her . . ."

He was even a better actor than she'd thought, or his feelings for his daughter were as powerful as any father's. She felt herself softening toward him, though all her internal alarms were screeching maniacally. "You want to be sure she's protected, too?"

"I don't think anyone's out to get me. But if they were, threatening Tara would be the best way to do it."

"What does any of this have to do with me?"

"I need a bodyguard. I want you."

She couldn't help herself. She snorted. "Me?"

"That's funny?"

"Hysterical." She slid off the counter and faced him. "Why?"

"Felice suggested it."

"And you always take her advice?"

"The reasons are good. You're trained to do this kind of work. I've already seen you in action, so I know you're no slouch. A woman would be less intimidating for Tara to have around. A woman would be easier to pass off as my constant companion."

"Whoa. I get it. You don't want the world to know Griff Bryant needs a bodyguard. So you'd pass a little woman off as, what? A lady friend? Your hairdresser? No one would think I might be packing a gun, and your macho reputation would remain untarnished?"

He stood quietly for a moment, then he shook his head. "It's not going to work." He looked at his watch. "I'll call Suzy's editor and tell him exactly what happened. Thanks for the coffee."

He was halfway to the door before she stopped him. "Are you leaving because I made a point or because I didn't?"

His smile was perfunctory and as cold as his eyes. "You decide."

"Don't bother to call the paper. I don't want my name in it. You were right about that."

He nodded. "Fine."

"Thanks for stopping by to explain."

He was gone before she could say anything else. Not that she would have known exactly what to say. She was rarely unsure of herself, rarely unsure what she was feeling. But as she watched him get in a white Volvo and drive away, she felt the emotional equivalent of yesterday's assault. She didn't know what was happening to her, and she didn't know why. She just knew that she didn't like it. Not at all.

Chapter 5

Felice's new house looked like an armed camp—not that the "armed" part showed. Only someone with Kelley's experience would know that most of the people striding in and out the front door had at least a .38 strapped somewhere on their bodies.

She was rarely armed herself. The gun-toting detective, ready to whip out his revolver and shoot random bad guys on the streets, was a myth. She owned a gun, but since becoming a private investigator, she had only shot at targets. Most of her jobs were perfectly safe, and she was skilled enough to keep safe while doing the occasional job that wasn't.

Today she wore her .38 under the jacket of a linen blazer.

On the sidewalk she passed Simon and his wife, Tate, and exchanged greetings. They were an interesting couple, Simon blond and regal, Tate small, dark and very pregnant. Kelley hadn't met either of them before yesterday, but now they felt like old friends. A little gunfire was a lot more effective than chitchat at bringing people together.

Felice was waiting by the front door. "They're heading back to D.C." She waved her last goodbye to the Vandergriffs, then shut the door behind Kelley. "Everyone thinks it's better if Simon and Josiah aren't in the same place for a while. Simon's furious, but Tate's calming him down.''

''I liked them both.''

''There are some terrific people in the world. Then there's the other kind.''

Kelley followed Felice into the living room, cataloging the remodeling that had been completed since she was last here. The house had been in sad disrepair when Felice and Gallagher had made an offer on it. Since then they had performed miracles. Carpets had been removed, and the floors beneath had been refinished, walls had been replastered and painted. The house was sun flooded and welcoming now. They had made it theirs.

''How's your mother?'' she asked.

''Well, Mother and Daddy left for home about an hour ago, with some of the relatives. We told Mother she would be more useful making sure everyone kept calm and didn't have serious aftereffects from the ruckus yesterday. Hopefully that will keep her busy for a while.''

''Does she blame you?''

Felice gave a little smile. ''Actually I think she's in her element. Nothing this exciting has ever happened to her. She pulled herself together immediately and started ordering everybody around.''

''And you wondered where you got your taste for excitement.''

Felice, still paler than Kelley had ever seen her, flopped down on a sofa and motioned for Kelley to join her. ''Did Griff show up at your house yet?''

''I understand you sent him.''

''He came to find out who you were. We talked.''

''Whatever made you suggest I might want to be his bodyguard?''

''Come on, Kell. You're perfect for the job.''

''Come on, Felice,'' she mimicked. ''You've got something up your sleeve.''

''You think I've got time right now to play Cupid?'' Felice leaned back and closed her eyes. ''My wedding was annulled by a few thousand blanks yesterday. My relatives will never speak to me again, the church is going to excommunicate me, the newspapers are having a field day, Josiah and his FBI buddies won't tell me anything they've found out, and I'm still not an honest woman!''

"I think if you were hanging from a cliff by one fingernail, you'd still be plotting and manipulating."

"Look, Griff's an actor. Who knows his kind of life and the demands on it better than you do, Sammy O'Flynn? And you could pretend to fit yourself into his life in a way that a man never could."

"Now *you're* doing it."

Felice sat up and frowned. "Doing what?"

"You're trying to protect him from looking like a wimp. He wants me to be his bodyguard because no one could guess. What's the big deal if the world sees some beefy male following him everywhere he goes? So he needs a bodyguard. Who cares? He's not the bulletproof stud he plays on-screen. Why doesn't he just face it and go on from there?"

"Boy, are you wrong."

"Am I? I know you're really taken with this guy."

"I'm taken with him because he's an honest, decent person who's more interested in setting the world to rights than in shooting it full of holes."

"Maybe he is, and maybe he isn't. But he still wants me following him around because I'm little, cute and female, and I don't look deadly."

"When I suggested you, he hit the ceiling. He doesn't want to put a woman in danger—"

"So he's a sexist pig on top of everything else?"

"Listen to yourself!" Felice pushed her hair off her forehead. "You're upset if he wants a woman, and you're upset if he doesn't! Griff doesn't want to put anybody in danger, male or female, but he has to have a bodyguard. He said you'd been through enough already, and he wasn't going to subject you to more. I told him that you'd be safer following him around than just going about your business. That's why he asked you."

"You've lost me."

"Look, I don't think anyone was aiming at you yesterday. For that matter, I don't think they were aiming at Griff, either.

But there's a small possibility one of you was the target. Now, I know you. You won't take that threat serious for long. You'll carry a gun for a day or two, then you'll figure it's more trouble than it's worth. You'll make some stupid remark about Neuf protecting you and let it go at that.''

Kelley realized she had done just that with Griff early this morning at the station. Felice knew her too well. "All right, so maybe I can be arrogant sometimes. But how is following Griff around going to help me?''

"If you're watching out for him, you'll automatically be watching out for yourself.''

"And he believed this bull?''

"Kell, think about it! The guy needs you. He's going to pay you to take care of him. You can take care of yourself at the same time. What could be more perfect?''

"If I'm in danger, why does he want me anywhere near him or his daughter?''

"I think he believes the biggest danger to Tara would come from the constant reminder that her father wasn't safe. She's confused and insecure. That's why he doesn't want a man. And don't forget, Griff saw the gunman's face, too, though not clearly. If the guy tries to eliminate you because you can identify him, he'll go after Griff, too. You'll be safer together than either of you would be alone.''

"My head's spinning.''

"Your head's empty, except for a few leftover prejudices and knee-jerk reactions.''

Kelley winced, but she and Felice had been friends too long to be offended at anything the other said. "Think so?''

"Know so. Now, help me figure out how to get Josiah to tell me what he and his buddies are doing.''

Kelley stood. She had something else she had to do, and she'd planned to do it even before she'd talked with Felice. "I'll pass, thanks.''

Felice followed her to the door. "Josiah put a little pressure on the phone company. We'll be getting a phone up here today. I'll call you as soon as I know the number.''

"You'll be calling me to see what I've decided to do.''

"We're still partners. Whatever you do affects me.''

"Just worry about you and Gallagher. You've still got a wedding to get through."

Felice moved aside to let yet another in the procession of clean-cut men in suits into her house. "You think we'd try to get married again? You've heard of omens?"

"No. Are they anything like true love and happily-ever-afters?"

Felice gave her a bear hug.

Griff's house was palatial. The sight of it was enough to make Kelley want to turn her station wagon around and start back down the winding road that led into Palm Springs. There was no room to turn around, however, not without going into Griff's driveway. And if she drove up to his front door anyway, she might as well stop and apologize.

She had always prided herself on giving everyone a chance. As a cop she had never assumed, as some of her fellow officers had, that a suspect was guilty until proven innocent. She had been careful, but she had never made up her mind about someone until all the facts were in. Apparently though, she, like everyone, had her vulnerable spot. And Griff had jabbed his profession right smack-dab in the middle of it.

The woman who opened Griff's door was formidable. The word *large* just didn't get the job done. There was a large frame and about six feet from the soles of her feet to the gray frizz on top of her head to accommodate double the calories anyone else could consume. Kelley wondered why Griff needed a bodyguard when he had this woman.

She explained who she was and asked to see Griff. She was left to wait on the front porch, a towering, shake-roofed, architect's showpiece. She had considered leaving twice and was working on the third time when the door opener reappeared and ushered her into a sunny room graced by a white-and-gold piano decorated with ornate candelabra.

She wandered around the room, but there was little to see other than the piano. Furnishings were minimal. Almost everything was white—white marble floor, two straight-backed wooden chairs and a white deacon's bench to go with them. In the corner a granite statue of a bird with no wings passed for decoration.

When no one arrived, she sat down at the piano and tried to pick out a one-fingered tune, but all the notes sounded alike to her. She was just about to start on another when she heard voices outside the door. Immediately she knew she was eavesdropping on an argument.

"You said you'd be bringing her next week, Joanne. Her room's not even ready."

Kelley recognized Griff's voice. The woman's that answered was unfamiliar.

"So sorry," she said. From her tone, Kelley guessed she was anything but. "I hate to mess up your orderly existence, but I've had it with our little girl. You deal with her for a while. You're her father, though I'm not sure she remembers. I've raised her by myself all these years, and now it's your turn."

"What's wrong?" Griff asked in his cynical screen voice. "Can't you dress her up anymore and parade her around? Or does she remind Pierre that you're past thirty?"

"Maybe it's just that I'm tired of raising her alone! Did you think of that? I'm not a great mother, but I'm a better parent than you've been! At least I've been there most of the time."

Kelley expected a denial, but there was silence. "There's no point in trading accusations. I want her here," Griff said at last. "I always have. But I think there were better ways for us to make this transition."

"I'm fresh out of patience."

"You didn't even say goodbye to her."

"I doubt if she noticed."

"Will you at least give her a call before you leave the country?"

There was another silence. "I'll call," the woman said at last.

The voices grew dimmer. The music room had a view of the front sidewalk. Kelley told herself she didn't need to see the woman to whom Griff had spoken, the woman who was obviously his ex-wife. She told herself she didn't care what his taste in women had once been, but she found herself at the window, anyway.

The woman heading down the sidewalk was blond and tanned. Neither the shade of blond nor the tan looked as if Mother Nature had had anything to do with it, but the woman was still stunning in a Beverly Hills sort of way.

Kelley wondered what Tara looked like with Griff and this woman as parents.

She heard voices in the hallway again. She turned just as Griff opened the door. She had been caught spying, but she didn't care. She cared more that he looked pained to see her, as if he expected her to shred whatever part of him the past few minutes had left intact.

"Since I had no choice but to listen, I thought I might as well get the full impact," she said.

He stopped in the doorway and leaned against the frame, folding his arms. "Did you?"

"She's quite glamorous."

"Joanne didn't have much of a childhood herself. I think she's tried with Tara, but she could only manage some semblance of coping when Tara couldn't talk back."

"And she talks back now?"

"Like a pro."

"Is Tara glad to be here?"

He shrugged.

"Well, I'm not glad to be here." Kelley walked toward him. "And I'm not glad I heard all that. Your personal life's none of my business."

"Why be any different than the rest of the world? My personal life's everybody's business."

She nodded sympathetically. "I remember how that was."

He didn't react. "What are you doing here?"

"I came to apologize. Which is why I'm not glad, by the way. I don't like apologizing. I don't usually have to."

"Why not?"

"Well, when I make mistakes, I usually bear the brunt of them myself. I don't involve anybody else, so I don't have to say I'm sorry."

"You could try a practice run, just to be sure you get it right."

"Thanks, but once is enough."

She hadn't come to admire him; in fact she had made a conscious decision not to admire him since the day she'd discovered he was to be at Felice's wedding. Now, however, she gave in to temptation. He was wearing jeans, without a designer label in sight. His green T-shirt was faded, and the pocket needed a few more stitches to keep it in place. His hair was rumpled, as if he'd recently run his hands through it in frustration; his feet were bare. He wasn't trying to impress anybody. Apparently until just minutes ago he hadn't realized anybody would be there to impress.

He looked like a man thoroughly at home with himself. She realized for the first time that this confidence, this comfort with who he was, shone through on the screen. It was this, as much as his rugged good looks and his pirate swagger, that appealed to his fans. He was the man he was, and apparently fame hadn't affected that.

"I misjudged you," she said. "I was wearing my Hollywood blinders. I'm sorry."

"What did you misjudge?"

"I realize now that you weren't trying to save face by hiring me. I jumped to conclusions."

"Unprofessional of you, wasn't it?"

"Yeah. Rule number one in investigation. If you jump to a conclusion, it's going to be wrong."

"I'll rub it in and point out something I think you forgot."

"I guess I deserve this."

"You survived Hollywood. Do you think you're the only person in history who has?"

"But I got out."

"Intact, too. Or isn't that true?"

She didn't have to think about it. "Intact."

"Then use rule number two and put the facts together slowly and carefully."

"I get the point."

"Good." He was about to say something else when a girl's voice called from somewhere behind him.

"Griff?"

He turned. "I'm in here, Tara."

The child who came to stand beside him and stare at Kelley looked nothing like her father or what Kelley had seen of her mother. Her hair was light brown and straight, her features indistinct, as if they were waiting for some inner signal that would come in late adolescence. She wasn't plain, and she wasn't pretty. A frown or a smile might have edged her toward one or the other, but there was no expression on her face except boredom.

Griff made the introductions, and Kelley walked forward and extended her hand. Tara took it, then dropped it as fast as she dared.

"How's your room coming?" Griff asked her.

"It's all right."

"Your mother says if you make a list, she'll have your things sent from her house."

Tara shrugged. "I don't care what she sends."

"You must have something you want. How about that stuffed-animal collection I saw last time I was there?"

"I don't want it anymore."

"If you change your mind, the staff will be there to send things after your mother and Pierre leave. Or we can drive in and pick up anything you want."

She gave no sign she had heard. "May I watch TV?"

"Sure. I thought we'd go for a swim before dinner."

The girl didn't answer.

Kelley realized Tara was staring at her. The effect was chilling; the eyes were Griff's. "Well, I've got to be going," Kelley said. "I'll let myself out."

Griff shook his head. "I'll walk you to your car."

Kelley watched Tara disappear down the hall without another word to either of them. She told herself to keep quiet; she told herself that rule number three in her line of work was never to get involved. But there had been something about Griff's daughter that had hooked her and reeled her in so fast that she hadn't even had time to realize she'd been in the water. "That's one unhappy kid."

"I know."

"She calls you Griff."

"That's what she hears her mother call me."

"Does she ever smile?"

"Her smile would scare you to death."

Griff started toward the front door, and Kelley walked beside him. She couldn't make herself drop the subject of Tara. "I'd say she's thirteen."

"She'll be twelve after Christmas."

"I was twelve when I quit acting. It's a tough age. You want stuffed animals, but you don't want anybody to know it. Later, you compromise. You let boys give you stuffed animals, and that makes it all right."

"So I should find some twelve-year-old hunk to buy up her collection and give it back to her?"

"You should take a deep breath and prepare," she warned. "You're going to have a hell of a year."

"I don't know her. She isn't going to come to me with her problems. I'm a stranger."

Kelley was surprised he had revealed so much. "Not a stranger. You're her father. No matter what she calls you."

She didn't say anything else until they reached her car—she was surprised it hadn't been towed as an eyesore. Griff opened the door for her before she could stop him. She started to get in, but at the last moment she faced him. Her words surprised them both. "Do you still want a bodyguard?"

"I still *need* a bodyguard. I've never wanted one." He hiked his thumb toward the road behind her. "Case in point."

She looked over her shoulder and saw a white sedan cruise slowly by. She recognized the man behind the wheel. "He's a good cop," she said. She hesitated before she spoke again. She hadn't come to Griff's house to tell him she'd changed her mind about his offer. She had come solely to apologize—or so she'd thought. She wasn't even sure what had changed her mind.

"If I take the job," she said, "who am I going to be?"

He shrugged.

"I'd have to be someone who went everywhere with you and someone who made sense tagging along. I'd have to be able to live with you without raising eyebrows."

"Then you'd have to be my lover."

Her eyes didn't flicker, but her insides were twanging a tune even she could recognize. "Your *pretend* lover."

"I can live with it. Can you?"

She asked herself if she could. Had she jumped into something here that wasn't going to be a good arrangement for either of them? "I'm not exactly your type," she pointed out.

"Really?" He surprised her by flashing his famous grin. "What is my type?"

"I think it walked down the front sidewalk a little while ago, tanned and gorgeous."

"I was nineteen when I married Joanne. I'm thirty-two."

"Then you think I'd be believable?"

"I think you underestimate yourself." Griff touched her shoulder. "And you definitely underestimate me. Still."

He touched easily, spontaneously. She liked that, and she liked the weight of his hand, the connection it signaled. She wasn't going to let him know, though.

She started dictating the rules. "I'll do it but for a limited time. If this goes long-term, you'll have to find somebody else."

"It's not going long-term, because I'm not the person they were trying to kill yesterday."

She ignored that, since she wasn't sure it was true. "As soon as the press gets wind of this, you'll introduce me as Sammy O'Flynn, not Kelley Samuels. We'll have to lie about where I've been and what I've been doing since I quit acting. If some reporter tracks down my past and finds out the truth about my real line of work, you could look pretty silly."

"I've always wanted to do comedy."

She smiled. "While I'm with you, there can't be any other women in your life. Nothing that will make our arrangement look suspect."

"If you're following me everywhere, there certainly *won't* be any other women."

"There's no one in your life who's going to be hurt?"

He shook his head.

"I agree that Tara shouldn't know who I am and why I'm here. She's going to be scared to death if she thinks you need a bodyguard. You've already introduced me as Kelley, but she probably understands how names get changed in this part of the world. We'll tell her I'm a friend who's sold her house and needs a place to stay for a little while. We'll make it clear we're not lovers, no matter what the gossip is.''

"That would be best," he agreed.

"I'll need your schedule for, let's say the next three weeks. Hopefully this won't go on much beyond that. And I'll need a blueprint of the house, information on your security system." She ticked off a few more items. "I'll want to be in the bedroom closest to yours. That will do for a start."

"Thorough, aren't you?"

"If I'm not, you might die to regret it."

"When are you moving in?"

"I've got to get down to the station and help them put together a composite picture of the guy I wrestled with yesterday. Then I'll go home to get a few things and feed Neuf. I can come back up then."

"We need to be seen together in public. Somewhere to start the rumors so it won't look odd when people find you're living here."

"An announcement?"

He nodded. "Of sorts." He thought for a few seconds. "I'm invited to a party in Laurel Canyon tonight. I wasn't going to go, but maybe we should go together."

The idea made her stomach turn, but she saw the logic. "What about Tara?"

"I'll have dinner with her before we leave. Mrs. Robbert can probably stay overnight. She has a room here."

"I'll ask the police to keep an eye on the house while we're gone." She shook her head when he looked pained. "We aren't going to take any chances, not while I'm in charge. They're discreet. Tara won't even know she's being watched."

"I don't want to take any chances. Not with my daughter."

"Good." She got into the car and let Griff close the door behind her.

"I'll pick you up at seven? It's a long drive."

"I'll be ready." She slid her key in the ignition. "By the way, what kind of party are we talking about?"

"Cocktail. Just short of black-tie."

"Gotcha." She started the car before he could ask whether she had anything to wear. "I'll see you at seven." She waved goodbye and pulled out of his driveway.

Halfway down the mountain she asked herself what on earth she had gotten into. But *why* was a different matter. The reason had something to do with a child with ice blue eyes and a father with bewilderment in his. She told herself she wasn't going to get involved. She was just going to be there; somebody had to be.

It might as well be her.

Chapter 6

Seldom worn but never out of style, the collection of cocktail dresses in Kelley's closet could have been the envy of a game-show hostess. They came from her mother, a free-lance costumer who had worked on close to a hundred movies before she and Kelley's father moved to a small town on the Oregon coast where he sold antiques, and she ran a vintage clothing shop.

The dresses she'd gotten for Kelley had all been worn by actresses, famous and not-so-famous, or by stunt women and extras. Each dress had a history. One had been worn by a movie murder victim, another by a prostitute. Several had been worn by James Bond's vamps, and one special dress, purchased at a studio auction, had been worn by Jean Harlow.

Kelley loved all of them as she loved the other Hollywood nostalgia pieces in her house. Her father, who had worked as a set decorator for twenty years, had found it difficult to say no to any negotiable prop or furnishing, large or small, that "spoke" to him when a movie was completed. There had been times in Kelley's childhood when the family home had been so crowded she had needed a map to get from one end to another. Now her own house was much the same way.

The dress she chose for her debut as Griff's lover was dull gold oriental brocade. Tiny pleats flowed away from the high neck and bared her shoulders. The pleats were caught and cinched at the waist, then sprang free again until they ended just below her knees. She had never had the chance to wear it herself. A reed-slender man, padded in just the right places, had worn it when he had doubled for a famous actress in a romantic thriller. The dress had survived unscathed; the man had broken an arm.

She chose hose of the same gold cast and topaz drop earrings to wear with it. Her last accessory, her gun, went into a bronze mesh bag the color of her sandals.

She was trying to reason with her hair when the doorbell rang. Neuf sounded the alarm. She tossed her brush on the dresser and picked up her purse.

Griff was standing on her porch. He was wearing a light gray sports coat that looked handwoven and hand tailored. She was sure that in her days as a costumer, her mother would have loved to stretch fabric over Griff Bryant's broad shoulders.

"Did the police follow you down?" she asked in greeting.

Griff didn't answer. He wasn't sure what he had expected, but it wasn't this. Kelley looked as expensive, as notable, as the dress she was wearing. Her hair was pulled back from her face into a rioting mane of curls, and the face itself had been artfully shaded and enhanced.

She watched him stare at her until she couldn't help but smile. "You like?"

His answering smile was the same one that sent actresses onscreen tumbling into bed with him. "I like."

She ignored her very female rush of pleasure. "Bet you thought I didn't have a dress I could wear."

"It occurred to me."

"I have a wardrobe suitable for any part I have to play. Mostly that means jeans or dresses that no one would ever be able to remember, but I could do Suzy Slander better than she does herself."

"You're still acting, aren't you?"

"I suppose. Once it's in the blood . . ." She shrugged.

"You really are perfect for this."

"I'm glad to be perfect for something."

She lifted the small suitcase she had packed and started past him, but he barred her way. "At my house you were so busy asking me questions that I didn't ask you an obvious one. Is there a man somewhere who's going to be unhappy that you're living with me?"

"Most definitely. My father."

"Your father?"

"You think *I* don't like actors?"

"If your parents didn't like actors, why were you allowed to act?"

"I fell into it." She edged past him, and he took her case so that she could lock the door. "Literally."

He was growing more curious by the second. "Is this story going to take us all the way to Hollywood?"

"Maybe. If you want it to." She touched his arm, an ingenuous gesture that had served her well in *Strawberry Finn.* "Look, we don't have to be friends or even friendly. My job's to protect you. We don't have to chat, and you don't have to get to know me. I'm not going to be offended if you like silence."

"You'll just sort of disappear into the shadows?"

"I do it well."

He paused just long enough to make the next words important. "I don't subscribe to the people-as-objects school of thought."

"I'm not implying you do. But nobody enjoys being shadowed twenty-four hours a day. Some of the time it might just be easier if you could pretend I'm not here."

"You'd be a hard woman to ignore."

She had an internal debate on the reasons why as she followed him down the sidewalk and got into his car. They had traveled nearly thirty miles and begun to hit heavier traffic before he spoke again. "Tell me how you got into acting."

She had given him an out, and he had refused to take it. Kelley reminded herself that he was paying her; it wasn't up to her to set the ground rules.

"My parents both worked in the film industry. By the time I was six, my father was lead man on a set-decorating crew. Then the director on a film he was doing had a falling-out with the decorator and fired him. There wasn't time to call anybody else in, so the director asked my father to take over. Daddy wanted everything to be perfect so he'd be called to be decorator again.

"The film was about some genius kid, and there was this one scene where the kid walks into his bedroom. It was just a flash, but in those ten, fifteen seconds, the camera had to make an absolute statement about this kid's life. Daddy knew what adults would expect to see in the room, but he wanted to be sure that kids—it was a family film—would be impressed, too. So one evening he took me and my three brothers down to the set to see what we thought."

"Three brothers?"

"Older brothers. I was spoiled rotten."

He flashed her a smile, the first since they had gotten in the car. "I can believe it."

"Well, I was interested in the set for about three seconds. I wasn't allowed to touch anything, so I just sort of wandered off. There was another set not too far away that was a lot more interesting. I was in my Tarzan phase—actually I think my brothers only let me play Cheetah, but I'm sure I wanted to be Tarzan—"

"Not Jane?"

"Jane was a girl."

"Makes sense to me."

"Anyway..." She stopped and turned to look behind them. She was silent for a full minute.

"Anything wrong?"

"No. Good."

"Good?"

"A car's been following us for a while, but it just turned off."

He hadn't noticed she was paying attention to anything besides him. "We're on the freeway. Cars have to follow if they're behind us."

"This car switched lanes every time you did. And you switch lanes more than anybody I've ever seen."

"I learned to drive here. I'd switch lanes on a two-lane road." He switched again, as if to prove his point. "The whole time you were talking you were watching the side mirror?"

She turned around again. "That's what I'm paid to do. Watch cars, remember license plates, entertain you with stories of my childhood, shoot to kill. You know, the usual detective stuff."

"You can't shoot to kill if you're not wearing a gun."

"Notice I carry my purse on my right side? The latch is just fingertip level and takes one click to open." She glanced at him long enough to watch his lips compress in a grim line. "Sorry, but I never got beyond green belt in judo. And even a black belt doesn't stop a bullet. I'll be pals with this gun for the duration."

He didn't like to be reminded that she wasn't just an appealing woman he was taking to a party. And he particularly didn't like knowing she was carrying a gun. A gun drew the line between them with indelible ink. He sped up and switched lanes again. "Finish your story."

She heard his irritation and thought she knew the cause. What man wanted to be escorted anywhere by a gun-toting female sworn to protect him? It violated all the stereotypes that men were so comfortable with, especially a man whose movie roles thrived on them.

She knew better than to address that, though. Her life story was safer than a discussion about male chauvinism. She picked up where she'd left off.

"The set I found when I wandered off was supposed to be the interior of an old movie theater. There were steps going up to this dark, creepy balcony, and there was a rope hanging just off the edge of the railing that the key grip or gaffer had left there. I decided that I could climb up to the balcony, grab the rope like Tarzan and swing down to the floor. It looked easy."

"And did you?"

"Well, I tried. I swung off, but I ended up dangling from the rope because it stopped about twelve feet from the floor. This man came running up, shouting for me to hang on. I thought it was very exciting. The rope was knotted at intervals, so I could even wrap my legs around it while I waited. I made it swing back and forth and did a few practice Tarzan yells. Somebody moved a crane, and the guy who'd spotted me got up on the camera platform and grabbed my legs.''

"You should have been banned from the lot forever.''

"But it was Hollywood, land of make-believe. Remember? The guy who grabbed me was Tom Fortney.''

Tom Fortney, director of numerous award-winning films, had been a Hollywood household name. Griff, like everyone else, had his own Tom Fortney stories. "I knew him,'' he told her. "I worked on one of his pictures as an extra before he died. He was quite a man.''

"He was looking for a rambunctious little girl to play a scene in his next movie. He'd had his heart set on a redhead. Letting me play the part was the only way my father could get out of disgrace for losing sight of me.''

Griff glanced at her, but her eyes were on the mirror. "From playing Tarzan to becoming America's tomboy sweetheart.''

She shrugged. "Directors liked working with me. My parents weren't pushy. In fact they were happier if I didn't get a role.''

"Do you miss it?''

"Sometimes. I thought about doing stunts for a while.''

"Don't.''

Kelley was surprised at his tone. She didn't know much about Griff other than his on-screen persona, but she pulled out what she did know and tried to piece it together. Her facts were deficient.

"You sound convinced,'' she said tentatively.

He realized the correlation between bad memories and the Volvo's burst of speed. He forced himself to let up on the accelerator. "Movies are movies. They're entertainment. They're not worth risking lives for.''

"You must have seen some accidents.''

"A close friend of mine was killed on the set of my last film.''

She searched her memory again. "*One Way Ticket* was one of yours?''

"Yeah.''

She remembered hearing about the accident. The fact that the movie had been one of Griff's had completely escaped her notice. "I never heard many details, just that someone had been killed. But was the man who died a stuntman? I thought he was an actor."

"He was. His name was Drake Scott. *One Way Ticket* was his fifth film. He had a small role, but a good one. We expected him to get a lot of notice for it."

He didn't have to complete his thoughts out loud. Both of them knew that Drake had gotten more notice dead than he ever would have received alive.

"Does talking about it upset you?" she asked.

"No more so than not talking about it."

"What happened? I remember something about an explosion, but that's all. I was immersed in work all the way up to my eyeballs while it was news."

"The film's about a select group of fighter pilots during World War II, sort of the American equivalent of the kamikazes. The men in this unit are always given an escape route, but they know that the odds are they won't be able to pull it off. In Drake's big scene, he manages to find a way back from his mission, although he and his plane had been shot full of holes. He gets out of the plane and starts crawling away from it, but when he's just a few feet from safety, the plane explodes. I'm running toward him, and I get blown off my feet by the explosion. Drake dies instantly. Unfortunately he really did."

She heard a man trying to be matter-of-fact when he obviously didn't feel that way. Her voice softened in response. "What went wrong?"

"The explosion went off too soon. Drake crawled too slow."

"Were you hurt?"

"I would have been if my timing had been just the least bit off. It wasn't."

"There was an investigation, wasn't there?" Kelley stopped watching the cars behind them and turned to Griff. "What did they find?"

He shrugged. "It was just one of those things. There wasn't much left after the explosion for anybody to sift through, but they investigated as thoroughly as they could. Everyone was satisfied that all precautions had been taken by the special-effects department. The powder man who set off the charge had set a hundred others. Nobody really blames him, but he won't work in Hollywood again.''

"Somebody had to be responsible, huh?''

For just a moment his eyes flicked to hers. "We take a lot of chances to bring the public what they want.''

"This hit you pretty hard, didn't it?''

"I have some real questions about what I do for a living.''

Kelley sat back and waited, but he didn't say anything else. She focused on the side mirror again to give him privacy, although by now it was obvious they weren't being followed. Whatever questions Griff had, though, she was certain he wasn't in the mood to discuss them now. She was sorry she had inadvertently brought up such a painful subject, but she was glad to know a little more about what made Griff Bryant tick.

They didn't exchange more than small talk again until they had gotten to Laurel Canyon, west of Hollywood. Griff wound his way along the base of a mountain, then turned off on a small residential street and started up. "I can't promise the party will be fun," he said, "but the views from the house are spectacular.''

Kelley focused on him. "How close are we?''

"Five, six miles. Ten minutes.''

"Well, that's just about right. I've been saving my recent history to tell you just before we arrived.''

"Oh?''

"I went it to be fresh in your mind because you have to remember every word.''

"You'd be surprised. I'm capable of retaining what I hear. Sometimes for as long as an hour or two.''

She ignored the sarcasm. "I graduated from high school and went to UCLA for two years. That part's true. This part isn't. I dropped out of college because I had a chance to work for a hospital doing public relations. I've made that my career. Now I have a low-profile job in an upscale company in Desert Palm, but I don't give any information about that because my employers wouldn't appreciate the publicity.''

"Low-profile, upscale. Or was that low-scale, up-profile?''

He shot her a smile, and she was glad to see he could, after relating the tragedy of his friend's death.

"Anything else?" he asked.

"We've known each other for five months, but we've been keeping our relationship very private. I don't want you to go into my part in Felice's wedding, but if it somehow becomes known that I was the woman you 'rescued,' you're to say that you went after me because you were afraid I might be hurt."

"Actually that's true."

"Then it won't be a lie. So much the better."

"Where did we meet?"

"Let's see. At a friend's house. A small party. Our living arrangement is private—we're not advertising how serious we are."

"How close are we supposed to be?"

"Very. We just make it clear we're not after publicity." She thought of a new, possibly difficult angle. "Have you been seen a lot recently with another woman?"

"No."

"Have you been seen recently with a lot of different women?"

"One—no, two."

"How serious have you looked?"

He laughed. "What does that mean?"

"Did you act cuddly and smoochy, like you were going to take them home for the night?"

"I didn't like either woman very much. Both were business."

"Great. I'd have to change the story a little if it looks like I've got competition out there."

"You can keep it like it is."

"Tell me about the party. I'll be expected to know where I am."

"It's just one of an endless round. Joe Burke is giving it. Do you know him?"

"No. Who is he?"

"He's a producer. He was probably around when you were acting, but I doubt he was doing films with kids. His stuff runs to the seedy and sordid. He thinks it's high art, a lot of reviewers think he borders on porn."

"Why are we going, then?"

"His parties are legendary, and everybody comes, even people who wouldn't work for or with him. It'll be a good place for you to be seen."

"Sammy O'Flynn grows up?"

"Something like that."

"And you'll remember to call me Sammy?"

"When we walk through that door you'll be Sammy O'Flynn, my hush-hush live-in, low-profile, upscale woman."

"If you're asked anything you don't know, don't make up answers that might not agree with mine. Just smile and say something like 'I bet Sammy would rather answer that,' or 'I'll defer to Sammy on that one.'"

"Relax. I'll be fine. I lie for a living, remember? Look out the window."

She sat back, confident he wouldn't forget the story. "It's beautiful up here, isn't it?"

"You pay a few bucks for the privilege of roosting this high."

"I grew up down below."

He guided his car along the winding road, past elaborate houses that shared exorbitant price tags in common, if not architecture. "Your folks didn't become millionaires when you became a star?"

"They invested what I made, and I used most of it to help open the office in Palm Springs and buy my house." She saw lights ahead and cars stopped on the road. Men in white sports coats were helping the guests from their cars, which they then drove away to park. "Looks like we're here."

"Worried?"

"You pay me to worry."

He pulled in line to wait for a valet. When he turned to her, his voice was hushed, the kind of hush that made people snap to attention. "I meant worried about the party. You've reminded me frequently tonight that I pay you. I just thought you might have some feelings about being here, like how it's going to feel to see people you might not have seen in years."

She ignored the warning sign. "Who's taking care of whom here?"

"Does it have to be that way?" He flung his arm along the back of her seat and cupped his hand over her bare shoulder.

"You've got the gun, so I'm not supposed to have any feelings toward you? I'm paying you, so I'm not allowed to be considerate or interested in your past or..."

"Or?" she prompted.

His voice got even quieter. "Anything else."

"Want to define that?"

"It's a catchall category. Use your imagination." His fingers stroked her bare skin, a slow, deceptively casual rotation that reached every nerve ending in her body.

She sat very still. "I told you before, you don't even have to act like I exist. You owe me cooperation and a paycheck, not consideration or interest or anything else."

"I heard you before. You've absolved me of all guilt and shooed away any human instincts that you think acting may have left me. But I don't choose to be absolved or shooed. I choose to be interested."

"Look, it's going to be easier for me if you aren't. Okay? I can protect you best if we keep a distance."

"What kind of distance can we keep if you're only a few feet away? And what kind can we keep if you're supposed to be my lover?" He pulled her closer, moving closer himself as he did. "Don't you know how easy it is to mix fantasy with reality? There are people watching. I'm about to kiss you. When I've finished, will you be able to tell where fantasy started and reality intruded? Or if it did?"

She shut her eyes and forced herself to relax. She could feel the heat of his skin, smell the faint citrus tang of his after-shave before his lips even touched hers. The night was warm, but his lips were warmer. They took possession of hers, promising more than illusion. Her hand crept to his jacket, then inside to rest at his neck. She could feel his pulse beat unsteadily. Hers leapt in response.

He pulled away just a little. "Ready?"

She wished she could see him better, but even if she could, she didn't know if she could trust what she would see in his eyes. He was a consummate actor. "Ready." The voice belonged to a calm woman. The heart thrumming sonic rhythms did not.

"Kelley," he said, pushing a corkscrew lock of hair back from her face.

"Sammy," she reminded him.

He shook his head. "I know who you are. I just wonder if you do."

Chapter 7

Griff's house was impressive from the front, built with swooping lines and odd, eye-catching focal points compatible with the stark mountains behind it. Like most homes in the area, it was the color of sand, but there was natural wood and brick trim to relieve the expanses of stucco, and a weathered cedar shake roof to warm it.

It was the back of the house, however, that was most impressive. A brick terrace edged toward a grotto complete with waterfalls emptying into a huge pool and spa. The grotto was built into the side of the hill and overlooked the valley below. Lush tropical landscaping softened the stark rocky hillside and thrived on the mist rising from the pool.

Kelley would have been more impressed, however, if she had seen it after 7:00 a.m. At six-thirty a visit to the White House wouldn't have made her take much notice.

Suppressing a yawn, she let herself out French doors and walked to the edge of the terrace, her arms folded. "You in the pool," she called. "Listen carefully. Bodyguards guard bodies. The bodies aren't supposed to go sneaking off without the guards."

Griff surfaced and shook the water out of his ears. At the edge of his pool stood a woman with hair the color of the sun just lighting the horizon. A man's shirt tickled her thighs—and his imagination.

"What are you doing here?" He swam to the side of the pool closest to where she stood and pulled himself up, dripping wet, to sit on the edge.

"I'm supposed to be with you, remember? Everywhere you go."

He reached for a towel. "In my own backyard?"

"'Fraid so."

"Where's your gun?"

"This is just a warning. Next time I come fully armed, guns blazing."

"I thought you'd be wiped after last night. We haven't been home for much more than a couple of hours." He dried his face and hair before he slung the towel around his shoulders. "How did you know I was out here?"

"I'm an amazing woman." She sat beside him and dangled her feet in the pool.

He told himself that silent questions about what she was wearing—or wasn't—under the shirt were ungentlemanly. "I suppose this means that from now on if I think you deserve to sleep late, I have to sleep late, too."

"Can you?"

He shook his head. "I guess I'll have to pretend, or at least promise not to come outside."

"You'll still do what you want. I already know you're the kind of guy who'll just sneak off whenever you feel like it."

"I love the impression you have of me."

"Am I right?"

"I'd prefer to think of it as just living my life the way I always have."

"You don't take any of this seriously, do you?"

"You're here, aren't you?"

"Strictly because you don't want to take any chances with Tara's safety."

He didn't deny it. "Apparently you've recovered somewhat from last night."

"Do you go to parties like that very often?"

"As few as I have to. Luckily my reputation supports me. I'm supposed to be the strong, silent type."

"A hermit with an Uzi?"

He grimaced.

"You seemed to be well liked," she said. "Silent type or not."

"*You* were a smashing success."

She stretched her legs out and kicked. The water was warmer than the air and inviting. "I gave an award-winning performance."

"Did you?"

"You don't believe me?"

"You were genuinely glad to see some of those people."

"How do you know?"

"Are you going to deny it?"

She kicked again. "No."

"Sammy O'Flynn was a special little kid. A lot of people loved her."

Kelley wasn't about to admit that it was possible she might have lost sight of that through the years when she'd worked so hard to put distance between Kelley Samuels and America's tomboy sweetheart. The party had been both less and more than she had feared. Less staged and insincere, more a place where friends met friends and enjoyed a rare smogless September evening together.

"What are your plans for the day?" she asked.

"I've canceled all my appointments. I want to spend the day with Tara and register her for school so she can start tomorrow."

Kelley felt a twinge of guilt that she was going to be interfering with this all-important bonding between Tara and her father. As if he had read her thoughts, Griff responded.

"Don't worry that you'll be in the way. It might be better for us if you're around."

"Did you tell her about me last night?"

"Yes."

"And she didn't take it well?"

"How am I supposed to know? She didn't say a thing. She got this look on her face that's hard to describe. She probably looked that way when Joanne told her she was marrying Pierre."

"It's pretty understandable. She thinks I'm going to come between you."

"There's room between us for all the extras on a Cecil B. deMille epic."

"If you haven't spent much time with her, she probably doesn't know you very well. I bet she's frightened."

"I've wanted her with me more. Legally I'm entitled. But joint custody is one of those ideas that's only good on paper."

"You have joint custody?" Kelley was surprised. If nothing else, that kind of arrangement indicated commitment.

He sent her a look that told her he knew what she was thinking. "I insisted on it, but it didn't help much. When she was little, I had to pry her away from her mother. Joanne's second marriage was a bust, so Tara was her little doll, something to play with while she waited for her husband to come home between lovers. When Tara was older, Joanne divorced hubby number two and found other interests. By then Tara was rooted to school and activities in Bel Air. I'd go to pick her up, and she'd be off with her friends. If I found her and insisted she come with me, she'd sulk or find some other way to sabotage our time together."

"Well, you've got time now. A year."

"No. I've got her teenage years. She's not going back to live with Joanne. She can visit, but she's not ever going to live there again."

"Isn't that a little—"

"She needs someone she can count on to get her through the next years. Me."

Despite herself, Kelley was impressed. She only knew a little about the situation between Joanne and Tara, but it was clear from what she had heard yesterday that Tara was no longer wanted by her mother. She was glad Griff was going to stand by his daughter, even if the next years were tough. Too many rebellious kids ended up with nobody caring what happened to them.

She swung her legs out of the water and stood. "I'm going to spend part of the day checking the situation here. But I can tell you right now this area's not safe. Anybody who wanted to could come up the hill the hard way and use any one of a dozen vantage points as a place to shoot from."

"So I don't swim until I find out I'm not a target?"

"You don't swim until I check the area thoroughly. And you don't swim unless I'm here to watch."

He stood and finished drying himself. Viewing her legs from the ground up was an enticement he didn't need. At least standing, he could put them in some perspective.

"Has it occurred to you that anybody who wanted to kill me could have done it anytime, then?" he asked as he handed the towel to her. "Why wait until I was in a church full of people? Why rain blanks and throw smoke bombs for distraction? Why not just come up the hill quietly one day and—" he made a gun with his finger and pointed it at Kelley "—bang?"

"You come up with an answer, you let me know."

"I'll work on it."

Kelley dried her legs and told herself that the incredibly perfect body just an arm's length away was probably incredible because its owner spent hours perfecting it every day, hours a regular working man didn't have the time to spend. She lectured herself about health clubs and weights, about swimming pools and masseuses, rigid diets and personal trainers. When she'd finished, she found that her mouth had still gone dry.

"Are you hungry?"

She realized the perfect body had spoken. "Apparently more than I'd thought," she said ruefully.

He slipped a T-shirt over his head. "Mrs. Robbert will have breakfast ready by eight. She's an early riser, too."

"I can wait."

"I'll make coffee and toast to hold us over."

"I thought you said you didn't cook."

"Why destroy your stereotypes before I had to?"

"I'd better change."

"I don't know, I kind of like the view."

She looked down and realized her shirt completely covered the shorts she had hastily pulled on under them. With studied nonchalance she lifted the tails and tied them at her waist. She gestured to her spattered shorts. "I painted my house in these, but they don't go with your house. Not nearly elegant enough."

He didn't show his disappointment. "I like your house."

"Come on."

"No, I do."

"My house would fit in your living room."

"I *don't* like this house."

"Then why are you here?"

He opened the door. "For the view and the land."

She followed him, scanning the horizon in all directions first. Inside she paid closer attention to the interior than she'd had a chance to before. The house could be interesting. There were nooks and crannies usually only found in older homes, and the construction showed master craftsmanship. The major problem was the furnishings, or lack of them.

Everything was starkly simple, and although she could appreciate simplicity, austerity—bone-chilling austerity—was another matter. "There's nothing wrong with this house that living in it a little wouldn't cure," she said.

"It came like it is, with every furnishing in place. I'm too intimidated to touch anything."

"Someone sold it to you like this? With all their possessions in it?"

"A retired stockbroker and his wife. They got tired of it and wanted a change. They moved to Arizona and started all over."

"I could never leave my stuff behind—not that there's much chance anyone would want any of it."

"Your house gives me a feeling of history."

"My house is a museum." She stopped in the doorway to the kitchen. "This is awful."

He was forced to entertain from time to time. His job required it. Of the hundreds of people who had come through the house, however, not one had ever told him any part of it was awful. He felt like the emperor who couldn't see that the new clothing he was so proud of was simply air. He looked around. "Why is it awful?"

"Well, just look at it. It's all steel and plastic and marble. Lord, I could eat off of any surface in here and be sure it was antiseptic."

He pulled out a drawer and retrieved a loaf of bread. "I could leave the garbage out for a few days if you think it would improve things."

"You even hide the food, for Pete's sake. Kitchens are supposed to have food in them. It's nothing to be ashamed of."

"Well, what would you do?"

She squinted, taking in the whole room.

"Short of a match and a gallon of kerosene," he qualified.

"What do you know about the people who lived here, other than his profession and their destination?"

He shrugged. "Nothing. Why?"

"Let's put two and two together."

"Always working, aren't you?"

"Put lots of butter on mine," she instructed as he opened a cavernous, immaculate refrigerator. "Do you want me to make the coffee?"

"My coffee maker's not in the hallway," he warned.

"It's probably hidden somewhere. We probably don't even get to smell the coffee brewing."

He pointed to a corner cupboard. "In there. Coffee's in the freezer." He opened a cabinet and revealed a toaster on a roll-out platform.

She busied herself finding a new place for the coffee maker as she deduced. "First of all, why do people move to Arizona?"

"To retire? To cultivate cactus?"

"Because the air is cleaner."

"The air's plenty clean here."

"If you come from L.A., you believe that. But what if even a trace of smog made you sick?"

"Personally I thrive on smog."

"You wouldn't have moved to the desert if that was true."

"So?"

"So, let's just say your stockbroker and his wife left Palm Springs because they needed cleaner air. Let's just say that they weren't moving to one of the bigger cities, where the air's full of pollen from flowers and trees homesick residents transplanted from other parts of the country. Let's say they moved to a small desert town.''

"You're guessing."

"Bet I'm right."

He nodded. "You are, but what are you getting at?"

"Look around. There's not a rug in sight anywhere, hardly a piece of furniture with upholstery. There isn't a thing in this house that couldn't be washed or wiped down with a damp rag. Even the food gets hidden, in case it molds.''

"You're saying I'm living in a house designed for allergy sufferers?"

"Have you sneezed once since you moved in here?"

He looked around with new eyes. "I've been bored with the house," he admitted, "but never sick."

"You never considered having a decorator come in?"

"I had a couple draw up their ideas. One thought I ought to turn my bedroom into a sultan's tent. The other thought I ought to use swatches of army camouflage to make a statement about my films.''

She turned on the tap to fill the coffee maker. "Bet the water and the air are filtered.''

He nodded again and wondered why he had never paid attention to the house for long enough to figure this out himself.

"What about Tara's room?" Kelley asked.

"She won't miss any school this year from colds."

"Poor baby."

"Well, what do we do about it?"

Her breath caught at the "we." She wasn't sure she liked being included. "I'm really not trying to take over."

"Really? I thought by the end of the day we might be serving coffee in the hall and tripping over furniture."

"You should be so lucky." She turned to reassemble the coffee maker and saw Tara standing in the doorway. "Well, hi," she said. "Did we wake you up?"

"May I watch TV?" Tara eyed the kitchen scene with displeasure. Kelley noted that her satin pajamas and robe were stiff with embroidery, a fashion statement not meant for sleeping comfort.

"I thought girls your age slept till noon if they could," Griff said.

"I always get up early."

"We were just making some toast and coffee," he said. "There's plenty of toast for you. And there's juice in the refrigerator."

"I don't eat breakfast."

Griff frowned. "You're growing. You need food."

Kelley jumped in. "Come sit with us anyway."

Tara slowly assessed her, ignoring her father. "Griff says you act, too," she said after a thorough going-over.

"I used to. I haven't in years."

"Couldn't you make it?"

"Nope," Kelley said, knowing better than to give Tara what she wanted and take offense. "Didn't want to, either. I was about your age when I quit. I discovered . . ." She lowered her voice, as if to exclude Griff. "Boys."

Tara's expression didn't change, but Kelley hadn't expected it to. "Then why aren't you married?"

"Tara," Griff said firmly, "Kelley's a guest, not a punching bag."

"No, it's a good question," Kelley said. "I'm not married because . . ." She poured coffee in two fragile white porcelain cups that didn't hold nearly enough to suit her. "I don't know why." She handed a cup and saucer to Griff. "It must have something to do with not meeting the right man, or being too busy, or enjoying life alone. Or maybe it's just that nobody's wanted to put up with me so far."

Tara stared at her.

"And I have this dog . . ." Kelley shrugged.

"Kelley was just telling me she thought the house needed some redecorating," Griff said. He picked up the plate of toast and started toward a sterile white breakfast room without even a curtain softening the window. "What do you think?"

"I don't know." Tara sounded as if she couldn't care less.

"I'm not trying to get you to redecorate," Kelley told Griff. "Just soften it up, liven it up a little."

"How?"

"I don't know. It's your house. Rugs, maybe. Some plants. Bright pillows on the sofas, vases with flowers on the tables. Maybe some color on a wall or two. Bowls with fruit on the counters in the kitchen, dish towels, pot holders, bulletin boards. I don't know." She shrugged.

"For somebody who doesn't know, you've got a lot of ideas."

"Can you think of anything else, Tara?" Kelley asked. Tara had followed them, but at a distance, as if she was going to turn and leave at any moment. "What about your room?"

"I was going to have it painted," Griff said when Tara didn't answer. "I thought you were coming a little later, though. Maybe that's good. This way you can tell me exactly what you like. I was going to have it painted pink, like your room in Bel Air."

"I hate my room in Bel Air."

"Then it's good you came when you did."

"I don't care what color you paint it."

"Let me guess. It's white now. Right?" Kelley asked.

Tara's nod was almost imperceptible.

Encouraged, Kelley continued. "Do you like posters?"

The second nod was a copy of the first.

"White's great if it's covered with posters. Maybe you could put some up for instant color. Then, if you got tired of that, you could paint it later, when you know what you want."

The third nod never happened.

"It's your room," Griff said. "You can do whatever you want. When you want."

"May I watch TV?"

"Of course. This is your house." Griff watched every step that Tara took until she was out of sight.

"If you expect miracles," Kelley said softly, "you're going to be disappointed."

"A smile would be nice. One that looks like it didn't ascend from the depths of hell."

She rested her hand on his arm. "You might not see one for a long time. That doesn't mean you're not winning."

"Watch it."

She pulled her hand away. "Watch what?"

"You're getting involved."

She shook her head. "Not a chance. That's unprofessional."

"You talk mean, but you're squishy inside."

She smiled at him over her coffee cup. "Like you?"

His smile was sad. "Maybe."

By late evening Kelley had worked out strategy for protecting Griff's house, and by then there still wasn't any reason not to go ahead with her plans. Around noon Felice had called to say that despite the excess of clean-cut, competent-looking men investigating what was now fondly called "the case of the shotgun wedding," no one seemed to know exactly what was going on.

After dinner Kelley cornered Griff in the kitchen. He was thoughtfully plopping fruit into a green-and-white Mexican pottery bowl.

"Good start," she said, walking up to stand behind him. "Where'd you get the bowl?"

"I unpacked it this afternoon. I bought it for Tara when she was two. We were shopping, and she pointed at it and said 'pretty.'" He stepped back to admire his work and narrowly missed her feet.

She couldn't be the one to tell him the fast-ripening cantaloupes belonged in the refrigerator. The look on his face had probably been worn by Van Gogh and Picasso. *Still Life with Melons* might not be museum quality, but it was all heart.

"We've got to have a talk about the house, then I'm going to go home and get a few more things to bring up," she told him. "Where's Tara?"

"On the phone with a friend from Bel Air. Probably telling her how much she's going to hate living here."

"This won't take long."

He turned and they were only inches apart. Her hair was perched on top of her head with fugitive curls tickling her neck and cheeks. She wasn't wearing one dab of makeup, but she was wearing a dark green blazer. Because he knew what it concealed, the illusion of wide-eyed innocence grated.

"Do you have to wear the gun inside?" he asked.

She sympathized with his obvious distaste, since she didn't like guns, either. But she wasn't about to tell him that, since he was paying her to carry one. "I'm going to need a nightstand with a drawer I can lock. I don't want to leave a gun around with a child in the house."

"I'll see that you get one."

"But get used to seeing the gun," she warned. "I'll still be wearing it a lot."

He ignored that. "What did you want to tell me about the house?"

She moved back to lean against a counter. Putting some distance between them seemed important somehow. "You're in luck. I've gone over the plans, and I've talked to the man who installed your security system. It's one of the best. No one's going to get inside without us knowing it."

"Good."

"He's coming tomorrow to make a few modifications. I also asked him about an alarm system for outdoors. He told me the best we could do on short notice is a dog. He can install something to monitor movement anywhere on your property, but to do it well might take as much as a week."

"So in the meantime we get a Doberman with fangs and rabies?"

"Actually I was thinking about Neuf."

"Does he work by the day?"

She smiled. "Just until we come up with something better."

"I was going to tell you to bring him up anyway. Is he still at your house?"

"Someone's letting him out regularly and feeding him, but I know he's lonely."

"Do dogs get lonely?"

"You've never had a dog?"

"Not since I was old enough to remember."

"Neuf will teach you everything you need to know." She prepared to leave.

"I assume I'm not supposed to go outside until you're back."

"It's your life. I can't stop you, but be sure you weigh the risks."

"They seem minimal to me. Who would want me dead?"

She recognized his frustration. He was already beginning to feel like a caged animal, and for no good reason that he could see. She turned his words around, hoping it would make him realize the necessity of taking precautions. "Who *would* want you dead? It's a good question. Any good answers?"

"Not one."

"What about Joanne?"

He frowned. "What about her?"

"Does she have any reason to benefit if you kick the bucket?"

"She'd have complete custody of Tara, and you heard first-hand how excited she'd be about that."

"What about money? You must be worth millions. Would Joanne reap any portion of it if you died?"

"I really don't want to pursue this."

His tone was as chilling as his eyes. Kelley shrugged. "I'm not a gossip columnist. I'm trying to get you to think about potential enemies."

"I don't have any. There were hundreds of other people in that church, and one of them was the target."

"Not hundreds. The target had to be in easy range of the man we went after, the man with real bullets in his gun. That only leaves a dozen possibilities, you and me among them."

"I make it a point not to make enemies."

At last night's party she had seen for herself how well liked he was. But she also knew Hollywood and its cutthroat politics. Hollywood the business was no different than any billion-dollar industry, except that sometimes hatred was more personal and more cleverly disguised.

"Will you give this some thought?" she asked. "It's not disloyal to protect yourself. Think about people who might benefit if you die. You're not accusing anybody, you're just giving a problem some rational attention."

"I went over this with the police. There isn't anyone."

She heard the finality in his voice, but she never took no for an answer. She just waited, then asked the question again, when it was least expected.

Turning her back on him, she started toward the doorway. "I'll be gone about an hour. Hook some pot holders. That should keep you busy."

His strong hands on her shoulders stopped her. "I like having you here. I just don't like the reason."

She tensed, remembering a similar conversation the night before and the kiss that had followed. "If there wasn't a reason, I wouldn't be here."

"Is it all job, Kelley? No feeling at all?"

"I thought we went over this last night. I'm here to protect you. If I let myself have feelings, I won't do a good job. And that's not the same thing as a waitress who drops dishes or a secretary who can't type. It's fatal."

"You don't stay objective. You're just good at looking like you do."

She faced him. "One actor to another?"

"I know the tricks."

"If you act long enough, you become. You should understand that. It's one of the dangers of your job."

"I'm not the man I play on-screen. If I were, I'd have blown holes in that gunman—"

"And I wouldn't need to protect you now."

He touched her cheek, a feather-light caress, then he dropped his hand. "I'm not that man, and you're not just a trigger finger and an eagle eye."

"Why is this important to you?" she demanded.

"Maybe I don't like a stranger living in my house."

"You've got strangers manipulating every piece of your life. You wouldn't have gotten so far if you didn't."

"But none of them has ever told me to hook a pot holder."

She had been prepared for a line powerful enough to reel in a whale. She smiled, enchanted he hadn't gone for the clichés. "Shape up, mister, or there'll be more where that came from."

He smiled, too, then he leaned forward. She knew, for one dizzying moment, that he was going to kiss her again. There was no one here to watch tonight, no one to fool. They were alone, and he didn't have to pretend anything he didn't feel.

His hand touched her cheek; his fingers were warm and slightly calloused. He lifted a curl and tucked it over her ear. It was so unexpected that she stood perfectly still for the seconds it took. She wasn't a woman who usually inspired tenderness. The simple affectionate gesture touched her in a way that a casual kiss might not have.

"I've just been trying to tell you that I like you," he said when he stepped back. "And I wish you weren't carrying a gun, and I wish I wasn't hiring you to do it. Very simple things, those. Nothing to be unhappy about."

"You make the simple sound complicated."

"Do I?" His smile warmed the ice blue of his eyes. "I'm glad."

Chapter 8

"Griff!"

Kelley was out of bed and running toward Tara's screams before she was completely awake. She was halfway down the long hallway before she realized she hadn't grabbed her gun and three-quarters of the way before she realized why Tara probably sounded so terrified.

She skidded to a stop in front of Tara's open bedroom door. "Neuf!" A wagging tail on Tara's bed greeted her. She dived for the dog, wrapping her arms around his massive neck. "Neuf! Bad boy! Down!"

Tara covered her face with her hands. Through the thicket of dog fur, Kelley could see she was shaking. She managed to push Neuf off the bed. He lay, head on paws beside it, thoroughly chastened.

"Sweetheart." Kelley scooted closer and put her arms around Tara, pillowing the girl's head against her shoulder. "I'm so, so sorry. He's my dog. I brought him up here last night after you were in bed, or I would have introduced you."

Tara shook harder. Kelley held her closer. "He wouldn't hurt a flea, Tara. I promise. I didn't realize he was going to explore. He was in my room with me." She didn't add that her door had been cracked in case there had been any noise worth hearing in the night.

"I hate dogs!"

"Well, even if you loved them, that was no way to meet one."

"I hate them!"

Kelley felt something twist inside her at the pathetic warble in Tara's voice. "Do you, honey?"

"I hate them!"

"Maybe we could pretend he's a bear? Do you hate bears, too?"

"Why'd you bring him here? I don't want him and I don't want you!"

Kelley didn't loosen her grip. Despite her words, Tara hadn't tried to pull away. "Well, I brought him up here because he missed me something terrible. Dogs miss people, you know. Once you get to know him, he'll miss you every time you go out the door."

"Dogs are dirty, and they make people sick."

"Joanne's house is always immaculate," Griff explained from the doorway.

Tara lifted her head. Only when she saw her father did she give Kelley a firm shove. Kelley unwrapped her arms and moved back to give Tara room.

"If I woke up and found this monster on my bed unexpectedly," Kelley said, "I think I'd have had a heart attack. Your daughter's braver than I would have been." She reached for a box of tissues beside the bed and got one for Tara, laying it in front of her.

"I told Kelley to bring Neuf up last night." Griff made no attempt to move closer. "I'm sorry if you were frightened, Tara. We should have warned you."

Kelley had the urge to kick him. He was being calm and rational when Tara needed hugs and sympathy. It occurred to her that she had never seen Griff touch his daughter. Not once.

"Will you give Neuf a day here?" she asked Tara. "Sort of a trial run? I promise he won't hurt you. And he's a clean, healthy dog. I'll even tell him not to shed. Then, if you still want me to get rid of him, I will.'' She put her hand on Tara's leg. "Deal?"

"I don't care what you do."

Kelley noted that the child hadn't moved away at her touch. "Well, I care what *you* think and feel. And if Neuf frightens you, then he's out the door. Okay?"

"Don't try to make friends with me." Tara still didn't move.

"Tara!"

Kelley held up her hand to silence Griff. "Why not?"

"You just want to be my friend so Griff will like you better!"

"Tara!"

Kelley shot Griff an angry glance. "Thanks for being honest with me," she said, turning back to Tara. "If we're really going to be friends someday, then we're going to have to be truthful with each other."

"You're just saying that."

"Nope, but if you're going to be honest, I get a turn, too. This is the gospel. First, your father and I are already friends, so I don't care if he likes me any better. Second, I'll be okay if you and I don't get to be buddy-buddy, but I really *do* care if you're unhappy, because I like kids and I think I'm going to like you."

Tara stared at her as if she were a creature from *Star Wars*.

"Third, I really am sorry about Neuf. And I meant what I said. You decide if he stays, but please give him a chance." She patted Tara's leg, then she stood. "Boy, does this household get up early!"

She whistled for Neuf to follow her and started toward the door. Just feet away from Griff she realized that he—in cutoffs and nothing else—was as furious at her as she was at him. She prepared herself for a fight.

Halfway back to her bedroom it began.

"Just in case you forget again," Griff said, his voice too low for Tara to hear, "Tara's my daughter. If I don't want her to be rude, I'll tell her so. With or without your permission. Maybe Joanne lets her get away with that kind of crap, and maybe you think it's okay, but I sure as hell don't!"

Kelley turned her steps to the kitchen, which was farther out of earshot. She waited until she was there to speak. "Now listen to me, macho man. That kid was scared to death! If she hadn't been, she wouldn't have said anything like that. But for once she was too shook-up to act bored, so she said the first thing that came into her head. And that first thing was what she was feeling! You should be jumping up and down that she has feelings! I'm not sure anyone else in her family does!"

He grasped her arm and kept her from reaching for the coffee maker. "What's that supposed to mean?"

"She was scared to death! She needed a hug. She let me hug her, and she doesn't even like me! So what did you do when you got there? You posed in the doorway. Did you think she was going to be so impressed by the Great Griff Bryant she'd just forget she was terrified?"

She glared at him, but the words hung between them until even she could see how unfair they'd been. "Jeez," she said when his hand finally dropped to his side. She turned and stared out the kitchen window. "I'm sorry. This is none of my business. You're right. She's your kid. I've got no right to interfere."

There was silence behind her.

"But if I'm going to live here, I'd like to work out my own relationship with her," Kelley went on when Griff didn't speak. "I don't mind her telling me what she thinks. I can tolerate that a lot better than I can tolerate silence."

"She's never liked me to touch her."

She heard just the slightest change in his voice. She wondered what it had cost him to admit that to her after what she'd said. "Do you know why?"

"No."

She faced him. His veiled expression reminded her of Tara. "But doesn't it make sense in a way?" she asked gently. "You've said yourself that you've moved in and out of her life. Maybe she just cut herself off from you a long time ago because she thought she couldn't count on you being around."

"I really don't want to talk about this."

She put her hand on his arm. "I am sorry. Pop psych isn't usually my thing."

"No?"

She smiled. "Can't tell, huh?"

He lifted his arm; the effect was to shake off her hand. "I think you find it easier to tell other people what they feel than to feel anything yourself."

"Ouch."

"I'll make the coffee. Grab a shower. I'm going to take Tara to school this morning, then I'm due at the studio at eleven. We'll have rush hour to fight."

Kelley knew the day's schedule, since they'd gone over it the night before. Griff was starting a new film in a week, and there were still a host of details to take care of first. She was glad for the change of subject. "Have you thought about how you'll explain me?"

"The Great Griff Bryant doesn't have to explain anything he doesn't want to."

She heard the sarcasm. And the hurt. She sighed. "I'm especially sorry I called you that."

He ignored her apology and reached for the coffee maker. "Don't bother getting too dressed up. No one else will."

She had a temper—she almost hated to admit it, since the temperamental redhead was such a cliché. Hers was usually under control, but if kids or animals were threatened, watch out, world.

Kelley didn't know why she was such a sucker. Maybe it was all the corny movies she'd starred in as a child. Maybe she'd absorbed so much silver screen sentimentality it had blocked the blood flow to her brain.

Maybe she ought to try one more time to start a conversation with Griff.

"Tell me about the people we'll be having lunch with." The question required a real answer, not a yes or a no. She was hopeful she had trapped him. They were almost to the studio, and he hadn't said a word with more than one syllable.

"What do you want to know?"

She was encouraged, although the sentence had been grunted. He reminded her of the guy he'd played in *Victims No*

More, a real sweetheart who had interrogated terrorists while suspending them by a slender rope from the Statue of Liberty.

"Little things," she said. "Names. What they do. If you'd like to fire me."

"Michael Donnelly's directing the new film. I'm sure you've heard of him. Dwayne Fagan's my personal manager. Eddie Sexton's my agent. Cam Johns may show up. She's producing." He paused. "No."

"No, you don't want to fire me?"

He didn't spare her a glance. "No."

She settled back in her seat. "What kinds of relationships do you have with these people?"

"None of them have a contract out on me, if that's what you're asking."

"Lighten up. It's a perfectly good question."

"Our relationship is professional. Fagan and Sexton make a lot of money off me, and so does Michael, though I'm certainly not the only star he directs. But I've done a run of films with him lately. We complement each other. Cam is . . . Cam. You'll probably hear that we lived together for a while several years ago. We're still close."

"I thought you said there wasn't anybody—"

"We were always better friends than lovers. She's married now, has been for a year, and she's pregnant. She's the only woman I've lived with since Joanne. It was her idea for me to have a bodyguard."

"Don't come off your seat, but is there any reason to think one of them might be angry with you about something?"

"No."

"Your manager and agent have anything to gain if you die?"

"They're friends. They don't want me dead."

"Have you made life rough on Michael Donnelly? He was your director for *One Way Ticket,* wasn't he? Did you blame him for Drake Scott's death?"

"He was the last person I could have blamed. He's a perfectionist—he takes everything to heart. I think Michael felt like he had set the charge himself. He sobbed when Drake died, like Drake had been his own son."

"And Cam?"

"What's that supposed to mean?" he asked coldly.

"Do I have to tiptoe on eggshells, or can I spell it out?"

"You'd grind eggshells to dust under your feet."

"Is there any reason to think Cam might be a woman scorned?"

"None."

"Well, I guess I've really made your day, huh?"

He turned the wheel, and they settled into a line of traffic that hardly seemed to move. "I'll put it down to nerves."

"Nerves?"

"Your first day back on a studio lot."

She was surprised he had realized that. "I'm looking forward to it. After all, I'm not the one who's acting."

"You'll be acting from the moment you step foot on studio property."

"But not for the cameras."

"No, what you'll have to do is harder. You don't get a break between scenes."

She thought about that as they drove through the studio gate and Griff gave his name to the guard. She would be acting, although the part was one she'd played before. She had never really been Sammy O'Flynn. Sammy had always been an act. Sammy hadn't had a care in the world; Kelley had struggled every day to give her best performance and live up to adult expectations. Sammy had been gloriously free to hitchhike freight trains or ride rafts down the Mississippi; Kelley had endured rigid schedules programmed in five-minute segments. The little girl others had envied had never really existed.

Griff Bryant, the man the world knew as the reformer from hell, didn't exist, either. She, at least, had been blessed with parents who understood the conflict between her roles and reality. They had nursed her through the tough times, reminded her of the real world when it seemed too far away, shepherded her through the worst dangers.

Who provided an anchor for Griff? He certainly wasn't a child; he didn't need the same kind of protection. But everyone needed someone to come back to after a visit to fantasy land.

They parked in a choice section of the lot. Enough limos surrounded Griff's Volvo to remind her that he, too, could spare himself the hassles of traffic jams and hire a chauffeur. That he hadn't, said something about lack of pretension.

Although Kelley had never made a movie here, the lot and buildings on it seemed familiar. The studio was neither the largest nor smallest in the Los Angeles area. It was covered with buildings, some sturdy and permanent, some that looked as if they'd collapse the next time the earthquake-prone ground gave a friendly burp. There was a small back lot with some standing sets, but Griff had already told her that no filming would be done here. Almost the entire picture was going to be shot on location, not far from Palm Springs. One reason Griff had accepted this role was that he could live at home with Tara while he was working.

More familiar than the studio was their first stop. Of the four meetings Griff had scheduled that day, the first was with the head of the wardrobe department, the costume designer for the new film, *Teardrop Creek*.

Molly Zayre greeted them with real warmth. Kelley knew her slightly as one of her mother's cohorts. Molly, like a lot of people in Hollywood, had started at the bottom and worked her way up through the ranks. Now, at forty, she was the designer of choice for a number of producers. Her costumes were imaginative, pleasing to both the camera and the actors wearing them and cheap enough to stay within her budget. She obviously worked well with everyone or she wouldn't have reached the peak of her profession. She seemed to work particularly well with Griff.

"I've always wanted to dress you for a Western," Molly gushed. She was tall and reed thin, with a startling streak of red in her coal black hair. She had already greeted Kelley like a long-lost friend, and now she was pulling out costumes to show them both.

"I have never wanted to *do* a Western," Griff said. "Don't tell me you expect me to wear those spurs?"

"Authentic details, sweetie pie. You know Michael, he'd blackball me from every picture in town if I didn't give him au-then-ticity!"

Until that moment Kelley hadn't thought much about the fact that *Teardrop Creek* was a Western. "Can you ride?" she asked Griff.

"Oh, Griff can do anything, can't you?" Molly asked. "Fly, ride, kick, jump, shoot. He's a director's dream. A-a-a-nd a costume designer's." She held up an outfit that looked as if it had been some long-gone cowpoke's sole attire on a cross-country cattle drive. "Like?" she asked Griff.

"Did you stretch it out on the Hollywood Freeway during rush hour?"

"Close."

They argued good-naturedly about the costumes, but Griff didn't ask for any changes. Kelley had heard enough war stories from her mother to be impressed by his nonchalance.

He was impressive during their next appointment, too, with a representative from the studio legal department. His questions about the terms of his contract were astute but few, his demands none. Since his agent and attorney had already gone over it thoroughly, he signed.

When they had finished, Kelley was surprised to find it was time for lunch. Dwayne Fagan had chosen a small Greek restaurant not far from the studio as a meeting place. From both the outside and inside it seemed comfortable, but not a site for power lunches.

They were ushered into a private room where everyone else had already been seated at a large round table. All the men rose when Kelley walked in. The woman who remained in her chair examined her without smiling.

Griff made the introductions. She knew that two of the people there, Dwayne Fagan and Cam Johns, understood her real role in Griff's life, Dwayne because he had engineered Griff's finding a bodyguard and Cam because Zephyr had insisted Griff have one to protect the movie. The others, Eddie and Michael, believed her to be just whom Griff indicated: Sammy O'Flynn, his newest lover. She had insisted to Griff that her real identity remain secret. The fewer people who knew why she was staying so close, the safer he would be.

Kelley answered a few questions, effectively turning on the charm, but as the focus of the conversation turned to Griff, she settled back to watch. There was an aura of mutual respect in the room. Everyone there had made it to the top of his or her chosen profession. The game now was to stay there, and to amass more personal wealth. She understood and respected the game, although she had never wanted to play it herself.

She assessed the players. Dwayne Fagan was a nervous man, with hands that either clutched an icy tumbler of imported mineral water or fluttered. His counterpart, Eddie Sexton, Griff's agent, was older and, by contrast, reserved. He listened more than he talked, but when he said something, no one interrupted.

Of the three men other than Griff, Michael Donnelly was the most dynamic. Kelley thought he had a presence that would film well, an intensity that came from focusing his energy on the subject at hand, like a magnifying glass focusing sunlight until the surface under it ignited. He was a large man with a silver lion's mane of hair and rosy unlined skin.

Cam Johns, who Kelley guessed might be as much as five years older than Griff, was neither nervous like Dwayne, reserved like Eddie or dynamic like Michael. She was dark-haired, with olive skin and limpid dark eyes. She was dressed in a pay-attention red smock, and the pearls around her neck and in her ears looked real. She was classy, self-possessed and unmistakably brilliant.

The purpose of the lunch was to be certain everyone was clear about plans for *Teardrop Creek*. The talk flowed around Kelley, but as she worked on her Greek salad, she picked up the currents without much difficulty. Cam and Michael were united on what they wanted, a hard-driving, action-packed adventure film without the usual Western clichés. Michael particularly was bent on portraying the town of Teardrop Creek without any of the romance of television cowboy epics. It wasn't to be a prettied-up Dodge or Virginia City. He wanted dust and flies, sweating horses—and actors.

Fagan—who nobody called Dwayne—was united with Eddie to be sure that realism didn't eclipse Griff's star power. By the time Kelley had gotten to her last olive, there had been a meeting of the minds. Griff's fans wanted him tough; a little dust wasn't going to bother them. Those same fans also expected him to be larger than life, however, and Michael had to assure everyone that Griff's presence would still shine. He promised Griff would be the quintessential man of the West, the stuff that legends are made of.

As Michael expounded, Kelley unexpectedly caught Griff's eye. He seemed amused by the whole conversation, and his smile asked her to share his amusement. She smiled back at him, oblivious for a moment to the others. She had obviously been forgiven for her gaffe of the morning. She was warmed by his gaze, and for a moment she lost track of what was being said.

"Sammy, Griff tells me you'll be on the set with him, watching us shoot," Michael said.

Kelley tugged herself back to the conversation. Michael hadn't addressed any comments to her before this, other than a cordial "hello."

"I hope I won't be in the way." She made certain there was no question in her voice. She was going to be on the set whether she was in the way or not.

"You're a pro. You won't be any trouble at all," Michael said graciously.

"Well, I haven't been a pro for a while. It will be fun to see how things are done now."

"I have a collection of all your movies," Eddie said. "I show them to my grandchildren when they visit."

"Destined to remain a gap-toothed, freckle-faced tomboy forever."

"Hardly," Cam said. She openly assessed Kelley, but there was nothing malicious about the way her eyes narrowed or her fingers tapped on the table. "Michael, I wonder..."

"You don't even have to. I've been wondering enough for us both."

"Then you see it, too?"

Griff interrupted. "See what?"

"Carolina," Michael said.

Kelley was lost.

Griff shook his head. "She's not interested."

"She's not, or you're not?" Cam asked.

"Are you still in the guild?" Michael asked Kelley.

She guessed he meant the Screen Actors' Guild, since that was the only guild she had ever belonged to. "No."

"Well, it won't be hard to get her back in if you're willing to foot the bill," Michael told Cam.

"I think we could probably even make a case for getting her back in without having to Taft-Hartley her."

Kelley sat and waited.

"Have any desire to act again?" Michael asked her after he and Cam had exchanged a few more enigmatic sentences.

She leaned forward eagerly. She smiled engagingly. "Not . . . one . . . bit."

Griff laughed.

"She's going to be perfect," Michael told Cam. Cam nodded in agreement.

"No, I'm not."

Michael assumed the role of spokesman. "Listen, this is a great part. We had it cast until last week, when the actress backed out. She claims she didn't like our terms, but rumor has it she was offered something better at the last minute."

"I'll bet there's still an actress or two who can do it."

"Only if you won't. We haven't been able to agree on anybody we've seen." Michael held up his hand to interrupt her response. "Let me tell you about it, and frankly, I might as well give you the angle, too. Carolina's a Teardrop Creek tomboy, a Strawberry Finn all grown-up. And that's the angle. Can you see the publicity? Your return to the screen, playing the character you always played, but an adult version?"

"It's not a big part," Cam said before Kelley could refuse, "but it adds humor to the movie, so it's imperative we get someone who's just right. Carolina's eighteen and in love with Griff's character, Travis Jones, but she's not his love interest in the film. Carolina chases after him, she even joins the posse he's leading to get the outlaws who murdered the sheriff and his family. There's a sweet, tender scene toward the end where Travis kisses Carolina. It's one of the best moments in the script. If Michael doesn't object, we could shoot all your scenes first. In case you don't want to stay on the set for the entire film," she added meaningfully.

"Do you ride?" Michael asked.

"Not that it matters, but yes."

His whole face smiled, but she had seen less calculating eyes on the pythons at the Los Angeles zoo. "The part calls for some hard riding and some minor stunts. Of course, if you'd rather, we'd use a stuntwoman. You probably aren't up to doing stunts yourself."

She knew a challenge when she heard one. "You've very good at figuring out how to get what you want, aren't you?"

"Absolutely the best," he said.

She had listened, and she had even heard the sultry blues note of temptation. Still, she would have refused on the spot, except that instinct told her to wait. Cam knew her purpose for shadowing Griff because Zephyr was paying for her services. Why was Cam asking her to play this role, unless she had a reason she hadn't yet declared and couldn't declare at this table?

"Tell us you'll think about it," Cam said. "You could let Michael know this evening."

Since Michael didn't know she was Griff's bodyguard, Kelley could only assume she really must be perfect for the role of Carolina. She felt a twinge of long-forgotten professional pride. It was nice to know she was still wanted in Hollywood by someone as prestigious as Michael Donnelly. More important, however, was what Cam thought and why, and for that, she would have to wait.

"I'll have to talk this over with Griff," she said. "I can let you know later this afternoon."

Everyone seemed to think that would be good enough, and the conversation drifted to other things. Kelley imagined Griff's gaze was boring holes through the middle of her forehead. She met that gaze and shrugged for the benefit of the others at the table.

His eyes were frostbitten blue. There were no traces of the smile they had shared. Whatever Cam and Michael thought, Griff obviously did not think the same.

Chapter 9

Molly stood back and squinted. "It works. The alterations don't show and the blue gives the right effect. Don't ever try to make a power statement with navy, Sammy. It's never going to be your best color."

Kelley viewed herself in the wardrobe trailer's big mirrors, ignoring the other actors and actresses streaming in and out the door. In the voluminous dusty blue split skirt and threadbare white blouse, she looked eighteen again and girlishly hopeful. She also looked scrawny, dirty and anything but a fashion plate. "Any man who saw me coming would take off running."

"That's what we're trying for."

Kelley shot her a mirrored grin. "You've succeeded."

"I'm still not sure about the shoes. Carolina wouldn't wear shoes most of the time."

Kelley wiggled her toes, and the cracked leather of her high button shoes puckered in protest. "She would when she was riding, especially if she was trying to keep up with men in boots and spurs."

"Are those comfortable enough to manage in, or are they going to rub blisters?"

"They look like hell, but they feel okay."

"We'll let Michael decide if they'll be all right."

"Does he pay attention to every detail? Even shoes?"

"That's how he got where he is today. Heck, Michael will expect to know what you're wearing *under* the shoes."

Kelley wasn't surprised at Molly's answer. In the week since she had been tapped to play the part of Carolina, she had seen Michael Donnelly at work enough to know that Molly wasn't exaggerating. The man was as total a perfectionist as existed in the business.

"Are you done with me?" she asked, turning away from the mirror. "I've still got hair and makeup." She looked at the clock at Molly's side. "Lord, it's not even six."

"Early to rise makes a director wealthy. Not a thing in the blooming world makes one wise." Molly straightened the collar of Kelley's blouse. "I won't tell you to break a leg. Better you on a horse than me."

"Better a stuntwoman on the horse than her," said a deep voice.

Kelley looked up to see Griff coming through the door. "The star deigns to visit the lowly peons?"

"The star wants to talk to you."

She met him halfway. "The star had his chance on the trip to the set. The star didn't take it."

He wrapped his fingers firmly around her arm. "I'll walk you to the makeup trailer."

She gave him a big smile for Molly's benefit and let him pull her along. Out of Molly's sight she pried his fingers loose. "Look, we've been over the stuntwoman thing before. I ride well. If I didn't, the stunt coordinator wouldn't let me try this. Besides, the talk is that you do most of your stunts yourself. How come you're being so pigheaded?"

"I don't want to go through the trauma of hiring another bodyguard."

"You won't have to." She lowered her voice. "And besides, I've told you why I'm doing the riding myself. I want to look like I'm serious about a comeback. I want people to believe I belong on this set."

"You've told me that before. It's bull."

"Well, maybe a little," she conceded. "I thrive on challenge. I'll admit that's a big part of it. But you fess up, too. You've been angry that I took this role since the beginning. Even after Cam explained why she thought it would be a good idea."

"I don't care what Cam thinks. You would have had access to the set and any part of it as my guest here. You didn't have to be in the film."

"But no one blinks an eye at my presence now. I can watch everything. I can ask all the questions I want. I'm one of the gang. And with the studio security guards keeping a special watch on you while we're here, you're still safe, even if I'm not with you every second."

He spoke with quiet intensity. "You don't need to watch anything, and you don't need to ask any questions. No one tried to kill me!"

"Then if I'm useless as a bodyguard, please leave me a profession I *can* excel at, since I'm on the studio payroll anyway!"

Griff dropped his hands on her shoulders to hold her there. His voice gentled. His thumbs caressed her neck; she wondered who was watching.

"Listen," he said. "I'm gun-shy. All right? I saw a man die on my last picture. I'm getting used to you following me everywhere. Tomorrow I want to look behind me and see you're still tagging along."

She didn't know what to say. She didn't know if she was looking at the man or the actor.

She hadn't been sure of Griff since the first day she'd met him, but as the days had gone by, she'd become increasingly uncertain. Griff hadn't wanted her to take this role, and even though her reasons for doing it made sense, he'd been moody and withdrawn since she'd agreed.

She supposed his moods were understandable. She remembered what starting a new movie was like. There was a transition period, even for a child, when some part of an actor became the person he was about to portray. And that wasn't all. Since Felice's abortive wedding, Griff's life had undergone significant changes: new movie, new relationship with Tara, new threat to his existence. Suddenly he had an armed woman following him everywhere, reminding him that the world might not be a safe place anymore.

"The worst thing that can happen is that I'll take a bad fall and break an arm or a leg," she said, gentler, too. "I'm not going to die. And if I thought I had even a ten percent chance of falling wrong, I wouldn't do it. But I've gone over and over the stunt, and short of putting it all together, I've proved myself."

"You're not going to change your mind."

"You can insist. We both know you can tell Michael to get me a stunt double, and he will."

"You're a grown-up."

"Thanks for noticing." She smiled at him. Despite the disagreement, she was touched he was concerned. For the past week he had treated her like a piece of household furniture. He had never been impolite, never patronizing, but neither had he shown the slightest hint of intimacy—except when others had been around to watch his performance.

She had missed this more touchable Griff Bryant. Now she was surprised how much. She had forced herself to think of him as nothing except a client, but conscious thought and unconscious yearning were different matters. She told herself to be careful, but her voice betrayed more feeling than she intended. "I promise I'll be careful. And if it looks like I'm getting into trouble, I'll just halt the whole thing."

"Sometimes you can't stop something once it's rolling." His hand lifted to her hair. His eyes were surprisingly warm as he leaned closer. "You can try. You can say all the right words, make all the right motions, but momentum builds and before you know it, words and motions don't mean a thing."

She knew she was supposed to respond. But for once she couldn't form a sentence, and she didn't want to move. She looked in his eyes and tried to fathom what was hidden there. Knowing who was about to kiss her, the actor or the man, seemed imperative.

Griff kissed her. His lips were warm and sure and very real. She moved closer instinctively, and her arms slipped around his neck. His tongue touched her lips, and she parted them in invitation. The kiss deepened and his hands guided her hips closer to his. The man was aroused; there were some things that the best actor couldn't pretend.

She felt his palms slowly stroking her cheeks, felt the heat of his body penetrate her clothing. Her heart sped faster, but every muscle in her body declared a holiday. For that moment she forgot they were anything but two people just beginning to find each other.

Griff lifted his head, and his eyes were the color of smoke. He dragged a thumb slowly across her bottom lip, as if to experience its softness in yet another way. "Do you see what I mean?" he asked. "Sometimes you can't stop what's already speeding out of control. Even if you want to."

As stunts went, the one Kelley was scheduled to do wasn't particularly difficult or dangerous. Griff told himself she could manage it, but some major part of him didn't believe it. His films, no matter the era or location in which they were set, always possessed elements of danger for those working on them. Until Drake's death, however, no one had ever been seriously injured on one, even though dozens of stunt people had performed feats of great daring.

He knew that under Kelley's skirts today there would be layers of padding. He also knew that the jacket she would don to conceal a jerk harness would be padded, too. In the past week she had spent hours with both the skeptical stunt coordinator and an animal trainer to prove that she was capable of taking the fall without injury.

He told himself she faced danger in her chosen career and that she was probably safer falling off horses than she had been walking some of Los Angeles's meanest streets as a cop—or walking down the aisle as Felice's maid of honor.

Telling himself all that proved one thing only. Talk was cheap.

Talk was cheap but feelings weren't. He had been furious when she'd decided to come on the set as an actress instead of his woman, even more furious when he'd discovered that she was going to take a few falls in the role of Carolina. He still wasn't sure exactly where the fury began and fear kicked in. At first he had been afraid that becoming an actress again would change her from the levelheaded, say-what-I-think person she was to someone who weighed every word in terms of what it could do for her, someone who tested every gesture by the reaction it got.

Now he was afraid she would be hurt. If she was, it would be his fault, just as he felt in the deepest part of him that Drake's death was his fault, too. Somehow he should have known. Somehow he should have demanded that the scene be eliminated or a double experienced with explosives be used instead. No matter how many times he told himself that this was not the same, that falling off a horse was a minor stunt, he still felt shaken with apprehension.

The sun warmed his hatless head, and as he stood silently waiting for shooting to begin, a makeup assistant dabbed sweat off his forehead and cheeks. As the cinematographer barked directions, the best boy adjusted one of the lights that had been strung to supplement the natural sunlight. On the other side the sound crew was lengthening the cable attached to the boom microphone. In front of him someone from special effects was sweeping the sand pit prepared for Kelley's fall so that it would look exactly like the rest of the narrow street.

Satisfied the lighting was now correct, the cinematographer came over to take a reading with a light meter, barking directions at his assistants as he did. Out of the corner of his eye Griff could see Kelley on horseback in the distance.

"She's going to be fine," Michael said, coming up behind Griff to clap him on the back. "I've seen her in action. She's quite a rider."

"I wish you'd used a stuntwoman."

"It's got to look real."

"It could end up looking too real if she breaks something."

"We've taken all precautions."

"I know you have." Griff knew better than to fault Michael. He always made sure that every safety measure was employed.

"Then look lively, we're going to start shooting in a minute. And don't look overly pained or worried when she hits the dirt, or we'll have to do it over again."

"Let's just get it over with, shall we?"

"You bet." Michael patted him on the shoulder, then started toward the camera where he would sit next to the operator as the scene was filmed.

The next thing Griff heard was a "let's go" from Michael, then a "settle down, please" from one of his assistants. A loudly buzzed warning sounded. Griff listened to the familiar preliminary announcements that indicated that film was rolling through the camera, then that the sound was in place. Someone snapped the clap slate in front of him. Finally Michael yelled, "Action."

The street of the small Western town seemed to come alive. Costumed extras began to walk along the wooden walkways in front of the shabby storefronts. A boy and his dog crossed the road just in front of a rattling buckboard. A crowd of men gathered outside a shop, pointing to three men across the street who were lifting a large pane of glass from a wagon. There wasn't a real window anywhere else in sight.

Griff ambled to his second position, stopped exactly on his mark outside an old-fashioned saloon and began to roll a cigarette.

The rapid beat of horse hooves signaled Kelley's arrival. He turned his head nonchalantly, as if he had little interest in who was coming. Another actor exited the saloon, stumbling a little, like a man who'd been inside too long. He pointed with an unsteady hand. "Well, will you look at that?"

Griff shaded his eyes. "Damn." He watched Kelley galloping toward them, and directly toward the men carrying the window.

"None of them Hortons have a lick of sense," the saloon patron said, spitting a stream of tobacco juice onto the walkway.

"That Horton doesn't have much luck, either." Griff knew that if all was going as planned, at the moment he said "luck," the camera would pick up Kelley's wild ride. He hoped to God that it did, so she wouldn't have to make the ride again.

He started down the steps, running toward her, waving his arms as if to avert a tragedy.

"Tra—vis!" she shouted happily.

"Car—o—lina! Stop!"

She hauled on the reins, the danger finally clear to her, but nothing happened. "Tra—vis!"

"Duck, damn it. Duck!"

In a last-ditch attempt to save the window, the men danced to one side. She swerved and ducked, covering her face with one arm, but it was clear she couldn't avoid crashing into the window. Griff hit the dirt to avoid shattering glass—the audience wouldn't know that the window was made from resin-based plastic and balsa wood and couldn't hurt him.

Kelley screamed as the window splintered, the horse reared, wearing a necklace of balsa wood, and she was launched backward—courtesy of a wire attached to the harness she wore under her jacket. She fell directly onto the area the special-effects department had prepared. The horse settled immediately.

Michael yelled, "Cut."

Then, and only then, did Griff fling himself at Kelley as one of the trainers grabbed the horse. She lay perfectly still. For a moment he was sure she had been hurt, and a sick feeling welled inside him. Then she opened one eye. "I hope there was film in that camera. I don't think I want to do that again."

He put his arms around her to help her sit up, ignoring the others converging to congratulate her. "Welcome back to show business."

She shot him a shaky smile. "I think it's safer to carry a gun for a living."

Michael seemed pleased, the stunt coordinator had promised her jobs if she ever wanted to give up regular acting and three child extras had asked for her autograph.

Kelley leaned back in a chair in Griff's trailer and closed her eyes. She wasn't even bruised, at least not badly enough to turn black and blue quite yet. She was finished for the day, although Griff still had some close-ups to film.

It was almost six. Making a movie meant long hours with relatively few breaks and many obstacles. Anything that could go wrong usually did. Although the scene with her fall had gone off without a hitch, the next part of the same scene, where Griff lifted her from the street and carried her to the sidewalk, hadn't gone as well. The first time he had lifted her, he tripped on the skirt of her dress and nearly dropped her. The second time, the script supervisor stopped them halfway across the road because she had just noticed that in repositioning Kelley to be picked up again, her hair had trailed across her left breast instead of her right, as it had after falling. There had been four other takes, all with relatively minor problems, but problems nonetheless. Finally one had been good enough to print.

She was exhausted, but she still had a job to do, her real job. The security team hired by Cam was excellent, but Kelley tried not to let Griff out of her sight any more than necessary. She still felt primarily responsible for him, even when others were covering.

"You look beat."

She opened her eyes to find Griff standing across the room. "I thought you had to do some shots."

"Technical problems. I'm off the hook."

"Tara's going to be glad about that. We'll be back early."

"Let's go home and celebrate."

She sat up straight and stretched. She had already slipped out of Carolina's clothes, showered and gotten back into her own jeans and shirt covered by one of her large wardrobe of gun-concealing blazers. "What are we going to celebrate?"

"You becoming a star again."

"Thanks, but you can have it." She stretched again. "This is my first and last film as an adult."

"Oh?"

"When the best part of your day is falling off a horse, there's something wrong with your job."

He gave her a one-sided smile. "That was the best part of your day?"

She smiled back. Lazily. "My *working* day."

He enjoyed the picture she made, orange blazer, yellow blouse, something gold holding a section of hair off her face. He believed what she was saying and wondered why he had worried. If she had wanted to act, she had made enough contacts as a child to have a start at a career as an adult. She had never even tried.

He felt relief, so strong it made him wonder about its roots. The feeling of impending doom that he'd been experiencing all day lifted. Today's stunt had been a success, and it was the most complicated and dangerous she would be called on to do. If nothing had gone wrong today, nothing probably would. The world suddenly seemed a better place.

"Champagne," he said. "And my famous chocolate mousse. After Tara goes to bed."

She heard the invitation. She knew better than to say yes. Champagne and chocolate mousse would lead to more of what they'd done this morning. She was his employee, his pretend lover. She was not the real thing.

She heard herself accepting anyway. "I won't be able to get back in my costume tomorrow."

"Molly will let it out."

"An invaluable woman."

"Let me grab a shower and change."

"Wake me up when you're ready to go." She closed her eyes, but exhaustion had fled.

By six-thirty they were in Griff's car, on the way back to Palm Springs. As a precaution Kelley insisted every day that Griff take a slightly different route. Repetition would be an asset for anyone bent on following them. She made sure they never left the house at exactly the same time, never took the same streets to get to the highway, never took the same exit off of it. Her maneuvers added ten minutes to the trip, but ten minutes seemed minor compared to a scene like the one they had experienced at the wedding.

Increasingly, however, she was beginning to believe that Griff had not been the assassin's target. There were still no concrete leads in the case, but the FBI had made some progress tracking members of the Knapp family. Indications were that several small-time criminals associated with the family's activities had been seen in Southern California in the weeks before the shooting.

If the Knapps or their henchmen were responsible for the scene at the wedding, then Simon, Gallagher and possibly their friend Aaron had been the intended targets. Not Griff.

"Did I tell you that Gallagher's collecting some photographs for us to look at?" she asked when they were no more than fifteen minutes from his house.

"Do you know if any of them look like the composite you made with the police?"

"I don't, but frankly, I don't think the composite's a very good likeness anyway. I look at it, and I know that something's wrong. I just can't tell them how to fix it. Every time we tried something different, it got worse."

"It's a reasonable facsimile."

"You think so?"

He shrugged. "I still don't think I could pick the guy out of a lineup. It was dark, and everything happened so fast."

"I can't believe I haven't figured out where I've seen that sucker before."

"You hate not being on top of everything, don't you?"

"Worse than anything."

"No wonder you and Michael get along so well. Perfectionists, both of you."

"Well, we both have lives at stake when we work."

Griff was silent for a few moments. When he spoke, his voice had grown serious. "Michael told me today that the answer print of *One Way Ticket* is almost finished."

Kelley knew that this meant the film was ready to be seen for the first time. "Are you going to the screening?"

"It's going to be at his house, next week sometime. He asked me to come. He thought I'd want to see it first with friends."

She rested her hand on his arm. "Are you going to go?"

"I think it's a good idea. Will you come?"

A week before, she might have reminded him that he was paying her to go everywhere with him. He wasn't asking for a bodyguard, though. He was asking for a friend, someone to sit beside him as he viewed the film that had been the last one of Drake Scott's short life. "I'd be glad to," she said.

She thought about his request as they drew closer to home. She had always made it a strict rule not to be personally involved with the people who hired her, but she had never been in a situation precisely like this one before. She and Felice did not routinely accept jobs providing security. They investigated, and usually there was no opportunity to grow close to anyone, even if they had permitted it.

Her feelings for Griff were entirely different from anything she had come up against before. She was undeniably attracted to him—as were half the women in America. But her feelings for him had grown rapidly beyond the bounds of movie-idol adoration. She was beginning to believe that the Griff she was most attracted to really existed, not just on film, not just in celebrity magazines, but in real life. Moments like these, when he obviously felt deep emotion, brought her closer to trusting her instincts about him.

Her eyes flicked to the mirror on her side of the car. Watching the road behind them was instinctive now. She imagined that long after this job was completed, she would still be checking mirrors everywhere she went.

It was twilight, the most difficult time to get a clear view. She had asked Griff to take a particularly winding route home, and the car was already beginning to climb the foothills edging along the town of Palm Springs. Lights were coming on below them, and as she turned to view them she noticed a van that she hadn't seen in the mirror.

"There's someone behind us without his lights on," she said.

"*I* don't have my lights on." Griff snapped them on. "Or, I didn't."

She waited for the van's lights to snap on, too, at this reminder. Instead the van slowed, putting more distance between them. "I think he's probably getting ready to turn off."

"People live up here, Kelley. He's probably going home."

"I know. You think I'm an overachiever."

"Your phrase, not mine."

"Do me a favor and just slow down a little."

"We're not exactly speeding as it is."

"Humor me."

He slowed. "Anything for a laugh."

She squinted, trying to get a better look. The van was dark green or possibly blue, and marred by patches of rust. "I don't think that van 'lives' up here."

"Why not?"

"It's not in great shape."

"You're trying to say something about the kind of people who live in these hills?"

"I guess it could belong to somebody's gardener, or somebody coming to pick up somebody's maid. Of course, the same could be said about my car."

"Why don't we just stop? You can flag down the driver and ask to see his 1040."

"Keep driving." She turned long enough to examine the road ahead of them. "Take a left as soon as you can, unless it's a dead end."

"Is this going to be a car chase? I've had more experience than anyone you've ever met."

"Look, we can laugh about this when we get home, okay?"

He passed one road, which didn't look promising, and took the next left. "Mission accomplished."

She was silent until they had reached the end of the block. "They turned, too." She punctuated the brief sentence by drawing her gun.

"Put that away!"

"Just drive. Turn at the next corner, and double back to the road we were on before."

"I'm a lot more worried about you and that damned gun than I am about the van!"

"I return fire. I don't start it."

He wrenched the wheel, and the Volvo hugged the ground, making a clean, quick turn. He sped up. "Guns kill people."

"If they didn't, every two-bit hood in this country wouldn't own one."

"You probably think every two-bit hood has the *right* to own one!"

"Buckle your safety belt."

"What?"

"You heard me." She pulled hers tighter. "And I've always supported gun-control legislation. Just wanted you to know in case one of us takes a bullet before I had a chance to tell you later." She rolled down her window.

"What are you doing?"

"Drive. They're still tailing us."

"Maybe it's a carload of my fans. There are tours of celebrity homes in the area. People find out where we live, what we drive. I've been followed before."

"Let's hope it's just an autograph they want."

"Nobody is trying to kill me!"

"Let's see some speed there!"

He concentrated on his driving, trying to put enough distance between his car and the van to calm Kelley.

"I don't believe it!"

"What?" He gripped the wheel harder, ready for the worst.

"After all that, they turned off."

He didn't know whether to shake her or kiss her. "Great," he muttered. He lifted his foot from the accelerator and let the car resume a normal speed. "Can we go home now?"

"I was just doing what you pay me to do."

"Not that again."

"Well, it seemed to matter."

He took a deep breath and exhaled slowly. "Home. And put the gun away."

"The quickest way home might be nice." She slid her revolver back into its holster.

"Yeah, a nice change." He followed the road they'd been on for another quarter of a mile, then began to wind his way up again.

He thought about the differences between them. He had every reason to be suspicious of people. Hollywood was a cutthroat town, and he'd been victimized from time to time, just like everyone else there. But basically he was optimistic about people and life. He saw the problems, but he saw the possibilities, too. Kelley, on the other hand, looked for shadows under rocks.

He glanced at her and saw she was still looking for shadows behind them. "Can't you just relax?" he asked. "It was nothing. Maybe you're just keyed up from our scene today."

"If I'm keyed up, there's usually a better reason than that."

"Well, you were in a lot more danger falling off that horse than you were from that van."

She faced him and opened her mouth to tell him to stop trying to keep her from doing her job when she saw the van partially concealed by shrubbery in a driveway just ahead of them.

"Jeez!" She was reaching for her gun again when the van shot out of the driveway, right toward them. She grabbed the wheel and wrenched it, afraid he hadn't seen the danger.

He wrestled for control even as his foot stamped down on the accelerator. "Hang on!"

She let go of the wheel and fumbled for her gun. The Volvo fishtailed back and forth across the narrow mountain road. She slammed against the door, then pitched forward over the gearshift. It was seconds before she realized that they had narrowly escaped being hit and seconds more before she realized what would have happened if they had been. The side of the road closest to her hugged the edge of the hill. One nudge and they would be over it and blazing a trail no one else would ever want to follow.

"Hold on tight!"

With no time to think, she obeyed orders, one hand on the dashboard, one gripping the edge of her seat. She felt the car shudder and heard the crunch of metal. The van was in the left lane, bumping them hard as Griff fought with the steering wheel. She released the dashboard and tried once more to reach for her gun, but the van hit them again, and the car spun out of control. All she could do was hang on and marvel at the way time seemed to disappear. She was suspended in some mysterious dimension with a long-forgotten prayer echoing in her ears and a helpless yearning to somehow comfort Griff.

Chapter 10

Griff's car took a wild plunge down the hillside, then rolled over twice and came to rest right side up against a barricade of boulders piled there when nearby lots had been cleared for million-dollar homes. The absolute stillness brought Kelley back into time, back into fear. She waited for an explosion of pain; she began to tremble.

"Are you okay?"

She turned her head, vaguely surprised her neck worked. She blinked as her vision cleared. The world slowed its spinning. "Are you?" she whispered.

He couldn't answer the question, either. He felt anything but okay. "We'd better get out of here."

She reached for her door handle, but the badly damaged door wouldn't budge. A flimsier vehicle would have caved in on her. "Can you open yours?"

He tried but couldn't. There was no window left to open; the glass had shattered on the first roll. "We'll have to crawl out."

"Your side will be easier to get out of. I've got the rocks over here." She wondered about the extraordinary politeness of their conversation. Someone had just tried to kill them and almost succeeded, yet they were discussing their exit from the car like an old married couple trying to decide which program to watch on television.

"I'll go first."

She didn't point out that of course he would have to go first, since she was trapped. She understood his need to voice every thought. It put order back in an insane world.

Griff turned to push himself off the seat, but he couldn't seem to move. He envisioned himself trapped by metal; he envisioned blowtorches and emergency crews—if the men in the van didn't get to them first.

"You've got to unfasten your seat belt."

Seconds ticked by before he registered Kelley's advice. She sounded shaken. Anyone else he knew would have been hysterical by now. "Thanks." He winced as the seat belt retracted, brushing across his chest. He was bruised and not yet sure that was the worst. But nothing was going to keep him from getting out of the car and pulling her out after him.

He hoisted himself out by gripping the top of the window frame and pulling his body through. He was standing on shaky legs reaching for Kelley when he heard shouts and the stampede of footsteps. He whirled, expecting anything. A group of small children came to a skidding stop just yards away.

"Griff Bryant!" one of the boys in the group shouted. "Look, Griff Bryant's making a movie in Grandma Marie's backyard!"

"Only Griff has enough Hollywood status to crash over a mountain ledge into Marie Winslow's backyard," Kelley said, her mouth just inches from a cup of hot tea. The tea was going down slowly. She was still trembling, although it was proof of her improvement that she could hold the cup, if not yet expertly guide it toward her mouth.

"What's she like?" Felice asked, her eyes flicking to the next room, where Griff was deep in conversation with Gallagher. The police had brought them straight to Felice's new house after a trip to the emergency room.

"Grand. I met her at the studio once when I was a little girl, and she still remembered me. That was back when she was the queen of Hollywood. Now she has chalk white skin, white hair, eyes still as clear a green as yours. She took one look at Griff and me and said, 'Really, Sammy dear, if you'd wanted to renew our acquaintance, there were easier ways.'" Kelley knew she was chattering, but she couldn't seem to stop herself.

"Palm Springs has its share of visible celebrities, but Marie Winslow's a recluse. You were one of the lucky ones who's gotten to meet her."

"Oh, yeah, I felt lucky."

Felice ignored the sarcasm. "What do you remember about the van?"

"It was old and green. It had some rust. That's it. There was no license plate on the front. We never saw the back. The windshield was tinted, but I think there were two men in the front. I can't swear to it, though."

"And the police arrived in time to put out an APB?"

"They got there in minutes, but you know that van's long gone by now. It's in somebody's garage getting a fresh coat of spray paint."

"Are you sure you don't have more than a few cuts and bruises? You didn't injure your neck? Your back?"

"My backside, but that's from falling off a horse." Kelley quit trying to manage the tea and set it on the table. "Somebody's trying to kill Griff, Felice. Now we know who the target was at your wedding."

"Not necessarily."

Kelley knew she still wasn't thinking as straight as usual, but Felice's reasoning escaped her completely. "What do you mean? You don't think this was a murder attempt? You think that van just brushed us by accident?"

"Of course not." Felice patted her hand. "Obviously somebody tried to kill either or both you and Griff tonight. But that doesn't mean either of you were the original target. It could mean you just saw too much. Both of you saw a face you could identify. It makes sense someone wants you silenced."

"But I helped the cops put together a composite. The guy's picture is already plastered all over California."

"Kell," Felice said patiently, "you and Griff are the only ones who could identify the guy if the picture turned up a suspect somewhere."

Kelley put her head in her hands. "My brain really isn't working right, is it?"

"You're excused."

"Then you still think it's the Knapps?"

"I didn't say that."

"Spell it out, okay? Slow—ly."

"The original target is still up in the air."

"Thanks."

"What we know for sure is that no matter who else these guys want, they want either or both you and Griff now."

One thing was absolutely clear to Kelley. "We need extra people covering Griff."

"Covering *both* of you."

She wasn't ready to deal with that. She was used to protecting, not to being protected. "Did you know that Griff used to drive stunt cars? That's how he got his first job as a regular actor. He knew just what to do when the car went over the side."

"Things like this happen in movies, not in real life. Griff's car getting bumped over the mountainside was the classic end to a car chase. My wedding was something out of a crime thriller." Felice began to hum the wedding song from *The Godfather*.

"Please!" Kelley rubbed her temples. "I've got to have a long talk with Griff."

"Seems like you've had plenty of time for long talks already."

"Well, maybe he won't be so resistant to answering a few questions now."

"Griff's a man who doesn't want to believe anything bad about anybody."

"That's not a Hollywood trait."

"Oh? You've got a list?"

"I grew up there. Remember?"

"Is making stupid assumptions on the list, too?"

Kelley lifted her head. "Lay off me, Felice. I've been thrown from a horse and thrown down a mountainside today. I don't need sarcasm thrown *at* me, not on top of everything else."

Felice shrugged, knowing better than to offer sympathy. "Have your talk with Griff, but just remember, it's going to be hard for him to see anyone he knows in a suspicious light. *You're* going to have to teach him that he can't trust anybody." She held up her hands when Kelley glared at her. "No sarcasm. No sarcasm."

"The next time I get in an accident, I'm going to have the police drop me off somewhere else, somewhere peaceful and soothing, like Dodger Stadium when we're getting creamed."

"If you want soothing, you could try a church around twilight time," Felice said. "There's a big Catholic church down in Palm Springs that I can recommend. Personally."

Champagne and chocolate mousse were traded for another pot of hot tea and three aspirin. Kelley was in Griff's kitchen swallowing the third when Griff came back after making sure Tara was asleep. She held out her bottle, but he shook his head.

"Screen heroes don't take aspirin?" she asked. "Afraid you'll look like a sissy?"

"I'm allergic."

"Great. If someone wants to kill you, all he has to do is dissolve a couple of these in your coffee."

"If someone wants to give me a rash," he corrected her. "Someone who wants to watch me scratch for twenty-four hours."

She looked at the deep V of bare chest exposed by his bathrobe and thought about all the women who would gladly volunteer to scratch any of his itches. He didn't look like a man who had almost died. He looked tan and strong and more alive than anyone had a right to. She thought about the evening that almost had been and felt a sharp pang of regret.

She made herself turn away to rinse her cup. "I know you got bruised. Don't you ache all over?"

He folded his arms and leaned back against the counter. "I'm going to get in the spa. You're coming with me."

There was only so much rinsing she could do. She faced him. "Not a chance. First thing we know, an old green van will come crashing through your little tropical paradise and hop right in with us."

"We'll take Neuf." He let her finish her protest before he continued. "The security people finished the outside alarm today. Mrs. Robbert told me when we got home."

"I should check it out before we take any chances."

"We're not taking chances. These guys are too thorough to have anything else planned this quickly. Besides, the police are driving by every half hour again."

"We could have been killed." She leaned against the counter beside him. Her knees seemed to have forgotten their purpose.

"I know."

"We almost were."

His arms came around her shoulders, casually, as if he knew she would reject an outright attempt at comfort. "I like the first part of that better. We could have been. We weren't, and 'almost were' doesn't count. Neither of us got more than scrapes and bruises. That's a long way from dying."

She didn't move closer, and she didn't move away. "We survived because your car's not a piece of junk and you knew what to do with it when we went over the side."

"I don't even know what I did. There were only seconds when I could still steer. Mostly I prayed."

She didn't know what to say to that. Things had obviously been worse than she'd even feared. "We've got to talk about who might have done it."

He turned her toward him and brushed a curl off her cheek. "We'll talk. In the spa."

"Do you always get what you want?"

"I'm just like everybody else in the world. You figure it out."

"I don't know enough about you to figure anything out."

"That's because you don't believe what you see." He gave her an intimate half smile, but he dropped his hand. "I'll be outside if you want to have a conversation."

After he left, she stayed in the kitchen and finished the rest of the tea before she realized she was being stubborn and stupid. He was right about safety. They would be fine now that a top-quality alarm system had been established outside. And Neuf, who still remained at the house despite Tara's dislike of dogs, would be good backup.

In her room she changed into her suit, a brown racing style with no pretensions. Her hair flopped on top of her head in a ponytail, and her freckles bloomed without benefit of makeup. If one thing had been made perfectly clear to her, it was that she had no business letting the strong attraction she felt to Griff interfere with her reason for being in his house. She was here to protect lives, something she could only do if she stayed objective and watchful. How objective could she be in his arms? He was a man who could drive all thoughts from her head, channel all her instincts into sexual fulfillment.

With this new, certain threat to his life came new knowledge. Now the need to protect Griff was clear. There was no longer any doubt he was in danger. She was in danger, too, both from the men who had tried to kill them tonight and from herself. If she let up her guard, allowed Griff to assume a different place in her life, then she was risking more than heartache. She was risking both their lives. She had to make that clear to him if she was going to stay.

The thought of the bubbling water soothing away the aches of the day propelled her outside—that thought and the one that reminded her she was still being paid to protect the man in the water. She whistled for Neuf, who nowadays could always be found outside Tara's door, a perennial Stage Door Johnny who was never allowed to put a foot across the sacred threshold.

"You have to carry that everywhere?" Griff asked when she set her gun under a towel on a poolside table.

She watched Neuf wander to the other side of the pool and take up his post. "You figure it out. The alarm goes off and Neuf starts barking. What happens next?"

"We cover our ears?"

"Wrong. A man comes charging into your little paradise, shooting at everything that moves. This guy doesn't care about a barking dog or an alarm. He figures he'll do his worst and get away before anybody pays attention to either."

"Do you stay up late inventing these scenarios?"

"If I did, maybe I'd have invented one about a van forcing us off the road." Kelley tried to ignore the broad-shouldered, muscular body within touching distance. Griff half-naked was difficult to ignore—witness the thousands of women who paid good money for occasional glimpses of less flesh than she was privy to right now.

She sat down on the edge of the spa and dangled her feet in the blissfully warm water.

"I'd have expected you to plunge right in," he said.

"You were just telling me I'm *too* cautious. This is in character."

He moved around the edge of the spa to be closer to her. From somewhere in the multitude of plantings surrounding the pool area, jasmine scented the air. The fragrance twined around the night breeze and wrapped itself around some nameless yearning inside of him.

"You're just cautious about some things," he said, "like protecting me and suspecting everyone who's ever drawn a breath. You're not cautious about what you say or do."

She slid into the water and took a seat beside him. "This was a good idea."

He watched the water cinch her waist, cup, then cover her breasts. He watched it caress her chin and he wished he could follow its path.

Instead he leaned back and shut his eyes. "Is that an apology, or are you trying to change the subject?"

"I'm not going to apologize for being too careful. I think today's fun and games prove that a little caution's a good thing. If anything, I haven't been careful enough."

"What does that mean?"

"Isn't it obvious? I should have realized the van turned off so that it could get ahead of us and pop out when we didn't expect it."

He opened his eyes and turned so he could see her. "You're not a fortune-teller."

"No. I'm a distracted private eye who almost got us killed tonight."

He started to protest, but she silenced him. "I can't do this job anymore. Tomorrow I'm going to find someone to take my place."

"I don't want anyone else."

"You need someone you can't charm."

He let the water bubble over him for a little while, thinking about her words. She looked both pensive and impatient, a combination only she could manage. "You mean I was getting through to you?"

"That's just what I mean. You need someone immune to you. Someone you take seriously."

"I take you seriously."

His deep baritone caressed her. She reminded herself that the line, said just that way, could have been the showpiece of a movie love scene.

"No, you don't." She stretched out so that she was facing him. "I ask you for information, you tell me I'm too suspicious. I tell you someone's following us, you tell me I'm—"

"Too suspicious," he finished for her.

"Anytime I'm doing my job, you tell me I'm overachieving. You look at me and you see a woman first, a warmed-over child star second and your security consultant third and last. You asked me, a woman, to be your bodyguard because you didn't *want* to take the idea seriously."

"Maybe that was true, but things have changed."

"No, they haven't. What did you do when I came out here a little while ago? You criticized me for bringing a gun, then you criticized me for listing reasons. And before that, when I was questioning the wisdom of coming out here at all, you told me you were going to do it anyway. When it comes right down to it, either you don't want anyone protecting you, or you don't want me. Whichever way it is, I'm off the case."

"Stay." He leaned forward so that they were almost touching. "I need you here."

"For what? Company? Trust me, Griff Bryant doesn't have to hire his company."

"Maybe you're right and I haven't taken this seriously. I haven't wanted to believe someone's trying to kill me."

"And?"

"It's pretty clear now it's a possibility."

"If you can see that, then you need someone you'll listen to."

He wanted to reach for her and tell her not to be foolish. But she wasn't being foolish. She was being honest, and unfortunately he could see that she was right on the mark. He had hired her because he had to hire someone and she was by far the most pleasing possibility. But his lack of commitment to his own safety had almost cost them both their lives. If he hadn't teased or criticized today, they might not have ended up in Marie Winslow's backyard.

"There's nothing wrong with you, and it's not your fault," he said after the silence had gone on too long. "I've made protecting me almost impossible."

"True enough."

"I won't put up any more roadblocks. Do your job the best ways you know how. You'll have my cooperation."

"There's more to it than that."

"What?"

She turned and swam to the other side. Resting her head on her arms, she stared through the feathery branches of a tree at the sliver of moon overhead. He joined her there after a minute.

"Looking for answers?" he asked.

"I don't think the moon can provide any."

"When I was a little boy, my mother told me I had to be very good and courageous, or the moon would disappear. At night I'd watch it get smaller and smaller and wonder if I'd be able to stop it. Then one night I'd see it seemed to be growing larger again, and I'd know what whatever I'd done had been good enough."

"An eclipse might have set back your entire psychological development."

"My mother wouldn't have let that happen. She would have made up another story to make it all right."

"She sounds interesting."

"She was a wonderful teller of tales. She named me Griffin because she said that when I was born she knew I would be as fast as the wind, that I would see far across the reaches of the earth and be a man of great strength. In Greek mythology the griffin was a creature with the head of an eagle and the body of a lion. Griffins guarded a vast store of gold, and they were always watchful in case someone tried to steal it."

"So you were both the swift eagle with eyes that saw all and the lion with superior strength."

"And the moon was the gold I guarded."

"What a wonderful gift to give a child."

He turned and leaned back against the side so that he could see her face. "She died when I was twelve. I still miss her."

She was touched. This was not the man who dangled villains from the Statue of Liberty. This was someone real, someone who wasn't afraid to admit his feelings, someone she liked much better.

She touched his arm before she'd thought better of it. "It's no wonder you became an actor. You grew up in the land of make-believe."

"We gave family plays when I was a kid, with costumes and props and scripts my mother or brother Jake wrote. Jake still writes plays. One was produced off-Broadway last year."

"Jake?"

"Jacob, after the biblical Jacob, who wrestled with an angel. My mother used to say that was what life was supposed to be about."

"She would have liked what you've become, Griffin."

He was silent, staring into a past that she couldn't see. "I don't know," he said after a moment. "I don't think so."

"No?"

"She wouldn't like the roles I play. I don't like them anymore, either."

"Tired of saving the world?"

"Tired of saving it by blowing half of it away. I represent death and destruction. That's not what I want to make people think about."

"I don't know. I've always thought you represented what we like to think of as the American spirit, might and right overcoming the forces of darkness, no matter what the odds."

"There are better ways to overcome anything, short of blasting it full of holes."

"That's why you didn't shoot the gunman at the wedding?"

"*Couldn't* shoot him. I intended to when I shouted at him. But I couldn't pull the trigger."

"And you wouldn't let me do it for you."

His smile was cynical. "If I had, maybe we wouldn't have met Marie today."

"You didn't want to shoot. You don't want to search your past for reasons why someone might want to shoot you. What do you want to do?"

He rested his hands on her shoulders, but she knew the lightness of his touch was deceptive. If she tried, he wouldn't let her move away.

"I want you to continue being my shadow," he said. "I don't want any more talk of someone else taking over."

"Look at us. Do you think this is the way the job is usually done? I'm soaking under the stars with you. You're being one hundred percent charming, and I'm falling for it."

"Are you?"

"I can't do my job if I'm not objective about it."

"You mean you're so overcome by desire, you wouldn't notice someone sneaking up on us?"

"You can laugh, but you know I'm right."

He traced a feather-light trail the length of her neck. "I don't know it. You've done a good job so far, despite my interference. And you're forgetting a couple of things. By protecting me, you're also protecting yourself. We still don't know who's being attacked and why. By being on guard, you're taking care of yourself, too. It only makes sense to stay here and do it."

She covered his hands to stop their wandering. "You said a *couple* of things."

"Tara's gotten used to having you around. If you leave and a man takes your place, I'll have to tell her why."

She turned away from him, moving to the spa's edge once more to stare into the night. "Tara's much brighter than anybody gives her credit for. She's certainly read about Felice's wedding—all of America's read about the wedding. And she'll hear about tonight's accident on the news tomorrow. A bodyguard won't come as a huge surprise to her."

"She's having a rough time right now. A man following me everywhere I go is going to make it rougher."

"What else?"

He rested his hands on her shoulders again, and his fingers began a slow massage. "Two reasons aren't enough?"

She sighed. "Well, you forgot to mention the one about my commitment to *Teardrop Creek.* I'm going to be on the set with you for a while, anyway, bodyguard or not. What else did you forget?''

''I didn't forget anything. I chose not to mention how much I like having you around. I know you don't want to hear it, so I'm still not mentioning it.''

''I'm supposed to be part of the scenery. You're not supposed to have any feelings about me at all.''

''You underestimate both of us.''

''I don't. That's exactly why you should get someone new.''

He turned her to him and pulled her closer. ''We're going to ride this out together.''

She waited until she was only inches from him to answer. ''On three conditions.''

He smiled. ''Why do I get the feeling this is what you've been wanting to tell me all along?''

''Because Tara gets her smarts from her father.''

He circled her with his arms, resting his hands at her waist. ''What are these conditions?''

''One, you let me hire someone to back me up, someone who'll stay out of sight but still be watching all the time.''

''Sounds like a good idea.''

She was surprised that number one had been so easy. ''Two, you treat this threat seriously and level with me about every person who might have even the most unlikely reason to want you dead.''

He stared at her, his lips tightening to a grim line.

''I mean it,'' she warned. ''I won't stay if you don't give me one hundred percent cooperation.''

''Done,'' he said at last.

''Third, you help me remember why I'm here. You're in danger and I can protect you. It's that simple. Not because I'm your friend. Not because your daughter needs a sympathetic woman in the house. Not to work my way into your bed.''

''Have you ever suppressed a thought? Even one?''

''This is no time to suppress thoughts, but it's a heck of a time to suppress what's happening between us.''

''And what is happening?''

"I'm acting like one of the women in your films. I turn to mush when you touch me. For God's sake, my knees get weak. And when you kiss me, I forget why you're doing it."

"You're sure about why I'm doing it?"

"Griffin, don't play the film hunk hero with me. Look, I'll tell you something. I'm twenty-seven, and there've only been a couple of men in my life who meant anything to me. I lived with one of them for a while and thought I was in love. I also believed everything he ever told he. Then one day I found out that none of it had been true, including the fact that he was divorced. It took his pregnant wife to convince me. Do you see? I fooled myself into believing he loved me. I could fool myself again someday. Don't let me."

"If you expect to be fooled, someone's going to try."

"Don't be the one. Okay?"

"If you expect to be loved, someone's going to try."

She sighed.

"Kelley." He covered the few necessary inches to kiss her. She sighed again, against his lips, but her body was as warm, as silken and fluid against his as the water pulsing around them.

He wrapped his arms around her and rubbed them against her bare skin. She made a sound deep in her throat that was beyond words, beyond language of any sort. It told him everything he needed to know. He clasped her tighter. She moved into his embrace as if she had always been held by him.

He could feel himself growing harder against her. Her hips fit perfectly against his; her breasts flattened against his chest. She tasted like desert rain, like a cooling summer breeze, like all of life's miracles. He felt desire shudder through him, testing his control and taunting his intention to go slowly. He wanted her with a speed that sucked him into its tail wind and carried him along with it until thought was feeling and feeling was everything.

She was the one who finally broke away. He held her against him at first, tighter, harder, unable to relinquish what he had found. She pushed with gentle force against his chest.

"I can't stay unless we put a stop to this."

His lungs seemed to catch with every breath. "Is that really what you want?"

"It has to be."

He saw the shudder pass through, although her words denied it. "For my safety or yours?"

She backed away. "I said three conditions. Are you willing to abide by them?"

He took a deep breath. Then another. "Until I'm not willing."

She lifted her chin. "Then that will be the moment I pack and go."

He didn't smile. "And that will be the moment I come after you."

She stared into his eyes until she realized he wasn't going to show her what he was feeling. She supposed it was just as well. She turned away. "It's time we both went to bed. We've got an early call again tomorrow." She climbed out of the spa, whistling for Neuf. Then she started toward her gun and towel without waiting to see if he was going to follow.

"There are two people who might want me dead," he said quietly.

The night was warm, and the dry desert breeze was already sweeping moisture from her skin. Still, she shivered at his words. She turned and found him close behind her. "And you haven't thought to tell me that before?"

"I haven't wanted to believe the scene at the wedding had anything to do with me."

She knew there was no point in telling him how stupid that had been. Two men in a green van had explained it nicely. "Who are they?"

"I don't know the identity of one of them. He writes me letters, threatening letters."

"Why?"

"Because I'm Griff Bryant."

"A crazy fan?"

"You could say that, I guess, though fan's an odd word to use."

"Do they come to you through the studio?"

"He's smarter than that. He has my home address."

She shut her eyes. "I don't believe this."

"He makes no sense. He rambles. He talks about his father. He talks about real men. In one letter he tells me I'm his idol and in the next he tells me I should die for my sins."

"Just your ordinary sort of fan mail."

"Obviously I toss the letters out when they come. But he writes frequently. I'll pass the next one on to you."

"Did it *ever* occur to you to turn some of these little love letters over to the police? Did you think they might want to check him out?"

"There's never a return address."

"There are ways to trace mail. You've worked in enough spy thrillers to know that."

He reached for her towel and tossed it to her. He didn't touch the gun. "The other possibility is an actor named Norris Roxey."

She got an instant picture of a man Griff's size with a big-toothed smile and a mop of golden hair. *"My Ghoul Friday?"*

"That's the one."

She didn't know much about Roxey except that *My Ghoul*, a second-rate horror-comedy, had become a camp classic that had hurtled him into the public eye. He was not an actor of Griff's stature, however. The films he starred in were low budget or made for television. She was almost surprised Griff even knew him.

"Why would he be after you?" she asked.

"He wanted the lead in *Victims No More.* I think he saw the film as a way to be taken seriously. Zephyr considered him for it because I was still working on another film when they wanted to start shooting. In the end they decided to wait for me. Roxey accused me of pulling strings to take the part away from him, although I couldn't have cared less. We were both guests at a party a few weeks after the decision was made. Between the hors d'oeuvres and the entertainment, Roxey took a swing at me."

"Did he connect?"

"No. In fact when he missed, he passed out in an alcoholic haze. It was big news for a while."

"In Suzy Slander's paper, maybe." She considered what he had told her. "Has he made any threats? Tried anything since?"

"He talks big. There's no reason to think he means anything he says."

"Is he capable of pulling off something as grandiose as the wedding?"

"He's an actor. He can stage a scene. But it'd be more his style to swing out of the choir loft like Douglas Fairbanks and try to plant a foot on my jaw."

"And fall into the congregation instead."

"Apparently you've seen his movies."

She shook her head in disbelief. "And you didn't think this was worth mentioning?"

"I still don't. But I'm mentioning it anyway."

"Anything else?"

"Yeah." He moved closer, until there was nothing between them except inches of fragrant desert air. "You can set all the conditions you want, but the moment we both know making love is right, all the conditions in the world aren't going to make any difference."

"And if that moment never comes?"

He smiled an intimate, caressing smile she had never seen onscreen. "Now who's living in a world of make-believe?"

Chapter 11

Two recently retired police detectives, with experience and skill at blending into shadows, skirted the edges of Griff and Kelley's lives. She knew when each man was working and where he was because she stayed alert to everything around her. She didn't think Griff was aware of them most of the time. She hoped that Tara wasn't aware of them at all.

The days after the incident with the van fell into a routine that made the brush with death seem like a distant fantasy. She and Griff got up before dawn and drove to the set, varying their routes and times of departure. One of the men routinely followed several car lengths behind. The cars the men used varied, although Kelley always knew what they would be driving, so that she wouldn't think the worst. Since Griff's Volvo was at the shop, he drove a variety of rental cars, trading them in every few days to help confuse would-be attackers.

A third man had been hired to come in as Griff and Kelley were leaving and stay at the house until it was time for him to drive Tara to school. Mrs. Robbert had agreed to pass him off as a brother who was doing her a favor. He picked Tara up after school, too, and stayed around to do gardening and other chores until it was late afternoon and time for the second detective to take up his station outside the house. The first detective followed Kelley and Griff home and left as soon as he was sure his replacement was already on duty.

A week after the accident, Kelley got up earlier than usual to make coffee before the long drive to location. Tara sat at a small oak table that Griff had recently added to the decor, staring out the window into the darkness. Neuf lay in the doorway watching her.

"Up so early?" Kelley asked. "You don't have to leave for school for hours."

"I couldn't sleep."

Kelley thought she heard leftover tears in Tara's voice, but she knew better than to mention her suspicion. She had backed away from Griff's daughter much as she had backed away from him. Strangely, though, the maneuver, meant solely to maintain objectivity, had somehow made it easier for Tara to reach out to her. It had happened so slowly, at times Kelley hadn't been sure she wasn't imagining it. But little by little some of Tara's hostility toward her had disappeared, replaced by something that, on the surface, looked much like yearning.

Now Kelley went right for the ordinary, as if she hadn't noticed anything unusual. "Would you like some juice?"

"That would be nice."

The positive response was a small thing, but relationships had been built on less. Kelley poured orange juice into two glasses and took them to the table. "I used to like to get up early sometimes when I was your age. The house was always quiet, and I could think without anyone bothering me."

"This house is always quiet."

"It is, isn't it?" Kelley sat down across from Tara. "When you live with your mother, is there more going on?"

"Sometimes she lets me have friends over."

Kelley swallowed the "sometimes" right along with her first sip of juice and concentrated on the rest of Tara's sentence. "Have you made friends here yet?"

"No."

"I know how hard it can be."

"You probably always had friends."

"Think so?" Kelley tried to remember. "Nope," she said at last. "Remember, I used to work in the movies, and while I was filming, I was taught on the set. When it was time to go back to my regular school, everybody already had friends and didn't want somebody new around. Besides, I always had to prove I wasn't Strawberry Finn. It always took time. My mother called it the six-week rule."

"Six weeks?"

"She told me that it would take six weeks to find new friends in my class. So we'd make a chart, and I'd mark off days on it. Sometimes she was wrong and it only took five and a half."

"Did it ever take longer?"

"Nope. Never. I found out that if I was nice to people, they'd kind of look me over. That took about two weeks, and that was a pretty lonely time. Then for the next two weeks they'd start remembering I was there and maybe include me in things once in a while. For the last two weeks they'd stop thinking about me as someone new and think about me as someone they *knew*. They'd start inviting me places and coming when I invited them. By the end of that, I was on my way to being part of the gang. It always helped to know it would work that way, so I wouldn't be too impatient at the start."

"I'm not impatient."

Kelley risked a smile. "Good for you."

"I mean, I don't care if anybody likes me. These girls are dumb and the boys are even dumber!"

"Are they?"

"I don't care if they make fun of Griff, either."

Kelley's heart went out to her. She could just imagine what being Griff's daughter must be like. "I'm sure you don't. I mean, you're smart enough to know that they only do it because they're jealous, right? I'm sure you don't brag or make a big deal of who your father is."

"I never brag."

"And you're smart enough to know that in a few weeks no one will remember who your dad is anyway."

"They won't?"

This time Kelley forced herself not to smile. Every once in a while Tara forgot to sound bored and sounded just like the scared kid she was. "Absolutely not. They'll forget you're new, too. It's just that you're in the toughest part of it now, so that's hard to see." She reached across the table and lightly touched Tara's arm, withdrawing her fingers before the girl could object. "It'll get better."

"I don't care if it does or not."

"Well, you know, you're allowed to, if you want."

Tara looked up from her juice and frowned.

"Allowed to care, I mean," Kelley went on. "It's okay to wish things were different. It's part of being alive."

"It's boring here. I'm bored. That's all."

"I've got something you could do with me late this afternoon, if you wanted."

Tara looked suspicious.

Kelley sighed and promptly backed away. "I bet you'd hate it, though."

"Probably."

Kelley stood. "Want more juice?"

"What could I do?"

Kelley reached for Tara's glass. "Well, I'm taking my Cub Scout den to a friend's swimming pool. I thought maybe you'd come with me and help me keep an eye on them."

"Cub Scouts?" Tara sounded horrified.

"Let me tell you about these kids. Three of them don't have fathers, one of them lives with an aunt and uncle and another one lives in a foster home. They can really raise the roof, but they're great kids. The pack is special. It meets in a police station, and the leaders are police officers who volunteer their time. All the kids have been recommended by their teachers because they're having problems in school."

"How come you work with them?"

Kelley took her time walking over to the sink with the glasses. She couldn't tell Tara the truth, that her connections with the law enforcement agencies in the area were so solid she had been an automatic choice. She didn't want to lie, either. "Well, when I lived in Los Angeles, I was a police detective."

"Really?"

Kelley peeked over the counter at her. "Surprised?"

"I thought you were an actress."

"I've done both." She wrinkled her nose. "Frankly I liked police work better."

Tara fidgeted in her seat. Since she was usually absolutely still, as if life weren't worth moving for, Kelley knew something big was coming. "Kelley," Tara said softly, "if you used to be a policeman—woman, then maybe you could keep an eye on Griff."

Kelley looked away. The concern on Tara's face was both wonderful and painful to witness. "Are you worried about him?"

"Bad things have been happening to him."

"I know."

"Do you think somebody's trying to hurt him?"

Kelley knew better than to lie to this child who could sense the truth with the instincts of a bloodhound. "I'm afraid so."

"Somebody needs to protect him."

"That's being taken care of," Kelley promised. "Both the police and security guards at the studio are watching him carefully. Someone follows him everywhere he goes." She didn't add that that someone was her, although she was tempted. She just wasn't sure if it would upset Tara to know that the situation was so serious she was being paid to live with Griff. She didn't want to admit they'd been lying about her identity, either.

She compromised with a little of the truth. "I do keep an eye out. And someone's keeping an eye on you, too," she added. "There's no reason in the world to think anyone wants you hurt, but just so you won't be worried, I want you to know you're safe."

"I'm not worried about me. It's Griff. He's the one—"

Griff entered the room. "You don't need to worry about me. I'm going to be fine."

Tara wiped all expression off her face. "I'm not worried."

Kelley wanted to shake them both. She restrained herself. "I was just telling Tara about my Cub Scouts. Since we're getting off the set early this afternoon, I'm going to take my den swimming at Felice's condo after school. Want to come? Tara might."

"I'll come if Tara comes. We can protect each other from you and your kids."

Kelley saw Tara glance at her father. Her expression was inscrutable, but when she looked away, she nodded. "There's nothing else to do."

Kelley glanced at Griff to see if he was pleased. The look on his face was brighter than the sun edging over the horizon. She told herself that this was not her concern, that she wasn't getting involved. She told herself that if having strong feelings for Griff was unwise, having strong feelings for both Tara and Griff was catastrophic.

Tara walked past her on the way out of the kitchen. "I've been in school for two weeks," she said, as if to no one in particular. Neuf lumbered to his feet and followed her out of the room.

Kelley took a deep breath and urged the voices in her head to speak a little louder.

Griff insisted Kelley's den come to his house to swim. Since Griff's pool was protected by elaborate security precautions, Kelley gratefully agreed. She made all the necessary arrangements from Griff's trailer on the set.

At four o'clock she was back at Griff's house and ready for the onslaught. Tara had stayed after school to finish a social studies project, and Griff had walked through the door and straight to the phone for what seemed like a marathon call with Cam. She knew that having Tara and Griff there with the boys didn't really matter, but the disappointment she felt was more convincing.

The boys were dropped off, courtesy of her assistant den leader, Tony, a fifteen-year veteran of the Desert Palm force who was putty in the hands of kids. She convinced the boys to take off their shirts and shoes before jumping in the pool, but that was the most order she could bestow on the chaos. There were five little heads bobbing above the water in various stages of faked drowning when Griff came out to stand beside her.

He took in the sight of his pool filled with the churnings of a rainbow assortment of little boys. He took in the sight of Kelley's worried face. He wondered if she told herself she had to be objective about these kids, too. He had never seen more naked evidence of love than that shining in her eyes.

Something he had been trying to control for days slipped its moorings. He had told himself he could play along with her need to control their relationship. There was some merit in what she said about needing objectivity to do her job, even if he suspected it was mostly an excuse to keep from getting involved with him. She didn't trust easily, and she'd admitted to one bad experience to spur that distrust. But he suspected there was more to her feeling than one experience. She was a perfectionist. When Kelley did something, she did it perfectly, or she couldn't live with herself.

Some of her relentless striving had probably come from her early career in films. He knew for a fact that she had worked with some of the film community's most demanding directors. While other little girls were playing with dolls and jumping rope, she had done endless retakes of flawed scenes. She had learned to expect only the best from herself and to fear anything else.

He had witnessed the careers of enough child actors to understand what happened to them on a movie set. No matter how supportive their home environment, on the set they were still expected to be little adults. Directors instinctively used approval or lack of it to control them. Directors weren't evil people, but they had a job to do, and approval was the best way to get what they wanted. Money meant little to a kid, and future reviews meant even less. Friendship and love meant everything.

Kelley had grown up expecting perfection from herself, doing real-life retakes if she didn't get it right the first time or even the twenty-fifth. Add a childhood of watching Hollywood bedroom shenanigans to one bad experience with a man, throw in one apparently perfect relationship between her own parents, and her list of what the right kind of relationship entailed was miles long and so restrictive that she would never find what she thought she was looking for.

Unless he made her see what she was doing.

"Griff." She turned to him, glancing away from the pool just long enough to shoot him a smile. "I'm glad you're here."

"I told you I would be."

"I thought maybe you'd gotten tied up."

"I'm never tied up when someone's counting on me."

She heard his message loud and clear and felt properly chastised. "Well, thanks."

"Tara's not home yet?"

"Mrs. Robbert says she should be here any minute."

Griff pitched a beach ball at two boys who were trying to duck each other. As he watched, they started throwing the ball back and forth instead. "Tara likes you."

"How can you tell?"

"Because she's a lot like me. Her taste is excellent, but she's not always good at expressing it."

"She's a good kid."

"Like the kids in the pool? Good kids, not kids you're particularly attached to or anything?"

"Are you trying to make a point?"

"Just that you're not nearly as tough as you like to pretend."

"I'm made of steel."

"Which kid in the water is your favorite?"

"Every one of them."

"Softie."

"Go soak your head."

"My thought precisely." He slid his arm around her affectionately, then with one quick scoop knocked her into the water. She surfaced to retaliate, but he was already in the pool by then, under attack from five fierce eight-year-olds. By the time Tara arrived to join them, all-out war had been declared.

Tara, it turned out, was a master tactician. To Kelley's surprise, she didn't hold back at all, jumping into the battle and organizing troops with the skill of a general. By the time they all climbed out to demolish three huge pizzas courtesy of Mrs. Robbert, Tara, Griff and the boys were firm friends.

Much later, when the boys had gone home, Kelley lay out in the sun beside the pool, too tired to move. She considered herself temporarily off duty since Griff wasn't going anywhere that she knew of and the house was not only secure but under guard.

"Aren't you going to burn?" Griff asked, coming up beside her.

"I don't burn. I freckle, and I have this theory that if I get enough sun, my freckles will merge into one glorious tan."

"How long have you had that theory?"

"Since I was old enough to fantasize."

He spotted a bottle of sun block beside her and poured some into his hands. "Hold still."

"Why?"

"Because the sun's making a liar out of you."

She felt his hands on her shoulders and tried to squirm away. "Hey, I don't need that. It's late afternoon, and besides, I already used some."

"Not enough."

Knowing it was useless to continue her objections, she lay still. The instant he touched her again, she tensed.

"Either you have the firmest body in California, or you're about to jump out of your skin."

She wasn't going to tell him she was protecting herself. He touched her and all her nerve endings twanged the "Hallelujah Chorus." She had to allow him a certain amount of touching when they were with other people, but now that there was no one around to impress, she didn't have to allow what amounted to torture. "I'm just trying to get some rest," she said pointedly.

"Then relax and rest. I'll help the process along." He began to knead her clenched muscles. "I like your Cub Scouts. Who's the kid with the blond crew cut? Jared? He told me he'd seen one of my movies, but he didn't like it very well."

"That's Jared."

"Your kind of kid. Says whatever he thinks."

She bit back what *she* was thinking. "They loved being here."

"Some of those kids could hardly swim. I don't think they get chances like this very often."

"Some of them have had private lessons at their country club. Kenny's father is a millionaire, but Kenny's only met him twice. Apparently his dad's a swell guy. He sends Kenny's mother a big check every month and figures that's the price he has to pay for keeping them both out of his hair.''

"Bastard.''

"You probably know him.'' She named an actor who had been in the movies almost as long as they had included sound.

Griff repeated himself.

Kelley sighed. "The only things my kids have in common is that they've all shown signs of heading for trouble. Eight years old and they're on their way to jail already. The rich ones will get bailed out and the poor ones won't, but that will be the big difference between them.''

"You don't really believe that. You think if you help them now, talk about God and country and brotherly love enough, you'll change the path they're on.''

"Somebody's got to care.''

He gave up trying to untie the knots in her muscles and lay down beside her. "You care about everybody.''

"Don't be too sure.''

"But you hate to show it.''

"Let's talk about something else.''

"Tara's on the telephone with a girl from school. It sounds like they're making plans to spend the night together and finish working on some project they're doing for social studies.''

"Really?'' She turned on her side to face him. "She was just telling me this morning—well, sort of telling me, upside down and backward like she does—how lonely she was here.''

"Apparently her teacher assigned her to work with this girl today.''

"Did she?'' Kelley turned onto her back and shut her eyes.

"You wouldn't know how that happened, would you?''

"How would I know?''

"You were on the phone a lot in my trailer today.''

"I was setting up the swim party. I had to call Scout headquarters and let them know the location had changed so that their insurance—''

"Did you call Tara's teacher? Yes or no?''

"No, I did not.'' She was silent for a little while. "I called her principal.''

"Kelley.''

She heard both exasperation and respect in his voice. "What's wrong with that?"

"I should have been the one to call."

"When would you have had the time?"

"She's my daughter. I always have time for her. You assumed I wouldn't think this is important."

She thought about what he'd said and realized he was right. "I'm sorry, but after she talked to me, I just thought I should be the one to try to do something to help her."

"I wish she'd talk to me."

"You never tell her your feelings, so she doesn't think she can tell you hers."

He was silent for a long time. "That's what it takes?"

"I think so."

"Then how about if I tell *you* my feelings."

She wet her lips. "Well, I—"

"I need you with me tonight."

She turned back to her side and faced him again, completely taken aback. "What?"

"I said I need you with me. Will you come?"

"I go everywhere with you."

His gaze locked with hers. "That's not the same thing. I need you with me tonight. Not the detective, not the pretend lover. You. Kelley Samuels, the woman, the friend."

She felt the fragile truce they had made shattering around her. "I don't know, I—"

"Cam called to tell me they'll be screening *One Way Ticket* at Michael's house tonight."

She stared at him. "You must be—"

"No." He touched her lips to silence her. "Don't tell me what I'm feeling. I'll tell you. I'm scared. I don't want to see Drake up there, knowing he's not in the room watching it with me. And I don't want to watch the scene where some stuntman pretends to get blown to kingdom come, just like Drake really did. I don't want to go at all, but Cam and Michael are right. This is the time and place for me to see it."

"You don't ever have to see it. You don't have to go to the premiere."

"I can't ignore this. I have to get finished with that part of my life somehow."

She still wasn't sure why he had to see the movie. She wasn't even sure he knew why. But she had no doubt of his sincerity, nor of what he was asking of her.

"I want you with me," he repeated. "Will you come?"

A week before, she could have refused him. Now she could not. Despite everything she had told him, despite everything she still believed to be true about her role in his life, she was helpless to say no when he needed her. It wasn't pity, nor even compassion. It was a link between them that seemed to grow stronger every day. Each time he showed her the man he really was, she felt herself bound more surely to him.

"I'll come," she said.

He relaxed. "Good." He linked his fingers with hers and shut his eyes.

She saw clearly the path she was following. She grew tense when he touched her because it felt too good. She couldn't refuse him when he asked her to share one of his most emotional moments because she cared too much. She had demanded that their relationship be purely business, but now she saw there was no chance of that.

She should leave, find someone else to take her place and leave, just as she had threatened. But all the reasons why she should were less important than the one reason why she couldn't. She and Griff were bound together now, in some mysterious way and for mysterious reasons known only to the man or men stalking them. But even that connection was less compelling than the mysterious link that had nothing to do with the attempt on their lives.

She looked at him now, and she could almost see the world through his eyes. He touched her, and she could almost feel his heartbeat. The chance to pack and go had gone. With something that resembled fear she realized she was going to have to see tonight, and whatever came after it, to its conclusion. The choice was no longer hers.

Chapter 12

Michael lived in Rancho Mirage, not more than fifteen minutes from Griff's house. Kelley and Griff were almost there when she realized exactly what part of the small city they were in.

"Tom Fortney's house." She turned and touched Griff's arm. "We're not more than a quarter of a mile from Uncle Tom's house."

"Uncle Tom?"

She made a face. "Embarrassing, right?"

"You called him Uncle Tom?"

"I was special."

"If anyone else had called him that, they would have been barred from his set for life."

She was glad they were talking because she knew that at least temporarily it helped Griff take his mind off what was to come. "He was always kind to me, beginning with the evening he rescued me from the rope, right through to our last movie together."

"Fortney was well-thought-of in the industry. His funeral was huge."

"I was there."

"So was I." He turned onto a new street. "You're about to experience déjà vu."

It took her only a moment to figure out what he meant. "We're going to his house?"

He nodded. "Michael bought Fortney's estate after he died. He has a home in West Hollywood, too, but he spends all the time he can out here. He's a nostalgia buff. I think half the draw of this house was that Fortney had built it and lived in it for so many years. The other half was that it came with a lot of Fortney's possessions, including his film collection."

"He must have paid a fortune."

"Michael's worth one. If it weren't for him, a lot of us would still be playing bit parts and slinging hash for spare change."

She laughed. "Don't tell me you think you owe your success to somebody else?"

He glanced at her and was reminded how much he liked what he saw. She was dressed in the most-touchable fabric under the heavens, something between silk and velvet that hung and clung and guaranteed a man would be a basket case sitting next to her for the evening. The forest green pants and loose tunic covered every inch of skin, but didn't spare the imagination. Her hair, loose and riotous, was the perfect accessory.

"Well?" she demanded.

He forced his gaze back to the road. "Well what?"

"Do you think Michael made you a success?"

"He's one of the factors."

"And the others?"

"Luck. Ambition. Hard work. Talent. None of which would have done me much good if I hadn't had a director who knew how to showcase the talent I did have and focus my energy."

"Come on. You've worked with other directors."

"Michael was the first one who saw my potential and figured out how to use it. I owe him a lot." He turned onto Michael's street, an exclusive section of an exclusive community. The houses were more easily described as compounds, set back from the road and surrounded by acres of lawns and lavish gardens. Palms and elaborate landscaping shielded many of them from view, as did fountains of water spraying almost continuously to keep the lawns green.

Kelley was surprised to hear that Griff was so modest about everything he had accomplished. She wanted to argue with him about Michael's role in his success, but she knew this wasn't the night for an argument. He already had too much on his mind.

She returned to the subject of Tom Fortney. "Uncle Tom had a granddaughter my age. Whenever Sara was in town, he'd send a limo for me and I'd be driven out here to play with her. This was country in those days. A lot of these estates were just sand and cactus."

"Now every square inch of it's worth a fortune."

"I liked it better when it was desert."

He pulled into a drive bordered by swaying palms. He passed through an open gate, the only break in a tall fence surrounding the property, camouflaged by oleander and thickets of pine.

"The fence is a new addition," Kelley observed.

"Michael got tired of would-be actors coming up to his front door for impromptu auditions. He controls the gate by computer from the house."

"Trials of the rich and famous." She reached over and put her hand on Griff's arm when he stopped the car. "I'm with you tonight."

He didn't answer. He just covered her hand for a second, then got out to open her door.

Michael greeted them on his porch. He shook Griff's hand and kissed Kelley's cheek. "You make a spectacular couple. I want you together in another movie, something with a bigger role for Sammy. She's outclassing Miranda," he said, addressing Griff. "The scenes with both of you in them are explosive. You're going to have to work harder at remembering Sammy's not your love interest."

Miranda Lyle was *Teardrop Creek's* heroine and Griff's co-star. She was also one terrifically sexy woman. Kelley had found it difficult to watch the one love scene that Griff and Miranda had done so far.

"This is my final performance," she told Michael before he could launch into more compliments. "I told Uncle Tom that same thing, by the way, in almost this same spot."

"Well, you were wrong that time, and you'll be wrong this time, too. Odd, isn't it, that I live in Tom's house, and now I'm directing his favorite little actress?'' Michael put his arm around her and guided her through the house. She could hear the buzz of voices somewhere up ahead.

The house was huge, just as she remembered. As a child she had always felt as if the house were an elaborate movie theater lobby, and now she discovered little had changed. There were marble pillars, marble floors, high ceilings defined by ornate plaster cornices. Michael chatted nonstop as he took them through a thickly landscaped conservatory adorned with the same life-size statues of animals that she and Sara had played on as children. They emerged in the same screening room where she and Sara had once watched endless showings of *The Wizard of Oz*.

Cam was already there, and so were half a dozen other people who had worked on *One Way Ticket*. Griff, who had been silent until now, took over the introductions, making sure that Kelley was presented to everyone.

If the rest of the house resembled a thirties Loew's theater lobby, the screening room was the theater itself, the heart of a house built around it. It was small by commercial standards, but it could still easily seat seventy. The chairs were new, Kelley noted, royal blue plush and adjustable, with armrests and trays for drinks.

She settled herself in the third row and watched Griff make his way to the small bar set up on the other side of the room. His progress was slow because everyone wanted a word with him. Not as fans—these were people with no star adoration left in their hearts—but as friends and co-workers. She had noticed this before. There were no barriers between Griff and the people he worked with. She had seen stars freeze other high-ranking film professionals with a word or a glance, as if they truly believed they were too good to mix with anyone. Griff treated everyone courteously, from the extras to the studio heads.

As more people arrived, he returned with drinks and a plate of hors d'oeuvres. ''Cam says Suzy Slander's devoted her latest column to our romance.''

''Next week she'll have us married, and the week after that I'll be in Reno getting a divorce.'' Kelley held out her hand for the glass of wine she'd requested. Griff's drink looked ten times as potent. Since he wasn't much of a drinker, it said a lot about his state of mind.

"I always thought the tabloids were basically harmless, but after Drake was killed, they dug up all kinds of half-truths about his life and the way he died. They had a field day." Griff took a long swallow. "I wish Michael would get started."

Kelley looked around to see if anyone was listening. No one seemed to be. "Are you all right?"

"I just want this over with."

"Why don't you eat something? Everything looks good."

He took another drink and ignored her.

"Keep it up and I'll have to drive us home," she warned.

"You can't. You're riding shotgun, remember?"

"Men drink and women cry. Want to take bets which is healthier?"

"Shall I burst into tears to make you happy?"

She smiled gently at him and linked her arm through his, effectively making it impossible for him to drink with that hand. "Could you?"

"I wish Michael would get started."

"When I was a cop," she said, "I saw a carload of kids get hit broadside by a truck. Right in front of me. I pried the youngest kid out of the wreckage. The others managed to get out on their own. I held that kid and did everything I could to keep him alive, but he died in my arms. Months later, when I'd just begun to go for days without thinking about it, I had to go into court and testify. Someone on the scene had taken pictures and the kids' attorney had made them into slides. I got up after the third slide and left, but sometimes I still dream about it."

He didn't say anything. He just raised her hand to his lips and kissed it.

"We could still leave," she said. "Michael and Cam would understand."

"Drake wouldn't."

In some crazy way she understood. Griff believed he owed watching the film to Drake. It was up to Griff to see it to a conclusion since Drake could not.

Michael walked to the front and asked everybody to take a seat. He gave a little talk about the film. Most of the information was technical, relating to the editing and printing. He said a little about Drake and how the shadow of his death would always hang over the film, then he signaled for the lights to be dimmed.

The film began to roll.

Kelley was sure she wouldn't be able to concentrate, knowing how difficult watching the film was going to be for Griff. Ten minutes into it she was lost in the story.

Michael Donnelly's trademark was taking stories that had been done to death and redoing them until they were bigger and better than anyone had dreamed they could be. *Teardrop Creek* was his shot at a Western. *One Way Ticket* was his ode to the unsung heroes of World War II.

She watched in fascination as each scene built, as each actor gave a better performance than the last. Griff was stunning, reaching a technical perfection that outdistanced anything else she had ever seen of his. He was tough and aggressive, with an inner sensitivity that Michael and his crew caught again and again. She had fallen in love with him before the closing credits were finished, and she knew every woman who saw the movie would do the same.

Twenty minutes into the film she felt the real Griff grip her hand. A new character came on the screen, and she was familiar enough with Drake Scott's work to recognize him. He was a young man, no older than she was, cocky and self-assured. He was shorter and slighter than Griff, without his sexual magnetism or hard-edged good looks, but his acting was flawless. He spoke rapidly and moved restlessly, as if fueled by some inner flame. Unless it was Griff playing opposite Drake in a scene, he was always the scene's focal point.

In the darkness she stole a glance at Griff. His face looked grim. He hadn't dropped her hand, and she suspected if she tried to slip it from his, he wouldn't allow it. He seemed totally immersed in the movie, yet he held on to her as if she were a lifeline to reality.

Something turned over inside her. The man on the screen, a man any woman could fall in love with, was nothing compared to the man beside her. This man cared desperately about those close to him. Perhaps he couldn't always show it, but the caring was soul-deep and wide. There was nothing shallow, egotistical or demanding about Griff. Drake Scott had been his friend, and now he suffered because Drake was dead.

She wanted to demand that the film be stopped, that Griff take her home and try to forget what the film was soon going to show, but she knew she couldn't. She felt helpless; she could not soothe away any of his pain. All she could do was sit beside him and keep her fingers entwined with his.

The death scene came too soon. As little as she knew about the story, she knew Drake's plot line was building to a climax even before she felt Griff sit straighter. His tension was palpable. She could hardly bear to watch the screen. She saw Drake's plane come in for a landing, saw him leap free and begin to run.

She heard Griff make a sound deep in his throat, and she shut her eyes.

The explosion resounded through her head anyway.

The scene ended with merciful swiftness. One moment Michael's screening room echoed with the sounds of hell, the next it was silent.

She opened her eyes to Griff staring across an empty, windswept airfield. The camera zoomed out. Griff was little more than a dot on the horizon when he threw his arms up toward the heavens.

She counted the minutes until the film ended. She couldn't look at Griff. She wanted to comfort him, but his pain was her own. She didn't know what to say, what comfort to give.

When the lights finally came back on, he dropped her hand. Only then, with that link severed, could she face him. "Are you all right? Shall we get out of here?"

"I want to talk to Michael and Cam."

"Would you like me to leave you alone?"

"You can stay."

She watched him go through the motions as the rest of the guests discussed the film with him before they left. She listened to the accolades for his performance, the expressions of sadness at Drake's death, the technical comments related to the length and juxtaposition of certain scenes. She allowed herself a sigh of relief when only Michael and Cam were left.

"I need another drink," Michael said. He came back from the bar with two, one for him and one for Griff. "I should have asked you if you needed a refill," he said to Cam and Kelley. "I don't know where my head is."

"I suspect I know," Cam said. She refused his offer, as did Kelley. Griff took his drink and set it beside him.

"We want to know what you think," Cam told Griff.

"What do you want me to say?"

"You can just tell us what you saw tonight," Michael said. "Honest feedback."

"I hated it." Griff ran his hand through his hair.

"You hated the film, or you hated what happened on the set?" Cam asked.

"There's no separating them."

Cam's voice dropped to a more intimate level. Kelley was reminded of the relationship she and Griff had once shared. It wasn't a reminder she enjoyed. "I know how you must be feeling. It was a terrible tragedy to lose Drake."

"I stood there, and I watched him get blown away. I almost got blown away myself. For what? For two hours of film in a can. For a few vicarious thrills, a few tears, a jolt of patriotism."

"You used to think more of your work than that," Michael said. "You used to think more of my work."

"Michael thinks you blame him for what happened," Cam said.

"Hell, I blame myself for what happened," Michael said. "Why shouldn't you?"

"I don't blame anybody. I don't know what happened, why Drake wasn't out of the way when the explosives went off, but I know you're too much of a perfectionist to be at fault."

"I don't know what happened, either," Michael said. "I talked to Drake before his scene. I went over the instructions. I told him to be careful."

"I saw you," Griff said. "I know you talked to him. Damn it, I know Drake was being careful. Right beforehand he told me he was worried about the scene, that he had a bad feeling about it.''

Michael frowned. ''Did he say why?''

''We were interrupted. We never finished the conversation. I got the feeling it was the same kind of last-minute jitters we all get before a scene like that one. I was feeling them, too.''

''Are you going to be able to support the picture?'' Cam asked. ''The release is going to bring a fresh batch of questions about Drake's death. Are we going to be able to count on you, or are you going to tell the press what you told us tonight?''

Griff was silent.

''This is a good film,'' Michael said. ''One of your best.''

''And one of yours,'' Kelley told him.

''Do you think so?''

''I felt like I was living the whole thing.''

''You were. Film's no illusion. What's up there on the screen is part of a process, part of a chain of events. It's as real as anything else in life.''

''This time maybe too damned real,'' Griff said.

''You know Michael didn't use the footage where Drake died,'' Cam said. ''He reshot it with a stuntman. What the audience will see is not Drake's death. Cut us some slack on this, Griff. You must still have respect for Zephyr or you wouldn't be making *Teardrop Creek*. And you wouldn't be working with Michael if you thought he was careless and wasn't taking precautions.''

''I've never said anything about Michael being careless.''

She nodded. ''We know what you've been going through off the set, but on the set you're safe. Don't jinx *One Way Ticket* by bad-mouthing it to the press. Give Drake his due and let his last film be a tribute to his remarkable talent. That's all you can do for him now.''

''I don't want to make the rounds of the talk shows.''

''We won't ask you to.''

''I don't want to be at the premiere.''

''We've decided not to introduce it that way. We're going to release it in L.A. and New York just after Christmas, then follow that with a general release a few weeks later.''

Kelley knew that by the limited release in December they were assuring the film's inclusion in the Academy Awards competition for this year. She also knew that by not speeding up the film's general release, they were probably cutting their profit margin. She was surprised and impressed that they weren't going to try to make it a holiday spectacular. It was hardly a Christmas theme, but that had never stopped other companies from releasing far grislier films during the season of love and goodwill.

Griff seemed satisfied. "I'll keep my feelings about the film to myself."

"Thank you," Michael said. "I owe you one."

The drive home was silent, except for the whistle of a rising wind. Kelley knew that Griff needed silence as much as he had needed her hand during the screening. She wanted to reach out to him again, but she didn't know how. She could only guess at his thoughts. He had asked her to share this evening, but he had shared little of himself.

He parked his car, and she glimpsed movement in the car stationed unobtrusively across the street from his house. She knew their arrival home had been noted and that if someone came out of the shadows now, the man in the car would have the intruder covered immediately. Still, she clutched her purse to her side, fingertips dangling over the clasp. Seeing *One Way Ticket* had multiplied her concern for Griff.

Inside the house she breathed a little easier. The house was absolutely still, as if with Tara's temporary departure all the life had been sucked from the rooms. Mrs. Robbert had left lights on before she had gone home for the evening, but shadows still dangled and merged. Everything seemed menacing, even the shadow that preceded the sad animal who came toward them from Tara's room.

"Neuf." She knelt and put her arms around Neuf's neck. He made a sound that told her exactly what he'd thought about being left alone so long.

She rested her head against his neck for a moment.

"Do you remember when life was that easy?" Griff asked.

She looked up, puzzled.

"You could put your arms around a dog or play catch with your dad and everything was all right again, no matter what had happened."

"Come on down. I'll share."

He didn't answer. Instead he turned and left the room. She got up and followed him, with Neuf trailing behind her.

She found him in the sun room, gazing out at the pool. The image caught her by surprise. A man in moonlight, surrounded by glass walls, life and warmth caught inside a spectacular prism, a place where he could be seen in glorious Technicolor, but never touched.

She stopped in the doorway. "I don't know what to say to you."

"You don't have to say anything."

"But I do."

"There isn't anything anybody *can* say. Drake's dead. I'm alive."

"By the grace of God." She walked toward him. "You could have died with him. You told me it was close."

"That doesn't matter now."

Watching *One Way Ticket* had raised some questions in her mind, but she knew this wasn't the moment to explore them. "It matters to me." She stopped at his side and wondered if by touching him she could penetrate the barriers the world had erected.

"I'm not looking for sympathy. Maybe you'd just better go to bed."

The advice was good. She moved closer. "You don't ask for anything, do you?"

"If you have to ask, what you get isn't worth much."

"I want to help."

He folded his arms. "I know how much you like to make things better. But some things just can't be changed."

"Griffin, I'm not trying to be your social worker. I care about you. That's why you took me with you tonight. Let me in." She extended her hand. He was there, warm and hard beneath her palm. The length of an arm, the curve of a shoulder, the steady beat of a pulse at the hollow of his throat.

He looked at her. "I cared about Drake. We were friends, and now he's gone. He came to me before the scene. I think he wanted to talk to me. I should have listened, but I just mouthed all the old platitudes. He'd be fine. We'd drink a toast to the scene that night. This movie was going to signal the start of an upward swing in his career. Someday we'd be competing for parts." He laughed bitterly.

"Stop it." She began to understand more of what was eating at him. "Can you be faulted for trying to make him feel better? Isn't that what friends do for each other?"

"Maybe if I'd listened, he would have convinced me he was worried for a good reason."

"But you've said yourself there was nothing to worry about. You knew how careful Michael was, you've told me you knew and trusted the people coordinating the explosion. You had good reasons for reassuring him."

"He died."

"I know." Her hand slid to his cheek; her thumb stroked the strong line of his jaw. "And you didn't. And tonight you wished it had been you. You're a good man, Griffin Bryant, and you were a good friend to Drake. Don't eat yourself up about things you can't change."

He shut his eyes as she framed his face with her hands. "It was all so real again. Michael's too damned good." He laughed the same bitter laugh. "You know something? Drake's death would sell the film even if it wasn't any good. People will turn out by the thousands to see his last scene. And the attempt on my life won't hurt audience share, either, especially if the next attempt succeeds."

"None of that matters."

He opened his eyes. "Doesn't it? I'm in a business that sells blood. Drake's. Mine. Anybody's."

"That's not what your movies are about. They're about coming out on top, about winning against odds. And if people go to them, it's because they want to believe in the impossible. They won't go to see Drake die, they'll go to see him live, eternally, in that film and all his others." She turned his face to hers so that he was looking right at her. "But the man they'll see when they see *you* on that screen is nowhere near as sensitive or compassionate or unique as you are.''

His expression didn't change, but his hands lifted to her shoulders. Their weight was welcome. ''You made it bearable. I needed you with me tonight.''

Her hands dropped to his shoulders, but she didn't move away. ''I needed to be there.''

''As my friend?''

She hesitated. She could feel the change in him, see the light kindling in his ice blue eyes. Every rational part of her told her not to ask the question that had sprung to her lips. But in the end she asked it anyway. ''Are we friends, Griffin?''

He lifted a hand to her hair. He wound a curl around his finger, lingering over it as if it might provide him with a better answer. ''No.''

She tried to smile but failed. ''I didn't think so.''

''Maybe we would have been. If things had been different.''

''We've been catapulted from strangers to...'' Her voice trailed off. She didn't even know how to finish.

His hand slid back to her shoulder, as if to hold her there. ''You'd better go to bed.''

She yearned to read what she saw in his eyes. She didn't want to tell herself that she understood what she did not. She could feel their relationship changing, but the ground at her feet felt like quicksand. ''You said that before,'' she said. ''I don't seem to have gone.''

''You refuse to see what's happening between us, what's been happening from the beginning.''

''I don't refuse to see anything. I can't see what isn't there, and I can't see what you won't show me.''

''The camera sees what you don't.'' He pulled her closer. ''Michael said it tonight. Did you listen?''

''He said our scenes were...''

''Explosive,'' he finished for her.

''I don't know how they can be. I'm nothing more than—''

''The woman I can't take my eyes off. Damn it, I've seen some of the rushes! I know what he's talking about. And either you're a better actress than you think, or you feel something for me, too.''

She tried to deny it. "I told you. I care about you. I went with you tonight because I care what you think and feel."

"Compassion, Kelley? Just like you care about anybody who's hurting? Is that what you're trying to tell me?"

"I don't know what—"

"You can't talk about your feelings, can you?"

"That's your problem, not mine!"

"What is it? Can't you tell the difference between what you feel and what you think you're supposed to? Did all those years in front of the camera confuse you?"

She stared at him, wanting to protest, but the right words wouldn't come because there were no right words.

He hauled her closer. He stroked his hands down her back, but there was nothing of the wooing lover in their strength and tension. He was bending her to his will, even as he was bending her body to his.

She could have stopped his kiss. Instead her lips parted as if she had been waiting forever for this moment.

Chapter 13

Outside the sun room, the wind moaned a seductive accompaniment to the beating of Kelley's heart. Moonlight caressed but didn't soften the hard lines of Griff's face. When he backed away from her, she saw a man whom comfort couldn't touch, whose heart could only be eased by something deeper, surer, something freely given from her own heart.

Griff saw a woman who had believed herself to be above the simple, elemental needs of other women, above the hunger for warmth, love, the touching of soul to soul. He saw a woman who was no longer sure.

Kelley stretched out her hand; it stopped inches from his face. She didn't know what she had to give; she wasn't sure who she was anymore. But somehow, knowing, being sure, didn't seem to matter. She stretched her hand farther and stroked his cheek, then she lifted her hands to his hair, her lips to his in invitation.

He kissed her again. There was nothing tentative about his need for her. His demands were clear, but so was the fact that if she protested he would release her immediately.

She didn't want to be released. She had been free for enough years to know both its exhilaration and its emptiness. She could remain free and never know the bonds of love, the security of trust and faith in another, the power of commitment.

Instead she wanted to revel in Griff's touch, without fears that this was wrong. She wanted to forget why she was in his house and his life. For that moment she wanted only to be a woman, his woman, whatever that meant and whatever consequences it triggered.

"I need you, too," she said before fear and logic could intrude. "I don't care if this is crazy. We need each other." When he didn't answer, she could feel her own vulnerability deepen. "Or don't you need me anymore?"

"What do you need?" His voice splintered a silence that had seemed unending. "What do you need that I can give you?"

If there was a word for what she wanted, she didn't know it. She searched for a way to express her feelings. "I need to have you here," she said at last. She touched her fist to her chest and held it over her heart.

"Will you let me touch you there?"

"How can I prevent it?"

His fingers tunneled through her hair. Her words stirred something inside him, something winged and precious. He named it hope before he could remember that hope was something he had given up a long time ago.

His kiss no longer seemed filled with questions. Kelley realized that when they stepped apart, Griff was no longer the man alone, the man separated from warmth and life. His glass prison was nothing more than a room pierced by moonlight.

She let him lead her through the house. His bedroom wasn't far away. She had been there once to check security, but now it seemed familiar, an extension of the man. Here there were no austere, uncluttered surfaces. A Persian rug warmed the floor; graceful jade carvings lined a gleaming wooden shelf.

He stopped on the threshold and pulled her to him. The drugging pleasure of his kisses was growing familiar, yet each was more of an intimacy than the last. He fondled the fabric of her blouse, lifting and crushing it in his hands. She drew a deep breath as his hands settled at her waist, skin against skin. She had not let herself imagine the perfection of his touch. Now a flood tide of long-repressed visions overwhelmed her. Griff's hands in far more intimate places, Griff's lips following the path of his hands, Griff's strong body finding pleasure, taking pleasure.

Griff the man. Only the man.

She felt the slow slide of silk velour against her back, and she lifted her arms. The air against her skin was cool, but his hands were warm. She felt the release of her bra clasp, felt the warmth of his hands against her breasts.

She knew who she was, what she was. She was not Felice, long-limbed and delicately boned. She was not Miranda Lyle, lush perfection wrapped around a waist tiny enough for a man's hands to span. She was only Kelley. Slender and athletic, breasts just large enough to nourish a baby, hips just wide enough to bear one.

His gaze swept her; his hands trembled. "A wild Irish rose," he said. "So beautiful."

A smile built inside her. She lifted her hands to the top button of his shirt. "My lionhearted, farsighted griffin."

His smile bathed her in its heat. "Shall I show you how beautiful I think you are?"

"Oh, yes."

He lifted her against him, high off the floor so that he could taste what he'd uncovered. She gasped as his lips found a breast. Scorching, incinerating heat poured through her. She felt her body flush with it, felt all but the most elemental tension abandon her.

The sound that came from her throat was not her voice; the fingers that clenched his shoulders belonged to another. He found her other breast, and she melted from the heat until she was molten and liquid and yearning.

She arched her back to offer herself more fully to him. He murmured endearments against her breasts, her shoulders, her throat. Her eyes closed of their own volition. A fierce sweetness filled her at the rasp of his voice, the perfect simplicity of his words.

He whirled with her in his arms and carried her to the bed, kissing her as he lowered her to the navy comforter. He couldn't bear to leave her even for as long as it would take to undress. Still fully clothed, he stretched out beside her.

She pulled him closer and finished unbuttoning his shirt. The hair on his chest sprang in soft swirls as she brushed the shirt open. She smoothed the soft fabric over one shoulder and down one arm. His heart beat beneath her palm as she smoothed it over the other side of his chest. A simple thing, the rapid pounding of his heart, but a connection, an enticement she felt deep inside her. He turned to his back with a low groan of pleasure, and she explored the bare flesh she had uncovered, as he had explored her own.

His hands grasped hers and he pulled her to him until they were flesh against flesh, heat against heat. She heard him murmur her name, felt the glide of his lips, the thrust of his tongue against hers.

He felt all traces of resistance leave her. If she had doubted this was right, she no longer did. He pushed away thoughts that the doubts might return later, that nothing had been resolved, that *this* would resolve only the question that attraction, that feelings existed. He told himself that nothing mattered now but this moment. He gave up all traces of resistance, too.

Kelley felt her body sink into his, felt his flesh become hers, his heat invade some part of her she had never shared. Boundaries dissolved. She didn't, couldn't know who undressed the other, who touched, who took, who sighed.

She only knew she gave. She gave up her boundaries, gave up her fears, gave up rational thought. When he was naked beside her, she gave up patience.

He held her back. "I want to treasure this," he said. His words were a spark to the heat coursing through her. The flames licked higher, brighter.

She couldn't believe this moment was so valued by him, yet the trembling of his hands, the sweat on his forehead despite the cool room, the undeniable evidence of his arousal proved his words. She felt beautiful, treasured, valued.

"Treasure this." She stretched along the length of his body, her hair tumbling over his chest.

He caressed her as she searched for the secret places that would destroy what patience he had left. His hands molded her flesh, a sculptor joyous in his creation. His legs entwined with hers.

Her lips tasted the base of his throat; her tongue flicked, her breath warmed a hard male nipple.

He felt his self-control disappear. One moment he was sure he could wait to take his pleasure. One moment he knew he could wait forever to give her greater pleasure, and the next he knew that waiting was impossible.

She felt the thrust of his hips against hers, the seeking heat of his flesh. Triumphantly she arched her back and cradled him inside her.

He tangled his hands in her hair as he turned her onto her back. She was filled with his heat, his taste, his scent. He was filled with the unbearable perfection of her body merged with his. He threw back his head and thrust deeper still.

The leap of flames burned away everything until response was all that was left to her. She thrust, too, taking all of him inside her. They moved as one, and the flames burned brighter, higher than she had ever imagined they could. She gave into them with a rushing wildfire blaze of sensation.

When he wrapped his arms around her and cried out her name, she gave up her heart.

She awoke before dawn and realized what she had done. Somewhere in the distance a dog bayed an early welcome to the sun. The mournful howl made her clutch the covers tighter around her breasts. She turned on her side and stared into Griff's eyes.

He didn't speak. She didn't know what to say.

The dog howled again. From some distant corner of the house, Neuf barked a response.

She turned onto her back and sat up, still clutching the covers. "I'd better go check and make sure everything's all right."

He put a hand on her arm. "Apparently everything isn't."

She knew he wasn't talking about security. She pretended otherwise. "We won't know until I check it out, will we?"

"What could be safer? You're in bed with me. You can't get any closer."

She had been closer last night, but she wasn't going to remind him. She didn't want to remind herself, either, although there was little choice. She was overwhelmed with guilt. She had forgotten everything that made sense out of her life. "I'm supposed to be doing a job."

"There's a man stationed outside. Stop making excuses. Tell me what you're feeling."

There was no way she could tell him what she didn't understand herself. The baying of the dog hadn't awakened her to fear. The events of last night had done that. Under the spell of moonlight, in this bed, she had given in to her own needs and found they were a bottomless crater.

She couldn't tell him she was afraid. Fear was something she had only rarely known. An adventurous, foolhardy child had become a wiser but fearless adult. As a cop she had walked streets that tough men avoided. As a detective she had breezed through dimly lit drug havens, through back alleys and locked front doors.

Now the only answers she could find struck fear inside her. She was twenty-seven but she was not old enough for what had happened to her last night. She had betrayed the rules by which she lived when she allowed her relationship with Griff to come to this. But more important, infinitely more important, she had betrayed herself. She had opened herself up to yearning.

She couldn't have Griff, not on her terms. He had not offered, and she would not ask him for a commitment. She understood the world he lived in. Relationships were casual. Divorces were as common as marriages. Couples lived together and changed partners as easily as competitors at a bridge tournament. Griff had been married; Griff had lived with Cam. She was sure last night had meant something to him; she wasn't trying to trivialize his obvious pleasure in what they had shared. But it had not meant commitment.

She wanted commitment.

The thought was dizzying. Only once before had she thought about marriage. She had been younger, foolish, blind to the signs that the man she'd thought she loved was incapable of the same emotion. When that relationship had exploded, she had been shell-shocked, but she had survived intact. And she had learned something. If she ever gave her heart again, if she ever yearned for marriage and children, she would choose a man who wanted both as much as she did, a man who was capable of the same fierce love she knew she had inside her. A man whose world would revolve around his family.

She had thought of none of this last night. She had thought only of the pleasures of being held by him, of giving *him* pleasure and comfort. She had not understood the power of his attraction for her. She had not understood how he could make her yearn for the impossible.

"Was last night a mistake?" he asked when she didn't respond.

She went for the easy answer. "I compromised your safety. Neither of us can be safe if we're wrapped up in each other."

"I've heard this before."

"Apparently I didn't say it loudly enough for either of us to remember."

He didn't doubt she was telling the truth, but only a particle of it. He dropped her arm, but she didn't move. "And if I say I'll find someone else to offer us both protection, what will you say?"

"This isn't the right time for either of us to let this go any further."

"This? Further? What are you talking about, Kelley? The fact we ended up in bed together? You don't want to repeat last night? Spell it out."

She turned to look at him. It was almost her undoing. He had pillowed his head on one arm. His eyes were heavy-lidded, and his feelings impenetrable. He looked dangerous and seductive, exactly like the man who had given her the greatest pleasure of her life.

She tried to sound neutral. "Your life is in danger. My life is in danger. That does funny things to people."

"Let's take it a little further. If we weren't in danger, would you be in my arms right now?"

She didn't answer, but the thought made heat rise inside her in anticipation.

"I didn't think so." He turned onto his back and stared up at the ceiling. He hadn't expected her withdrawal, but then he was no different than any other man when he had believed in the impossible.

Funny thing, though. His impossible was another man's due. It was impossible for him to live up to the characters he played on film. Impossible to be real, to be genuinely human, to show his feelings. Other men could be who they truly were. They had no shadow image of themselves playing on screens across the nation. They had no lines they were expected to repeat, no wondrous feats to perform.

Last night he had believed she was a woman who could love the man he truly was. There were odds against them, a man or men stalking them, career choices that made commitments difficult, a troubled child. But he had been crazy enough to think she might brave the odds and go for broke against them.

Kelley couldn't guess what he was thinking, but she did know that she couldn't leave him believing that last night had meant nothing to her. "How can we guess what might be true if things were different?" she asked. "We're here because we are in danger. If we weren't, you wouldn't even know my name."

"I know more than your name, don't I?"

"Much more," she said softly. "More than you should. More than I should have let you learn. But I let myself take something I wanted very badly. And I'm not sorry."

He didn't understand her words. He only knew that she wasn't being completely honest.

Neuf barked again.

She swung her legs to the floor. "I'd better check this out. Neuf doesn't bark at every falling leaf."

He didn't answer. He watched her rise, watched as she bent, picked up her clothes and slipped them on. She paused at the door but didn't say anything else. In a moment he heard a click, then she was gone.

She leaned against the wall in the hallway, trying to get her emotional bearings. She wasn't as concerned with a breach in security as she had pretended. Neuf *was* a discriminating barker, but another dog's howling was one of the things that would set him off. Moments passed as she tried to pull herself together. She fought the urge to go back to Griff's bed and finish their conversation. Yet what could she say to him? That he had uncovered a wealth of feelings she hadn't even known

she had? That spending one night with him had made her yearn
for a lifetime of nights and days?

She had too much pride to tell him that. She also had too
much self-respect and common sense not to take some time to
mull over everything that had occurred. Hasty decisions made
on feelings were often regretted. She was only impulsive about
physical risk; emotional risk was another matter. As a child
performing for the camera, she had learned to protect her heart
from those who would use it, to keep an inner core untouched
so that she could not be manipulated. Now that lesson seemed
imperative to remember.

Neuf began to bark again. She straightened and started toward the sound. If nothing else, she could quiet him and keep
him from being an annoyance to Griff.

The barking grew louder as she turned toward the sun room.
Normally the glass doors leading in were closed, effectively
blocking Neuf from entrance, but she supposed that in their
rush to his bedroom last night, neither she nor Griff had closed
the doors behind them. Since the sun room was a giant window on the world for the dog, she imagined that he was enjoying the view and the enticements of roadrunners or a neighbor's
stray pedigreed cat.

She found him with his nose pressed against the glass. The
sky was still dark, although the stars had begun to grow dim.
She peered outside but saw nothing in the darkness that looked
suspicious. The pool sparkled in the fragments of light from a
crescent moon, and silhouettes of trees swayed against the horizon.

She crossed to the dog and knelt beside him, putting her arms
around his massive neck. "Silly guy," she murmured. "You
shouldn't be out here."

Neuf's tail thumped at the hug, but he gave no ground. He
whined, and one giant paw scrubbed uselessly at the glass.

"I'm not going to let you out," she said, her cheek against
his shining coat. "You'll be off in a flash chasing something,
and I'll be outside for the rest of the night trying to find you."

"That's one lucky dog."

She turned to see Griff clad in jeans and nothing else. She
hadn't expected him to get up and continue their confronta-

tion. Something stirred in her at the sight of him. Something more important stirred at the knowledge that he had cared enough about what she was thinking and feeling to follow her.

"Did you notice the electricity's off?" he asked.

Surprised, she squinted into the darkness once more. Lights flickered below them, but there were no lights in his yard. Floodlights normally illuminated the pool. She hadn't even noticed that they no longer did.

"Well, I feel stupid," she admitted, glad to have something commonplace to talk about. "I noticed how dark it was outside, but it never occurred to me why." She didn't elaborate on why she hadn't noticed. She could have told him where her mind had been instead, but she imagined he knew.

"This happens from time to time up here. The wind's been fierce enough tonight to knock out power."

"They've got power down below." Apprehension suddenly gripped her. "Don't come out here. Stay where you are!"

"Why?"

"The security system—"

A crash from the other end of the house confirmed her fears. Before she could stop him, Neuf lunged toward the doorway and past Griff. Kelley stood to fling herself after the dog.

A bullet shattered a glass pane just to one side of her, but the bullet went wild, ricocheting off a stone fireplace at the edge of the room. Another followed its path.

"Get down!" she shouted. Twenty feet and three potentially deadly seconds separated her from the temporary cover of the hallway. Staying as low as she could, she covered the distance, expecting each second to be her last.

She could hear the third bullet screech past the back of her head, feel the air part in its pathway. Fear gripped her chest; her lungs forgot to inflate; her legs trembled. While she was still yards from her goal, Griff grabbed her and pulled her into the hall with him.

"Someone's in the other end of the house," she gasped.

"Are you all right?"

"I think." She tried to think what to do. Her gun was in her room; she hadn't once considered getting it before investigating Neuf's barking. But there was no time to lament poor judgment. The crash of glass behind them supported her worst fears.

"Come on!" Griff grabbed her hand and pulled her toward the front of the house.

She realized immediately what he was planning. "They could have the front of the house covered, too," she said.

"We've got security out there."

"I doubt it!"

"Got a better idea?"

She didn't. Someone was in the process of invading the sun room. Someone else was coming in from the other end of the house. They were defenseless inside. If they weren't killed getting there, they had a chance of survival outside.

He opened the door of the room where she had listened to his argument with Joanne and pulled her in after him. Thick shrubbery obscured the lower half of two windows that stretched from floor to ceiling, the same windows from which she had judged Griff's taste in women.

"This way." He dropped her hand and reached for the lock.

She peered out the other window as he struggled. The car driven by her security backup was parked exactly where it was supposed to be. She swallowed dread, knowing what they would find inside it if they ever got that far.

There were no screens to worry about. The window was open, she followed him out, crouching behind the shrubbery as he closed the window behind her. They moved beyond the windows. At the same moment that she felt Griff's hands on her shoulders shoving her lower, she saw a dark-colored van creeping slowly toward the front of the house.

There was no possibility that they could make it to the car without being seen. Kelley weighed staying where they were against skirting the edge of the house until they were in the back portion of Griff's yard. On the side opposite the pool there was a steep drop-off where his property ended. Just below that was a narrow gorge that wound down the mountainside until eventually it wound past the boundary of someone else's land. She knew every foot of the gorge because its twists and turns had made designing an outdoor security system that much more difficult. She wished with all her heart that she and the security system expert had spent as much time worrying about a foolproof backup generator as they had about the gorge.

"Around to the back," Griff whispered.

She had to agree, even though they were barefoot and would find running and climbing torturous. They were sitting ducks where they were. Griff's house was isolated enough that no one was going to drive by at this time of morning. They could scream and possibly be heard at a neighbor's house, but the closest people who would hear them were carrying guns. If they stayed silent, the gunmen would probably still find them eventually. By going over the cliff they had a chance of escaping.

Every second they waited brought dawn that much closer. In the short time that had elapsed since she'd gotten up to check on Neuf, the horizon had grown lighter and the stars had faded. Darkness was on their side now, but soon it wouldn't be. She began to move, praying that they would encounter no gaps in shrubbery, no windows where they could be seen from inside.

There was a loud crash from indoors, followed by Neuf's furious barking. Her heart twisted as she realized the dog didn't have a chance of making it through the next minutes alive. She was surprised he had survived this long without someone taking a gun to him.

She could feel Griff behind her, but she didn't dare turn to look at him. She had failed him before; she wouldn't fail him again. She forced herself to concentrate on everything around her except him. She crouched and ducked, summoning every bit of her natural athletic grace to keep from being seen.

They reached the back of the house without incident, but one glance at the obstacles ahead canceled any satisfaction. Griff's backyard was landscaped, too, but much of it was bare, paths between elaborate gardens, patches of green stretching down to waist-high flower beds. They would be visible in most parts of the yard, and by now someone was going to realize they were outside and begin to search. They had to get to the cliff immediately.

"I'll go first," Griff said. "I can help you down." Kelley felt his hands on her shoulders as he pushed past her. There was nothing she could do to stop him. He had obviously realized that the longer they waited, the more danger they would be in.

And if there was going to be shooting, he wanted to be the one to find out.

He started across the yard. There was no response from inside. Seconds later she started after him, running swiftly toward the cliff.

Neuf began to bark. The sound unnerved her. He sounded frantic to get to her, as if he could see her running and wanted to be at her side.

A door slammed, and fear clawed at her. She knew they had been spotted, and they still had too much distance to cover before reaching the cliff. A crack shot could pick them both off with seconds to spare.

She heard the sound of feet somewhere behind her. A thin clump of trees screened the back door. She imagined a gunman clearing the trees to take aim. The whine of a bullet, from a gun fitted with a silencer, told her she'd been right.

Neuf's barking became even more frenzied. A crash and the shattering explosion of glass followed. She couldn't look behind her; she couldn't guess what had happened. She could only keep her eyes on the man in front of her and run.

There was another shot and a scream. Ahead of her she could see Griff nearing the cliff. He threw himself to the ground at its edge and swung his body over. She prayed he wouldn't be hurt when he made the substantial drop to the ground below. As she neared the cliff, she slowed, then stopped and did as he had, scraping her arms as she hit the rocky edge. Grasping for a handhold, she swung herself into midair, then let go.

Arms caught her, strong, sure arms that kept the fall from being endless. He clasped her to him for one brief moment, then, taking her hand, pulled her past a cluster of boulders to the gorge below.

The sharp stones against the soles of her feet were agonizing, but she had no time to think about the pain. They were safer, but still not safe. Biting her lip, she followed him, scrambling over rocks to reach the deepest part of the gorge where they would be harder to see. The ground was treacherous; rocks slid and crumbled beneath their feet. Once her ankle twisted, shooting pain all the way to her hip, but she held her breath and kept moving.

"We're almost there." Griff pulled her along, but his pace slowed as the climb down became steeper.

"Almost won't do it."

Griff swung himself down to a more level plateau and reached up to help her follow. They faced each other briefly, then he looked behind her. "No one's following."

"We'd better not bank on it."

"Let's go." He started along the last part of the gully, then, thirty yards farther, at the spot where the gully curled away from his neighbor's property, he hauled himself up the side, finding toeholds and rocks to grasp until he was in his neighbor's yard. He lay flat on the ground and reached for her, but she was halfway up already. He helped her the last few feet, pulling her up to lie beside him.

"We're not safe until we're inside," she said.

"Jean's probably got a security system, too."

"I don't care if we set it off."

"Let's go." He stood and held out his hand. She was hobbling by now, her feet bleeding, her leg throbbing mercilessly with each step. Despite her pain, she forced herself to keep up with him.

At the back door he rang the bell, then pounded with both fists until a frowning middle-aged woman in the process of belting a pink robe appeared. She took one look at them and flung the door open, motioning them inside.

Only when the door closed safely behind her did Kelley's legs finally give way.

Chapter 14

Harris, the man who had been guarding Griff's house, was unconscious on the ground beside his car when the police got to him. The wires connecting his radio had been severed. He was taken by ambulance to the closest hospital.

Griff and Kelley found Neuf in Griff's backyard. A quick examination showed a dozen small cuts beneath his thick fur and one large gash across the top of his head. He lay still, as if dazed, but his tail moved at the sound of Kelley's voice.

"Looks like he went through that window," one of the police officers said, pointing to a long French window at the back of the house. "Looks like he got some evidence for us, too." He lifted a scrap of cloth from the ground beside the dog's head.

"He must have been shut in that room when he went to investigate. He probably jumped through the window when he saw we were being chased," Griff said. "There was a scream. He must have attacked."

Kelley blinked back tears. She thought of the scene she had rehearsed so diligently. The glass in the window she had gone through had been fake. Neuf had gone through the real thing and somehow survived. "I've got to get him to a vet."

"I'll take you," Griff said.

"Somebody's got to stay here and answer questions."

"I'll take you," he repeated. "That dog probably saved our lives."

"I don't understand why they didn't shoot him."

The investigating officer found the answer on the ground nearby, half-obscured by bushes. "Apparently when the dog attacked, the guy dropped his gun," he said. He pulled out a handkerchief and gingerly lifted a revolver, holding it out for them to see.

"I hope this guy's getting expenses," Griff said grimly. "That's the second gun he's lost. At this rate we're costing him money."

"You're *not* all right." Felice settled herself in a comfortable leather chair opposite Kelley's desk at Cristy and Samuels, as if she was planning to be there for the long haul.

"I mean it, Felice. I'm fine. I'll be better when I get my hands around the neck of whoever's trying to kill me, but considering everything, I'm okay."

"Baloney." Felice leaned over and picked up one of Kelley's collection of globe snow scenes. She flipped it, then turned it right side up and watched the snow fall.

"What in the hell do you want me to say?" Kelley exploded.

Felice cocked an eyebrow. "Whatever you want."

"You drive me crazy!"

"As subject matter, I'm off-limits."

Kelley put her head in her hands. She wasn't sure which hurt more, her head, her feet or her bandaged ankle. "The vet says he thinks Neuf is going to make it."

"I understand they still don't know about Harris."

Kelley barely shook her head, but it was enough movement to shoot pain to her temples. "I've been calling every thirty minutes. They know my voice at the nurse's station. They're using my first name."

"He's a strong man, and he knew what he was getting into. You don't have to blame yourself."

Kelley squeezed her eyes shut. She couldn't share the full extent of her guilt with Felice. While Harris had been under attack out front, she had been cuddled with Griff like his favorite teddy bear. Somehow that made everything much, much worse.

"Whoever cut off the power knew exactly what he was doing," Felice continued. "The power and the supplementary generator were both disconnected by a master electrician. Griff's security system was the best. The guy or guys who circumvented it were better than the best."

"I love competency."

"You get to blame yourself for another minute or two, then you have to get on with figuring out what to do."

"I know what to do. I'm going to tell Griff to get another live-in lover."

"That's unwise." Felice traded one globe for another. "You are going to need more security, that's true, but it's pretty obvious whoever wants you, wants you both. It's easier and safer to hire protection for the two of you together. And you're scheduled to be on the set with him for a few days, anyway. Give it till then."

Kelley knew she was in no shape to make a decision about something so crucial. All of her conceptions of her job and of herself had been blasted away. She and Griff had almost died, not once, but several times. Luck had been on their side so far, but luck always ran out.

Then there was the question of her feelings for Griff, confused, powerful feelings that had been more important this morning than staying on guard against danger.

"I've been with him every time someone's tried to kill him—us—and I haven't been any help at all," she said. "I might be more help if I was doing the investigation instead. Nobody's been able to turn up anything on Norris Roxey or the fan who keeps writing threatening letters."

"I've been working on the Roxey thing myself."

Kelley looked up. "You have?"

"Well, don't act so surprised. This is my office, too."

Kelley felt a new surge of guilt. She had given little thought to how Felice was keeping up with all the work now that she was staying with Griff full-time. She and Felice had always hired skip tracers and part-time investigators to work for them, and when Felice had planned to take an extended honeymoon—in those happy days when they'd thought she was going to make it through her wedding ceremony—they had hired another full-time addition.

Now Kelley realized how far removed she was from her former world. Griff and *Teardrop Creek* had become her new life. She got up and walked to the window looking over the courtyard shared with a square of upscale shops and businesses. "Have you found out anything?"

"I've compiled a file for you to look over. I've interviewed about a dozen people who know him. The consensus is that Norris Roxey is all hot air. Incidentally he was in New York on my wedding day, and he doesn't own a van. I don't know where he was this morning. Yet."

"If he's behind this, he's not doing his own dirty work."

"That's why I thought we should meet him today."

Kelley faced her. "Today?"

"Why not? The police are tailing Griff everywhere he goes. You told me so yourself. And I'm sticking with you, no buts about it, so we might as well take a nice long drive into the city. Let's go look over Roxey and see what we think."

"What about the fan letters?"

Felice paused. "I have a lead."

"Why didn't you say something before?"

"Because you have enough to think about. I was going to tell you if it panned out."

"What do you have?"

"Apparently before this guy started writing Griff at home, he did write him several times care of the studio. Griff might have thrown away his letters, but the studio took them seriously. They had three on file. They're about a year old, but the paper's unusual, imported from a small factory in England. I've been able to trace it to just a few shops in the Fullerton area. That's where the letters are postmarked."

"Well, it's a start."

"It's a little better than that. The guy actually described himself in one of the letters, comparing himself to Griff. I've given the description to the clerks at the shops and asked them to pay attention to everyone buying this paper. They all agreed to call me about anyone who fits the bill. They're a nice cooperative bunch. I guess they grew up on *Magnum P.I.*"

Kelley leaned against the wall. Her ankle was not so injured that it couldn't bear weight, but for a while, between the ankle and the cuts and bruises on her feet, she would be reminded of the morning's adventures every time she stood. "Do you ever wish you had a job where you associated with nice, normal people? People who weren't trying to kill other nice, normal people?"

"Or skipping town with somebody else's money, or trying to avoid child support or alimony?"

"Right."

"I like to think I'm making the world the kind of place where those people can live without looking over their shoulder all the time."

"Is it working?"

Felice shrugged. "I'll feel like enough of a success if we can just find the guy who's taking potshots at you and Griff."

The first glimpse of Norris Roxey's home in an exclusive part of Pasadena was a lesson in Southern California mathematics. One successful starring role plus some fast talking at the bank could add up to a house with a mortgage the size of the Taj Mahal.

"If he's paying off this sucker, I can see why he was upset that Griff got a part he wanted," Kelley said as Felice drove her sports car right into the circular drive at his front doorstep.

"Looks like the man loves extravagant gestures and big gambles."

"Not evidence in his favor." Kelley got out on her side and came around to join Felice. "Whoever's after Griff likes the same."

"Well, Roxey wanted the role in *Victims No More,* didn't he? We could do our own version, hang him from that big palm over there." Felice inclined her head. "If the neighbors noticed, they'd just think it was performance art."

Kelley smiled. "Oh, let's not do it yet. Let's give him a sporting chance to confess. Say, three to five minutes."

"I don't think it's him," Felice said seriously. "But let's ask him directly and see what he says." At the top of the steps, she rang the bell.

"Did you tell him why we were coming?"

"I'm not sure the dear boy understood."

Kelley knew if Felice had wanted Norris to understand, he would have. "Who are we supposed to be?"

"Groupies."

"What?"

"Well, when I phoned I told him I'd seen every movie he's made—which is true, because I've been studying up on him—and I told him we were putting together some information on his life."

"Oh, brother."

"Don't be surprised if he comes to the door in the male equivalent of a negligee."

Kelley was still trying to figure out what that might be when the door opened. To her disappointment, they were ushered to the back of the house by a starched young maid complete with Cockney accent.

Norris, naked from the waist up and barely clothed below, was in the shade beside his pool, reclining on a lounge chair of white plush. Languidly he raised a hand in greeting.

"I still can't figure out how you girls got my phone number." He examined them as he spoke, and apparently he liked what he saw because he punctuated his sentence with a huge toothy grin.

"Anything's possible if you want it bad enough," Felice said in her best sultry tone.

His eyes widened. "You couldn't possibly have come this far just to talk. There are suits in the cabana. Why don't you play a little swimmy-swim with me."

Felice sat on the edge of his chair. Kelley took a seat beside him. "Maybe later," she said. She drew a fingernail up his arm. "But there are just a few little tiny things we've got to know first."

He lay back, obviously relishing the lavish attention. "Anything. My life's an open book."

Kelley sent him her best come-hither smile.

He smiled back.

"Do you want Griff Bryant dead?" she asked.

He sat up straight, blond curls bouncing. "Who sent you?"

Felice pulled out her identification and held it up for him to examine. "We're working with the authorities. You should know your name's come up as a possible suspect in an attempt on his life."

"I don't know what you're talking about!"

"Don't you read the papers, Norris honey?" Kelley asked. "Someone's trying to kill Griff Bryant, and you're already on record for taking a swing at him at a party a while back. Now add that up and tell us what you see."

"I want you to leave. I know my rights. I don't have to talk to you."

"You don't *have* to," Felice agreed. "But you would have to talk to the police if they called you in." She held two fingers up side by side. "And I'm like this with the cops."

"I didn't kill anybody!"

"Wish-ful think-ing," Kelley scolded. "We said an attempt on his life. He's still very much alive." More alive than this creep would ever be, she added silently.

"Sure, I took a swing at him once." By now Norris was screeching like a motherless baby chimp. "He cut me out of a picture I was supposed to do. He didn't need the part. *I* needed it! He didn't even want it until he found out it was going to go to me!"

Kelley tsked. "Now, that's funny. The way I heard it, he was the one they asked first, and you were a distant second."

"Bryant's a no-talent bum! I could have made something out of that film!"

"If I recall, he made millions out of it."

"He deserved a lesson. I gave him one. I knocked him flat. I showed him."

Felice smiled sweetly. "The papers I read said you missed, and then you passed out."

"Bryant controls the press!"

Kelley's eyes widened at this bit of paranoia, but even Norris realized he had gone too far. He held up his hands. "All right, so I didn't hit him. I would have if I hadn't drunk so much."

"It's always nice to see a man who can tell the truth from a lie." Kelley leaned closer. "Now tell us some more," she wheedled. "Why are you trying to have Griff Bryant murdered?"

"I swear I don't have anything to do with that! What good would it do me?"

"Maybe you'd like to have a chance at some more of the parts that go to him?"

"I don't need his parts! I've got plenty of my own!"

"Then maybe you're still mad? Maybe you wish he hadn't made you look like a fool at that party?"

"No! And you don't have anything to link me to him. Everybody's got enemies, even Griff Bryant. Dig a little deeper. You'll see."

"We've dug plenty deep. Guess who was at the bottom of the hole?" Kelley stood and Felice joined her. "Do you happen to have an alibi for this morning before dawn?" Kelley asked.

"I was asleep in my bed!"

"With anyone, perchance?"

"None of your business!"

"It could very well be our business . . . and the cops'."

"I can supply a name, if I have to."

Since Norris seemed like the kind of guy who might be able to provide more than one name—and colorful home movies, too—Kelley gave up for now. Besides, she knew too well that alibis were easily bought.

"Sorry about the swimmy-swim," Felice said. "Maybe another time?"

Norris made a visible effort to pull himself together. "Don't rush back."

"But this has been so much fun," Kelley told him. "I love to watch a grown man grovel." She wiggled her fingers in farewell, then she followed Felice out of the house.

They were silent until they were back in Felice's car speeding toward Palm Springs.

"I don't think so," Kelley said at last.

"Neither do I," Felice answered. "And it's a darn shame. It would be so much fun to watch him make a fool of himself in a courtroom."

Griff's street was protected by police now, as was the mountainside behind his house. The security system had been reconnected, and an addition to the backup generator had made it impossible to circumvent. Three men had been hired to take over and supplement the work Harris and his relief had done. Broken windows had been replaced only hours after the attack, and by three o'clock Mrs. Robbert had already taken care of the mess the intruders had made.

Kelley wished that the mess that was her life was as easy to put in order.

"Well, it'll be safe living here now," Felice said, flinging her purse on a hallway table after following Kelley inside. "A fly couldn't get past the ranks out there."

"I'm going to call the hospital." Kelley started toward the living room.

A voice stopped her. "You don't have to." Griff came into the hall. His hair was damp, as if he'd recently gotten out of the shower, and his clothes were casual, as if he didn't plan to go anywhere that night. Gallagher was beside him.

Kelley met Griff's gaze and thanked whatever good luck was still left to her that they weren't alone. She didn't know what to say to him. She wasn't sure she would again.

Felice broke the strained silence. "Have you heard something about Harris?"

Gallagher answered. "He regained consciousness about an hour ago. His vital signs are stable. He seems to know where he is and what's going on. The doctors are optimistic."

Kelley closed her eyes for a moment. "Thank God."

"The vet says Neuf can come home tomorrow," Griff said.

"You're kidding." Felice crossed the hall to kiss Gallagher, then Griff's cheek. "And you told him you'd let that monster back in your house?"

"I don't think I've got much choice. The vet says he can't afford to feed him."

"He's really all right?" Kelley asked.

"He lost blood, so he's going to be listless for a while. But the vet says he'll recuperate better at home with us than in a cage in the clinic."

She heard more than the good news about Neuf. She heard Griff using words like "at home" and "with us." She no more knew what they meant than she knew what she was feeling.

"Do you know if there's any information on the gun?" Felice asked Gallagher.

"There isn't."

Felice traded a weary look with Kelley. Both women knew just how little would probably turn up. When the registration on the gun from the wedding had been traced, the police had found that its real owner had reported it stolen months before. The same thing would probably happen again. The market for stolen handguns was enormous.

"Have you considered making new living arrangements for your daughter until this blows over?" Felice asked Griff.

Griff went back into the living room, and everyone followed him, Felice and Gallagher with their arms around each other's waist. At a liquor cabinet in the corner he poured them all drinks without even asking if anyone else wanted one. No one protested.

Kelley took hers, and her hand brushed Griff's. Something warm curled inside her before she could take her first sip.

"Tara's just beginning to feel at home here," Griff said, making a nominal toast with his glass before he swallowed half its contents. He waited, as if hoping the liquor would numb something inside him. Then he shook his head. "I'm not going to send her away. I've thought about it, but I don't think she'd understand why I was doing it."

"She might be safer here, where a pack of people are watching out for her, than she would be anywhere else. If someone wants to get to Griff, hurting Tara would be the best way," Kelley said, addressing Felice. She wondered what she would do when Felice and Gallagher were no longer there to address. Would she and Griff talk? What would they say?

"I don't think it's likely anyone is going to come near this house again," Felice agreed. "Not unless they're crazy. Of course, whoever's doing this is certifiable. We're not dealing with run-of-the-mill hoodlums.''

"Whoever it is has seen too many movies," Griff said. He finished his drink in one more swallow, but he didn't pour himself another.

"Grade B movies," Gallagher said.

"Except the bullets are real, at least some of them." Kelley finished her drink, too.

"But the guy or guys with the guns aren't going to win any turkey shoots." Griff took Kelley's glass and set it beside his. Then, as if it were the most natural thing in the world, he took her hand and drew her to stand in front of him. Before she could protest, he crossed his arms at her waist and pulled her back against him.

He continued talking as if nothing had just happened. "So the sum of what we know after all this time is that we're dealing with one or more poor shots who have a flair for the dramatic.''

Kelley risked one glance at Felice. Her eyes were narrowed, their message clear. Felice had just spent hours in a car with Kelley, and never once had this new, obviously intimate relationship between Kelley and Griff been mentioned. She would politely bide her time, but the next moment the two women were alone together, Kelley knew she had some explaining to do.

"That about sums it up." Gallagher handed his glass back to Griff. "Three highly dramatic but flawed attempts on your life.''

"And as loudly as my instincts protest, that could lead to Roxey," Felice said. "He's capable of these kinds of flamboyant dramatics. He's—''

"Four attempts," Kelley said.

"Four?" Griff's arms tightened around her.

"You may have been the target all along."

"Since before the wedding?" Felice asked.

"There haven't been any other attempts on my life," Griff protested.

"What about *One Way Ticket?*''

He was silent.

"What if someone was trying to kill you, and Drake died instead?"

He still said nothing, but she could feel new tension in the arms surrounding her.

"You're talking about the accident on the movie set?" Felice asked. "Do you know the one they mean?" she asked Gallagher. He nodded.

"It may not have been an accident." Kelley turned so that she could see Griff's face, even though he didn't release her. "What if someone wanted you dead then? What if somebody with access to the set tampered with the fuse. You told me yourself it went off too soon, and you were saved from injury by a few seconds. What if you weren't supposed to have them?"

"But I did."

"Let's just say that you weren't supposed to, though. What if someone connected with the movie wanted you dead?" Since the idea was new to her, although it had been forming since the screening at Michael's, she was still feeling her way. She paused as some fragment of logic dangled just out of reach.

"That doesn't make any sense," Griff said. "If they'd wanted me dead, it would have been after the filming was completed. That was Drake's final scene, but not mine. If I had died, the whole movie would have had to be reshot."

"Then who would have benefited?" Felice asked. "Would anyone be better off if you'd died before the film's end?"

The fragment slipped into place. "What if Drake suspected something was wrong?" Kelley asked before Griff could answer Felice. "You said he came to you before that scene was shot, that he seemed anxious and needed to talk. What if he was suspicious? Maybe he'd seen something that worried him, but he didn't want to sound foolish."

"None of this makes sense," Griff repeated. "I told you, the whole movie would have had to be filmed again!"

"With who in the starring role?" Gallagher asked. "Who would have taken your place?"

Griff shook his head.

"Roxey?" Kelley asked. "Norris of the big ambitions and the bigger mortgage?"

"I doubt it."

"But it's possible?"

"We're talking about Tinseltown. Anything's possible."

"So we throw Norris back into the suspect's pot. Who else might have profited if you'd died in that scene?"

"No one."

"The film must have been insured," Felice said. "*You* must be insured. Who stood to get something if you died?"

Kelley saw Griff bite back anger. He was a fiercely loyal man. Despite coming up through the ranks in a dog-eat-dog industry, despite multiple attempts on his life, he still believed the best about people. She touched his jaw; it was clenched tight. "There are lives in jeopardy," she reminded him. "We're talking about possibilities here, not accusations."

"I think we're going to leave." Felice held up her hand when Kelley turned. "Stay where you are. It suits you both." She set her glass down. "Make a list of people who might gain something from your death, Griff. Let Josiah and his cohorts look it over."

"She's right," Gallagher said. "Absolutely sure of it, too, as always, but right." His smile said what he really thought of the woman in his arms.

Kelley watched them walk away. She knew when she and Felice met again she would have some explaining to do about Griff, but how could she explain what she didn't understand herself?

"You didn't tell her, did you?" Griff asked when Felice was gone.

Kelley couldn't pretend she didn't know what he meant. She knew quite well. She tried to pull away, but his arms tightened around her. She stopped, but she didn't relax. "Some things are too personal to talk about."

"Talk to me."

She had no words to organize her confusion. She met his gaze. "I don't know what to say."

"Did last night mean anything to you?"

"Did this morning mean anything to you?"

"Funny thing about this morning. Getting shot at strips everything to the bone, doesn't it? We don't have months to play cat and mouse. I want you, and I'm telling you so."

"Does Griff Bryant get everything he wants? No matter the cost?"

"You've asked me that before. You know better." He stared at her, then he dropped his arms, freeing her to move. "You accuse me of seeing only what I want. You expect me to make a list of enemies I don't even have. But you're the one with the narrow view of the world. You only see what you can fit between your prejudices and your fears. You think you're a risk taker, but the risks that really count scare the hell out of you!"

She *was* scared, and she realized she didn't even have enough courage to admit it. She couldn't make herself speak; she couldn't make herself tell him what frightened her most.

The front door opened, and she heard voices. She turned away from him. "Tara's home."

"And if it hadn't been Tara, you would have found another reason not to discuss this."

She moved away. "We're under siege, Griff. I'm responsible for protecting you, even if I've done a lousy job of it so far. Whatever's between us is going to have to wait until we're safe."

"There'll always be reasons to wait. I can think of a few myself right now." He stepped around her, as if she were no longer there.

She watched him walk away. No words would form to call him back.

Chapter 15

Two mornings later they were driven to the set by a pistol-packing chauffeur in a limousine that could have passed for a tank. A plain white sedan discreetly followed several car lengths behind.

Halfway there Kelley tried for the third time to make conversation with Griff. They hadn't talked much in the days since their last narrow escape. They had rarely been alone now that so many extra security people were on the scene. More important, neither of them had seemed to know what to say.

"You never told me what Michael said about the attack."

For the first time since they'd gotten in the car, Griff faced her. "The cops called him. I was too busy giving my statement to worry."

"But he's called since, hasn't he?"

"Half of Hollywood's called."

"People are concerned."

"The same people that you think are trying to kill me."

"You know what they say about barrels and bad apples."

Griff lounged back in his seat, although he was anything but comfortable. He chafed at being driven by someone else, even though a lot of people would have considered it a luxury. The moment he'd been able to pay his modest bills, having money had ceased to be much of a thrill. The charms of being rich and famous weren't many, particularly when they separated him from the people he wanted to reach out to.

"I know you don't want to think about this," Kelley said, "but did anything Felice say the other day make an impression on you?"

"Yeah. I've spent all the hours between dusk and dawn screwing over my friends."

"It's not screwing them over, Griffin." She used his full name without thinking about it, but when he shot her a look as cold as the ice blue of his eyes, she felt herself blush. "You're protecting yourself, Tara, me." She looked away.

"If we dug deep enough, we could find a reason anybody would like to see me dead."

"I imagine some reasons are better than others?"

He didn't know. He really didn't. He'd lost all perspective. Once he had begun to dig for dark plots, he'd felt lonelier than he'd known he could. He wasn't given to self-pity. But last night he had added up the human warmth in his life, and he hadn't needed a calculator.

"You've figured out why Roxey might want me dead," he said. "There are other actors, too, who could be jealous of my success, but no one else who's ever made a scene."

"Do you have some names for me?"

He gave her several with whom she was familiar.

"I'll have them checked out," she promised. "Discreetly."

He went on with his list of names, determined to be finished once and for all. "Fagan, Eddie and I quarreled over the contract for *One Way Ticket*. I thought they were making unreasonable demands, but they were united against me. When I told them they were treading thin ice, they backed off. We've talked about it since, and I'm satisfied they understand my position. I have no plans to replace either of them." He hesitated, hating every second of this. "While I employ them, though, they'd both receive a share of my estate if I died."

"Why?"

"Because in order to accommodate my career, neither of them has time for many other clients, and if I died, their gravy train would end at my funeral. So each of them is a benefactor of a large insurance policy I carry. It's part of our agreement.''

She leaned forward. ''Call your attorney and have that changed immediately!''

His expression grew even colder. ''I'll talk to my attorney, but I'll decide what to do.''

''Look, I know this is hard, but tell me this much. Was either Fagan or Eddie on the set the day Drake died?''

He shook his head. ''But you've pointed out more times than I've wanted to hear that whoever is behind this probably isn't soiling his own hands.''

''Who else stands to benefit if you die?''

''Joanne would come into a lot of money to use for Tara. Most of Tara's inheritance is tied up in trust, but some of it would have to go to Joanne to manage.''

''Does she need money?''

''Joanne always needs money. She manages to spend more than she has, no matter how rich the men she marries.''

Kelley hated to keep pressing, but she hated being shot at even more. ''Would anyone else receive something from your estate?''

''No.'' He looked out the window again and considered whether to name the next person on his list.

''Are there other people who might want you dead? For other reasons?'' she prodded.

''I told you I lived with Cam.''

Something clutched at her heart. ''Yes.''

''I think I also told you we were more friends than lovers.''

''Yes.''

''That wasn't the way Cam wanted it.''

''She was more serious about you than you were about her?''

''I loved Cam, but not the way she wanted to be loved. She wanted a real home together, kids. I didn't feel the same way. I thought we parted with no hard feelings, but maybe I was wrong.''

She empathized with his spurned lover. More than she could say. And more than ever, she knew that her fears about Griff and his casual, Hollywood attitude toward relationships were real. She shifted in her seat and wished they were already on the set. "You said she was happy now."

"Her husband flew to New York three weeks ago. Nobody knows why, nobody knows if they'll get back together again."

"Could it just be business?"

"Anything's possible," he snapped. "That's what this is all about, isn't it?"

"You're suggesting she might have ordered you killed in a fit of jealousy?"

He turned to look at her. "She was there the day we filmed the scene when Drake was killed. And we'd had a fight the day before. She'd accused me of letting our past interfere with our working relationship. We'd been on a tight schedule, and both our tempers were short, so I didn't think much about what she said."

"Did she say something that could be considered a threat?"

"She told me that she wished she could do something to make me forget we'd ever been lovers."

"Damn it, Griff! Why didn't you mention this before?"

"Because everybody has fights. Everybody has disagreements. But when they happen, you don't think that maybe the person you fought with is going to hire a hit squad to go after you!"

She drew a deep breath and told herself to stay calm. She failed. "Cam's providing security for you at the studio. She's in charge of protecting you there, for God's sake."

"We don't know if the explosion was an attempt on my life. We don't know if the wedding was, either. Damn it, we don't know anything except that this is an impossible situation!"

"Cam knows what I do for a living. She's paying my salary." Kelley closed her eyes and wished she could block out the whole world. "She called me at the beginning of the week and asked me for a full report of what was being done to protect you."

"Did you send it to her?"

"Not yet. But I did tell her about your security system, and..."

He put his hand on her shoulder, but there was no comfort in the way he gripped it. "And what?"

"I told her there was always a man parked out in front of your house for protection."

Carolina was not the love of Travis Jones's life. She was young, foolishly gauche, hopelessly ignorant. She was a Horton, member of a family of ne'er-do-wells whose genes no one would choose to pass on to an infant.

But Travis was not a shortsighted man. Despite all of Carolina's foolishness, all her mistakes, he could see the woman forming. Perhaps it was this deference to the woman she would someday become that made Carolina throw herself at him again and again.

Perhaps it was this appreciation of her finer traits that made Travis want to teach her what it meant to be a woman.

"So you've got the idea, now?" Michael asked Griff for the fifth time. "You don't love Carolina. You don't erupt with passion just because she's offered herself to you. You know she's just a mixed-up kid, and besides, you've got your eye on luscious Kate over there." He hiked his thumb at Miranda Lyle, who was standing yards away with her real-life husband, bouncing her toddler son on her hip.

"But you're not immune. You're not immune," Michael repeated. "You see beneath the dust and the starry eyes, and you know what kind of heartbreaker Carolina's going to become."

"You know, Michael," Griff said quietly. "This is the desert, and it's hot as hell, even if the weatherman says it's fall, even if the sun's about to go to bed."

Michael shoved his hands in his pockets. "Okay. I'll give it to you straight. Stop looking at Sammy like she's a hot fudge sundae and you haven't eaten in a week. Do that for me, okay, Griff? Just that much. She's not your co-star. Even if it's hot as hell, you don't have to sizzle!"

Griff didn't know if it was the heat that made him want to connect a fist to Michael's nose, or just the horrors of the last weeks. His gaze flicked beyond the cameras, beyond the rows of special lights and the flock of professionals. Kelley stood in the shadows, talking to Cam. Pumping her, he imagined.

"Does Cam seem all right to you?" Griff asked.

"Sure. Why?"

Griff shrugged.

Michael shoved a lock of silver hair off his forehead. "She's out here in this heat, too, and she's five months pregnant. She's like me. She'd like to shoot this scene. She'll be even more all right when it's in the can."

"Maybe she ought to go to New York with Jerry and take a little vacation."

"Yeah. And maybe pregnant women shouldn't produce movies? Hell, I don't know. She's got a job to do. I've got a job to do."

"I know. I've got a job to do, too. I'm ready. Go yell at somebody else."

"It's got to be right on one take," Michael warned. "The sunset's perfect. We won't get these colors every night."

"Will you shut up and start this thing rolling?"

Michael sent him a look that told Griff he was feeling the tension, too. "One take. Just one." He stalked off.

Griff positioned himself as he listened to the familiar wind-up before the film began to roll. From the corner of his eye he watched Kelley move to the spot she would enter from.

She was dressed in a green the color of grass. For once in the film, reality had been sacrificed to romance and she was clean.

She looked so young. Of course that was the way she was supposed to look. He was an older man, hard-bitten and ter-rifying, off-limits to a fresh-faced girl. But she was too young to know better. Her eyes sparkled when she looked at him; she glowed with an inner light. She was head over heels, crazy in love, and his job now was to let her down easy.

Someone measured the light. Someone shouted that the camera lens needed a different filter. Someone unfastened the top button of Griff's shirt.

Kelley was looking at him now. Staring at him. He won-dered what the cameras would catch this evening. As Cam had promised, Kelley's brief scenes had been shot first. Unless something had to be reshot later, this was her last one. He wondered how she felt about that and how she felt about him. And if the camera locked on film for all time the sparkle and the glow of Carolina's love for Travis, what did that mean? Was

Kelley, not Carolina, feeling more than she could express? Had their night together meant more to her than she had let on?

He didn't know. Sometimes he thought she was falling in love with him. Sometimes he thought he had been an actor too many years and could no longer tell the difference between fantasy and real life. The last months had seemed like one long scene from one long movie. Only in her arms had he felt a return to something real and lasting, something that wouldn't fade forgotten in a movie studio vault.

He heard the snap of the clap slate and the familiar shouted litany of start-up commands. Finally he heard Michael's "action."

He stared out at the sunset for five full seconds. Then, at the sound of her footsteps, he turned and watched Kelley coming toward him.

"You don't give up, do you, Carolina?" he asked. He detected the glide of wheels on carefully laid track as the camera moved closer. It was the last sound other than her voice that he was aware of.

"I don't give up," she said. "What good would that do me? If I gave up, you'd never look at me."

He stared at her, then he turned back to the sunset. "That should tell you something."

"Why won't you look at me? I know I'm skinny. I know I'm not pretty. But I'm a woman! Ain't too many women around here to look at!"

He laughed. "So you want me to look at you because you're one of the few in the territory?"

"I want you to look at me because I love you." She threw herself at him and wrapped her arms around his waist. "I love you, Travis! I want to be your woman. I can cook. I can sew. I know how to take care of babies!"

"Do you know how to make them?" He pushed her away, holding on to her shoulders so she wouldn't launch herself at him again. "Do you know what happens between a man and a woman, Carolina?"

She looked confused.

"I didn't think so. You need a mother." He dropped his hands, but not before he'd shoved her an extra few inches.

"All you've got to do is love me," she said plaintively. "That's what happens."

"There's a small matter of mechanics."

"I could learn anything. Anything at all." She grabbed his arm. "I learn fast. Faster than Kate."

"Leave Kate out of this."

"I could learn better. She thinks she knows everything already. How can she learn what she thinks she knows? You could teach me anything you wanted. I'd pay attention."

"Oh, you'd pay attention," he agreed arrogantly. "No doubt about that."

"Teach me, then! Whatever you want, whatever I should learn!"

He turned to her. She was young and eager. And Travis Jones was no saint. "You ever kissed a man, Carolina?"

She clasped her hands in front of her. "Sure." Her gaze wavered under his. "I've pretended."

"Pretended?"

Her voice faltered a little. "I pretended it was you."

He stared at her, but as the seconds passed, his expression gentled. "Me, huh?"

"Only you, Travis."

"You're still a little girl."

Her hands touched her chest, bound almost flat under the blouse. "I'm turning into a woman," she said huskily.

"Maybe I'll help a little," he said.

"I want a lot!"

"I don't think so." He lifted his hand to her shoulder and cupped it, savoring the feel. "I don't think you understand enough to know what you want."

"I want you!"

"No." He lifted his other hand and pulled her closer. She didn't come as easily as she had indicated she would. "What's wrong? Changing your mind?"

"Course not."

"Maybe you didn't think you'd get what you wanted."

"Course I did."

He drew his hands along her shoulders and up her slender neck. His hands framed her face. Her eyes lifted to his. He saw the glow of something real and precious in Carolina's eyes.

"You can shut your eyes if you want," he offered.

"I want to watch."

He smiled. "I'll watch, too."

He bent his head, but her next words stopped him. "Does this mean you love me?"

"No. You're too young for me to love."

"Does it mean we'll have a baby?"

"No. It means I wish you'd been born a lot sooner." He lowered his head until his lips were almost on hers. Her eyes were expectant, with just a glimmer of fear. He swept her closer until she fit tightly against him. Then he kissed her.

She tasted familiar; she felt familiar. His response was familiar, too. He wished his jeans weren't so damned tight.

She moaned, something he didn't remember from the script. He swept her closer. Her body fit against his, lock to key. He could feel her giving herself over to him. He could feel himself taking everything from her. His tongue dived between her lips; his hand dived into her soft curls.

Too many seconds into the kiss he remembered all of Michael's warnings. He remembered the sunset that wouldn't be perfect for a retake. He remembered the camera peering over his shoulder. He remembered staring into Kelley's eyes in the earliest hours of a morning and wondering what was going on inside her head.

He straightened and pushed her away. She looked shell-shocked. Her hand lifted to her lips, and she rubbed her fingers across them. Then, with a small cry she gathered her skirt in her hands, turned and fled.

"Cut and print," Michael said from somewhere nearby. "Damn you, Griff, I told you not to devour her! But it will do," he added reluctantly. "It will do."

Griff watched Kelley continue her path off the set, even though she could have stopped anytime. He smiled. It was the first time all day he had wanted to.

"Sammy was a perfect choice. She sure as hell can act," Michael said.

"She sure as hell can," Griff agreed. "And she sure as hell can tell the truth."

"Tara's gone to the movies with her new friend. One of the security people is going to follow them." Griff passed Mrs. Robbert's note to Kelley. "You're supposed to call your office."

Kelley patted Neuf, then watched as he dragged himself back down the hall to his spot in front of Tara's door.

She was tired, emotionally depleted from a day on the set and all the undercurrents of her relationship with the man standing beside her. The last thing she wanted was to conduct business. "It's late." She sighed, knowing that was no excuse. "I'd better try anyway."

"I'll warm up our dinner."

"Don't fix anything for me."

"I'll warm up *our* dinner." He left her standing in the hallway, clutching the note.

She couldn't imagine what they would say to each other over a meal. They had hardly exchanged a word on the way home. Their kiss for the cameras had shaken her to her toenails, but Griff hadn't seemed to notice.

She yearned for a long, hot bath and a night in front of the television watching a knock-'em-dead Dodgers' game. She wanted to be in her own house, on her own sofa, with all the crazy souvenirs of Hollywood surrounding her. She wanted a Neuf filled with bounce and energy instead of the bedraggled stitched-up version they had brought back from the vet yesterday.

She wanted her old life. Except that she could never have the same old life. She had changed. An evening like the one she yearned for would seem empty, lonely. The Dodgers, a dog, a den of delinquent Cub Scouts, even her friends and colleagues didn't add up to enough to satisfy her anymore.

She had shared little pieces of herself, a fragment here, a larger slice there, but there was no one with whom she had shared everything. More than anything, that was what she yearned for. And not just anybody.

Still clutching the note, she went into her room to make the phone call.

Griff was bringing food to the table when she finally made it to the kitchen. The room was homier now. One step at a time he had added bright touches of color, a rug in front of the sink, ceramic canisters, pot holders and dish towels in plain sight. Tara's favorite bowl still overflowed with fruit. A teakettle shaped like a chicken perched on the stove next to a woven basket of rainbow-hued glass eggs on the counter.

The scene was unbearably domestic. His house was slowly becoming a home, and somehow that made everything harder.

"Are you all right?" Griff asked, pausing in transit with a salad bowl.

"I'm fine. Felice wasn't there, but I talked to the new guy we hired. He passed on her message. I'm afraid it's not good news."

"About the investigation?"

She nodded. Since there was obviously nothing left to be done, she took a seat at the table. "Felice located your letter writer. She had a lead on the paper he used from some old letters at the studio. A clerk at a store that sells the same kind of stationery called her today. Someone there remembered a guy a while back who bought reams and reams of the stuff. He fit a description Felice had given them. They located a copy of his bill. Felice traced him through his parents' credit card number."

She put her head in her hands, massaging her temples. "He's in a psychiatric hospital. Has been for weeks. You weren't the only person he was writing. When his parents found out what he was doing and what kinds of threats he'd been making, they had him committed."

Griff sprawled in the seat across from her. "He's not our guy, then."

"No. He's been out of commission. And he wouldn't have had the resources for the kind of grand-scale attacks we've been subjected to anyway."

"Well, at least there's one person in the world we don't have to suspect anymore."

She looked up. He didn't seem concerned. Something inside her snapped. "Damn it! Don't you understand? He was the best choice! A crazy fan doesn't really touch your life. Now it could come down to somebody you know, maybe even somebody you care deeply about!"

His expression didn't change. "We both knew he was a long shot."

"Why are you being so calm about this?" She stood up, shoving her chair behind her. "Maybe you find this whole thing exciting. Maybe you don't care if it goes on forever, but I do. I want to get on with my life."

He stood, too, the arrogant pirate stretching himself to full height. "What life do you want to get on with?"

"The one I had before all this happened."

"I don't think so." He came around the table, dinner forgotten, and grasped her shoulders. "Can you really tell me you want to go back home and forget what's between us?"

"What's between us?" she echoed. "It's pretty forgettable, isn't it? I've trailed you everywhere you've gone for weeks now. You haven't even been able to go to the bathroom without me watching the damned door! And I've failed you every step of the way!"

"No, you haven't."

"Where was I when your security system was being dismantled? Where was I when the power was being cut?"

The smile was a pirate's, too. "In my bed."

"That's the point! I haven't really been your bodyguard, I haven't been your lover. I haven't been an actress, I haven't been a private eye. I'm nobody anymore. I want my life back. I want to know who I am!"

"I know who you are." He hauled her closer. "Shall I show you?"

"Damn it, no!" She tried to back away, but his long fingers bit into her shoulders.

"Let me tell you, then, since you can't figure it out. You're not Sammy, and you're not Carolina. You're not the war-weary cop and you're not the private eye who never gets involved. You're Kelley. You're a woman. You're my woman!" His mouth came down on hers before she could respond. She struggled against him, but the struggle only lasted seconds.

He was wrong. She *was* all the things he had named and more. She was more complex than she had ever dreamed, and more in love. She had no illusions that Griff calling her his woman meant all of the things she wanted it to. But for this moment it was almost enough. She needed him, as he had needed her after the screening. The future, and whatever it did or didn't hold, could be damned.

His hands were suddenly rough, as if they no longer had the time or impulse to be gentle. She felt him cup her flesh and lift her so that she would know the intensity of his desire. She didn't care. She didn't want roses; she didn't want poetry. She wanted the explosion of passion, the blotting of reality. She wanted nothing but to feel him merge with her until everything they had been was changed forever.

"Not here." His voice was a hoarse rasp. She felt its vibrations stroke her, just as his hands were.

The moments it took to get to the couch in the next room were lost to her. There was no brief return to sanity. Some inner voice cautioned her, but she was deaf to caution. Whatever emotions Griff had set free were stronger than her ability to control them.

They undressed swiftly, their clothes forgotten in a heap in the dark room. She clasped him naked against her, and felt the heat that had enveloped her once before rise again. She heard the words he murmured, felt the hot graze of his lips against her cheek, her chin, her breasts.

"Help me slow this down!" He buried his head between her breasts, and his breath was warm against them. "I don't want to hurt you."

She wondered how he could believe he wouldn't, no matter how slow they took their lovemaking. She would be hurt, but she didn't even care. More hurt would come from denying this.

She arched against him, pleading with every movement. He groaned, and clasping her tighter, fell with her to the sofa. The fabric was rough beneath her, his hands were rough above. She was lost in the passion, swallowed up in her own needs.

"You're not helping." She felt his whisper deep inside her. She wrapped her legs around him, and opening her eyes, stared straight into his.

"I'm not a little girl. I'm a woman," she said, adapting Carolina's words.

His lips dipped to hers. "You can shut your eyes if you want," he said after a long, thorough kiss.

"I want to watch."

He smiled a little, but his eyes smoldered. "I'll watch, too."

She couldn't stop herself from repeating the next line. "Does this mean you love me?"

"Damn it. You tell me!"

It was answer enough. Kelley took what Travis Jones had denied Carolina, and gloried in the taking.

Chapter 16

Kelley took her clothes from Griff and slipped them on without a word. He dressed, too, although he couldn't cover enough of his body to quiet the thunder of her heartbeat.

"I need another shower," she said, turning away from him. Before she could move, he wrapped his arms firmly around her waist.

"You can't wash away what just happened."

"I don't understand what's going on!"

His laughter buzzed against her ear. "Are you still playing Carolina?"

She pushed against his hands, but he held her firmly in place. "Let me go."

He grew serious. "Not until we've talked this out."

"I don't even know what to say."

"Start talking and see what happens."

She pushed again, and this time she was successful. His arms dropped to his side. She considered leaving, but she knew this time he was right. They needed to talk.

She wished they could go for a walk, but security dictated they stay inside. She wished they could go somewhere neutral, somewhere that didn't tease her with the intimacy of their lovemaking or the warmth of the home Griff was trying to make for his daughter. But that option wasn't open to her because somewhere nearby a crazy man—or woman—plotted their death. She felt like a bird beating its wings against a gilded cage.

As if reading her mind, he took her hand. "Let's go outside."

"We can't. It's not safe."

He sighed. "Then let's stand at the windows and pretend."

"I hate this."

He walked to the French windows and pulled all the blinds so that the lights in the valley below were visible. He stared at them in silence. But when she made no effort to join him, he spoke.

"When you're struggling to get to the top, you think if you ever do, the world's going to be yours. The dreams you have." He shook his head. "You don't realize you'll be cut off from it just because you made it."

"This won't last forever. You'll be safe—"

"Damn it, don't go out of your way to misunderstand."

She had planned to maintain a distance, but she was beside him staring out the window while the echoes of his last word still sounded. "Look, I know this is hard, but—"

"You don't know anything."

"They've been shooting at me, too."

"Do you think that's what this is about?" He turned so he could see her profile. "I suppose no one could fault you for being obsessed with life and death. But if the cops had already caught the people trying to kill us, what would you find to be obsessed by? What would you find to keep you from talking about us?"

She heard the stress on "us." She wished she were more sophisticated. She wished she were less.

The lights below them twinkled, a fairyland of possibilities. She believed in possibilities, but she also believed in logic. She was paid well to be logical, to solve problems step-by-step, deduction by deduction. She hadn't been trained to believe in the impossible.

"I don't know what you want me to say." She didn't face him, but not because she wanted to watch the lights. "I think it makes sense that under these conditions we've turned to each other. I don't blame myself. I don't blame you."

"Thank you."

She heard the sarcasm. She wondered if she imagined the hurt. "What do you want me to say?" Her voice rose, but it seemed to be a separate thing, out of her control. "Just tell me what I'm supposed to say now? This is new to me, you know. I don't have a repertoire of lines for situations like this one."

"This one? Why don't you start there? What does that mean?"

"You know what's been happening as well as I do."

"Then I'll give you my version. You've been swept off your feet, but you haven't liked where you've landed."

"I don't know what you're talking about."

"Did you really think I was talking about being cooped up in the house a few seconds ago? I understand necessity. I don't go crazy when I have to conform to a few safety standards. I was talking about what it's like to get to the top and find out you're alone!"

She turned. His eyes were cold. They revealed none of the emotion of his words. "I don't understand."

"I thought maybe you would. That was crazy."

"What would I understand?"

"You were at the top yourself, Sammy." He watched her react to her film name. "Figure it out."

She grasped his arm so he couldn't walk away. "I remember what it was like. And I remember what it was like to reach out to people and wonder if they were reaching back because I was me or because I was playing in Technicolor all over the world."

"Good for you," he said cynically.

"But I didn't use people." She dropped his arm. "I never got to that point. I quit before I could!"

"I've never used you."

"What *do* you call it, then? And maybe I've used you. I'm not a starry-eyed fool. I'm not Carolina!"

"And I'm not Travis Jones, am I? I'm just a man. I breathe. I sweat. I pull my pants on one leg at a time. I'm a man, not a perfect film hero!"

She stared at him, dismayed he could ever have thought she had expected him to be one. "Do you think that matters to me?" she asked softly. "Griffin, how could you think I'd want anything but a man?"

"Why should you be any different from the rest of the world?"

"I've wanted you because you're a man."

"Apparently the man's not good enough for you!"

She couldn't find the words to tell him he was too good, too much of what she wanted. He must have seen it in her eyes, though, because he hauled her to him and kissed her hard.

There was no logic to this, but as always, in his arms she forgot logic. She wanted the heartfelt sweetness of the kiss. More, she wanted him to know that he was everything she could ever hope for, every possibility she had ever imagined.

There was a noise in the kitchen, then the room was suddenly flooded with light. "Griff, I . . ." Tara's voice faded until nothing was left.

Kelley pulled away from Griff, dismayed that she had not heard Tara come into the house. The girl stood in the doorway, the man posing as Mrs. Robbert's brother behind her.

"I'll be going now," he said.

Griff nodded, but his eyes didn't leave his daughter's face. "We didn't hear you come in, Tara."

Tara looked stricken. She didn't respond. Neuf limped in from the direction of the kitchen to stand beside her.

"I thought you were at the movies," Griff said.

"Sandy got sick."

"I'm sorry."

"You must think I'm a baby!"

Griff sighed. "You sound very angry."

"You told me you and Kelley were just friends. What's wrong, did you think I don't know how women chase you around? Did you think I was stupid?" She backed away from them, as if she couldn't even stand to be in the same room. "Why did you have to lie? Did you think I cared?"

"I didn't lie."

Tara looked straight at Kelley. "You're not any different from my mother! You chase after rich men and movie stars, just like she does! She loves a man if his movies make money. Is that what you love, too? Is that why you're here?" She bit back a sob, then she turned and fled.

Kelley felt shaken to the bone. She started after Tara, but Griff stopped her. "Go take your shower. I'll deal with her."

"Griff, she's hurting. Don't—"

"Don't tell me how to be a father, damn it! If I'd been one before, I wouldn't have shut my eyes to what Joanne was doing to her!"

Kelley watched as he disappeared out of sight. Even Neuf hadn't stayed behind. She felt completely alone. For seconds she had almost reached for the impossible. Now she knew how foolish she had been.

Griff opened the door to Tara's room. She lay facedown on her bed, but if she was crying, she wasn't making a sound.

He crossed the room and sat down on the edge of the bed. She didn't move. "Tara."

"Go away."

"Kelley and I did lie to you."

"You thought I was stupid!"

"Never." He touched her shoulder, but she shrugged his hand away. He put it right back where it had been. "I'm going to start from the beginning, and you're going to listen."

"Go away!"

"You know about Felice's wedding, don't you?"

She didn't answer.

"Kelley was there, too. She was Felice's maid of honor." He gave a brief description of what had occurred, and the circumstances under which he and Kelley had met. "Kelley's a private investigator," he finished. "She used to be a cop."

Tara stiffened. "So?"

"So, she moved in here to protect us. I guess you could say she's our bodyguard. We decided not to tell you because we didn't want you worrying about your safety or mine. Now I think that was a mistake."

"You lied."

"Only because I didn't want you to worry any more than you already were."

"I saw you kissing her! You're still lying."

"I'm in love with her, Tara." The words slipped out before Griff realized he'd thought them. Love wasn't something he'd had much time to be concerned with, nor was it something that just happened in the blink of an eye. In a few short weeks love had grown, slowly, cautiously, one step at a time.

Now, still nursing the revelation, he tried to explain that to Tara. "There wasn't one moment that I didn't love Kelley, then another that I did. She's not like anyone I've ever known. She's pigheaded and absolutely sure of herself, but she also cares more about people than anyone I've ever known. When I hired her to come here, I hardly knew her. We weren't even friends."

"You still think I'm a baby." Tara sat up, facing him for the first time. Her cheeks were tear streaked, but her eyes were angry. "Joanne's told me over and over that she loved people, too. Then they moved in, and after a while they were gone. That's what people do. They say they love somebody, so nobody'll be shocked when they start living together. Joanne even marries them sometimes. Is that what you're going to do? Marry Kelley so nobody'll care if she lives here?"

He felt sick at the revelation that Joanne had paraded lovers in and out of the house in front of Tara. He felt even sicker that he had let it happen, that he had believed his ex-wife when she'd promised that her affairs were discreet and that the home she made for Tara wasn't touched by them. He hadn't looked below the surface. "Why" was a question he would have to struggle with for the rest of his life.

Now he could only respond, move on, try to be the father she needed. "I am not like your mother," he said.

"I'm not a baby. I don't care."

She wasn't a baby. She was absolutely right. But he saw clearly for the first time that she was still a child, still capable of being hurt, still aching for love. Too many years had been spent with a woman who couldn't be the mother she needed, but she had more years ahead of her, years when she could grow into someone very special.

He touched her cheek and she drew away. He touched it again, then let his hand rest on her shoulder. She felt so tiny, so much the child that for a moment he was overwhelmed with the desire to pick her up and put her on his lap.

"It doesn't matter right now if you love me. Like I said, love grows, and maybe someday you will. But you'll have to show some respect, because we're going to be living together for a long, long time, and we have to believe in each other for it to work."

"I'm not going to love you! You don't love me!"

His eyes closed for a moment, and he wondered what he could say to that. "How do you know I don't?"

"Joanne told me." She wriggled away from his hand. "Joanne says you're only letting me live here because you have to. She made you take me. She said you didn't want me and never would."

And he had wondered why Tara didn't want him to touch her, didn't want to spend time with him, didn't want to be in the same room with him any longer than necessary. He had wondered why she couldn't accept his love. He groaned and grabbed her, doing just what his instincts had told him to do. She fought, but she ended up on his lap anyway.

"Now listen," he said, against her hair. "Your mother was wrong. Completely wrong. I wanted you. I always have and I still do. But darn it, Tara, I'm just learning how to be a father. I can't read little girls very well because I've never been allowed to have much practice. I don't know how long she's been telling you I don't love you, but it's always been a mistake."

She stopped struggling, but she held herself stiffly, as if she was afraid to believe him.

"And get something else straight right now." He turned her face up to his so that she wouldn't mistake him. "You are staying with me for good from now on! I've been cheated out of being your father long enough, and I know I can make you happy here. Your mother's lied to you. I'm afraid she can say things that aren't true when she's angry."

She looked pathetic, as if she couldn't grasp this complete turnaround in her life. "Why?"

He forced himself to be charitable, although very little charity was left inside him for Tara's mother. "Maybe she was afraid you'd love me and shut her out, I don't know. Maybe she wanted to hurt me. That doesn't matter now. In her way Joanne loves you, and she knows you'll be better off with me. She won't fight it when I tell her you're going to stay here until you're a grown-up."

"She said you didn't want me."

"If I didn't want you, I'd be a crazy man."

She stared at him. He could see her trying to believe, wanting to believe. He bent his head and kissed her cheek. Then he wrapped his arms around her and held her close against his chest. He felt small hands slip around his waist. He swallowed convulsively and hugged her harder.

He tucked her in a little later, after she'd washed her face and changed into her nightgown, although she pointed out that girls her age hardly needed someone to smooth their blankets. He smoothed them anyway, trying not to think of the thousands of times he hadn't. He kissed her good-night and felt the brush of her hands on his shoulders.

"Will you tell Kelley I'm sorry?" she asked softly as he reached for the door.

"I will." He wondered what else he was going to tell Kelley, or what Kelley would allow him to tell her.

He opened the door and Neuf lurched past him. The dog took him by surprise; Griff let him slip by before he realized that Tara had made it clear she didn't want Neuf in her room. "I'll get him out," he said, reaching for his collar.

"No, let him stay," she said. "I guess there's room on my bed."

He watched Neuf drag himself up beside Tara and settle in as if he was used to that spot. He smiled.

"I just feel safer," she explained defensively.

"Smart girl." He took one long final look before he shut her door.

In the hallway he turned toward Kelley's room. With every step he took, the world seemed to change around him. He wondered how he had gone for so long without seeing the truth about Tara. He wondered when his feelings for Kelley had evolved into love, and he wondered why he hadn't seen it. Now the reality of what he felt for her seemed as obvious as Tara's love for him.

He knocked on her door, but there was no answer. He tried the knob and found it unlocked. Kelley stood beside her bed throwing clothes in a suitcase.

"Apparently I've missed something." He crossed his arms and watched her start on her underwear.

"It's not the first time."

"No, it's not."

She tossed a handful of bikini pants in an empty corner of the case. "I'm getting out of here."

"I see that."

"I'm not going to make Tara's life any worse than it is."

"Leaving might do that."

"Oh, come off it!" She turned. "Nobody's ever been honest with her about anything! We lied to her right from the beginning. She's never going to believe anything I say to her."

"She told me to tell you she was sorry."

She stared at him for a moment, then she turned and started on T-shirts. "What did you say to her to make her apologize?"

"I told her the truth about who you are."

"And she believed it? That kid's been pumped full of stories since she was born. I grew up with kids like Tara. I know! I hate Tinseltown and what it does to kids and families. I watched my friends. I saw what happened to them. I've seen that look on Tara's face tonight on the face of other kids. Shoot, some of them are in my Cub Scout den! Casual relationships, casual love affairs. Casual apologies. Casual lies!"

"I didn't lie to her tonight. She knows it."

"Can you possibly think I'm going to stay around and break her heart a few months down the road when you decide it's time for me to leave?" She slammed her suitcase shut. "Here's to the crazies who people your life, Griffin! People who knife each other in the back!" She whirled, suitcase handle in hand. "People who send hit men to weddings, like it was a scene from a film they were making!"

He moved toward her, prepared to jerk the suitcase away. She dropped it before he could reach her. "Holy hell," she whispered.

He watched her grow pale. "Kelley?"

She fell to the bed, as if her knees wouldn't hold her. "Holy, holy hell!"

He wanted to shake her; he wanted to kiss her. He knew better than to do either, yet. He waited tensely.

"Griffin." She looked up at him, dazed. "I remember. Lord, I remember."

"Remember what?"

"Where I've seen the gunman from Felice's wedding."

She looked so shaken, so pale, that he could do nothing but sit beside her. Frustration filled him, but he knew better than to pour out his feelings now. "Tell me," he said.

"I was a little girl. That's why it wouldn't come back to me. He was much younger, too. He hardly looked the same." She stared at the doorway as if replaying a scene. "I don't even know how old I was, but I met him at one of the studios. I was trying out for a part. I probably would have gotten it, too, but my parents wouldn't let me take it. It was a murder mystery, an Alfred Hitchcock kind of thriller. I was supposed to play a flower girl at a wedding, only the wedding never happened because men came in shooting. A man drew a gun on me, and I had to plead with him."

His response was profane and to the point.

"When my mother found out what they had me doing, she threw a fit. She dragged me out of the studio, but not before I'd already read for the part."

He reached for her hands. "Look, there's a good chance it's not the same man. You said yourself you were a kid and he was much younger. The similarities between the movie and real life are there, but it was dark in the church. The connection may only be in your head. He might just seem like the man."

"No." She shook her head as he warmed her icy hands between his. "No! Griff, it's the same man. I would bet everything on it! Everything!"

"This is no time to make a mistake."

"I'm not. I'm not!"

"Okay." He lifted her hands to his cheek. "Tell me everything you remember."

"I'm afraid that's just about it. But I remember his face. It was so sinister and I was scared, even then, even just acting. He's an actor for God's sake. An actor!"

"Think hard. Do you remember the name of the film?"

She shook her head.

"Do you remember seeing it afterwards? Reruns on television maybe, when you were older?"

She shook her head again, desperately searching for another piece of the puzzle.

"The studio? Anyone who was there when you read with him?"

"Nothing. Nobody. I was so young."

"Would your parents remember?"

"I doubt it."

"You could call."

"They're off somewhere exploring for the next couple of weeks."

"I don't remember this film." He chafed her hands to warm them more. "I don't remember anything like what you've described in any film I've seen."

"Maybe it wasn't released. Maybe it wasn't even made. Maybe nobody's mother would let them play that scene!"

"Somebody will know." Griff went through his mental list of Hollywood historians, people he knew or with whom he had worked who prided themselves on their knowledge of film trivia. Normally he didn't find those people very interesting; now he'd give almost anything to talk to one.

"My agent moved to the Bahamas a decade ago. But maybe I could reach him. I still get Christmas cards."

"Cam might know." Griff felt Kelley jerk her hands from his. "She's a film history buff," he explained.

"She's a suspect!"

Grimly he realized she was right. Everything he knew about Cam told him that she would never try to hurt anyone, but he no longer trusted his instincts.

Kelley got to her feet, too worked up to sit quietly any longer. "Tom Fortney would have known."

He stood, too. "Was he going to be the director?"

She thought hard. "I don't think so. I don't think he would have let me play a part like that one. He was very protective of the kids who worked with him. But he knew everybody and every film they made and tried to make. He collected a copy of every film he could get his hands on. There was a black market in prints that led right to Uncle Tom's door."

"And now Michael has them all."

"Michael." She said the name like a prayer's answer. "Michael would know!"

"He's a place to start," Griff agreed.

"Call him. Please?"

"He may not be back home yet."

"Try him."

"I will." He didn't move. "And when I have, when you know the name of our mysterious gunman, when you've reported it to the police and the FBI and every other law enforcement institution in the U.S., you and I are going to talk. And it isn't going to be about gunmen and movies. We're going to talk about us."

"This is about us. It's about our lives."

He grasped her chin and lifted her face to his. "There's going to come a time in the next few hours when you can't play games anymore, Kelley. Get ready for it."

Her expression, a funny mix of fear, guilt, expectation, satisfied him. He dropped his hand and strode from the room.

Chapter 17

"*Twilight Shadows.*" Kelley tested the title out loud. "I'm almost sure that's it."

"We can hope." Griff turned off the highway leading to Rancho Mirage and began the last lap of their journey to Michael's house.

"We could have spent days digging through studio vaults or talking to professionals before we found what we were looking for. And with just a little memory jiggling, Michael remembered."

"He was upset he'd never made the connection before."

She digested this new bit of information. It made sense. Michael expected perfection of himself, as well as others. "But you said the film was never released."

"It wasn't, but like I told you, Michael thinks he has a copy, one that came with Fortney's collection, and he thinks he may have watched it once. You know Michael, he expects perfection of himself, as well as the rest of the world."

"And he didn't remember anything else? The name of the actor playing the hit man? The stars? The director?"

"Even Michael can't be expected to remember those details, not from a film that was never seen by anyone but a few studio heads."

"If Michael finds the movie, we may see Norris Roxey on the screen."

Griff was silent for the next mile. He knew she could be right. There were others who might have been connected with the film, too, including Cam. The climb up the Hollywood studio ladder had taken her years. Like him, she had been barely out of her teens when she'd begun. Cam could have been part of a production team, some assistant's assistant for *Twilight Shadows*. Stranger things had happened.

"If nothing else," he said, cutting off his own painful speculation, "we'll see the credits. We'll know the gunman's name." Kelley looked straight ahead, willing the already speeding car to move faster. She wanted this over with. Griff was right; they had things to settle between them. But nothing could even be discussed until this was finished.

She wanted to tell him she was sorry. But how could she without opening a conversation that might be the most important of her life? She was sorry. She had overreacted when confronted by Tara's pain. She, who prided herself on logic and rational deduction, had taken her cues from Griff's daughter and acted like an emotional child herself. The reason was simple. Nothing had ever meant this much to her. Logic had only a tiny place in her heart right now. The rest of the space was taken by love.

She loved Griff. Love was what she had been running from so fast and furiously. Not that she was afraid to love. She gave love easily. She was afraid to *be* loved, or more accurately, she was afraid she wouldn't be loved. She had let Griff's career affect her vision of him, but not in the way he believed. Somehow, for some reason, she had convinced herself that a life with her wouldn't satisfy a man like Griff Bryant. She had confused the man with the screen hero, just as he had said.

She understood a little of her mistake. She had seen too many film colony marriages fail. She had seen indiscretions and heartache, and she had seen the terrible price paid by those left behind. She had been left behind once herself, and the experience had made her wary, too wary. She had been fooled, and now she expected deception as a matter of course. Griff, with his fame and fortune, was particularly suspect.

Earlier tonight she had been desperate to get away from the heartache that she had been sure awaited her if she stayed with him. But now, calmer, she realized there was no place to run, no place to hide. Logic should have told her that. Love finally had. She couldn't change the way she felt. She could only take the risks that came with feelings. She was an emotional coward who was going to have to be taught courage one step at a time.

"I wish you'd tried to get a catnap," Griff said.

"I'm all right."

"I'm not. It's nearly midnight."

Kelley looked at her watch and realized he was right. They hadn't been able to leave the minute Griff's conversation with Michael was finished. They had been forced to wait until a cranky Mrs. Robbert came back up to stay in the house with Tara. They'd had to map out security strategy, decide if any of the troops guarding the house should follow them, call Felice and Gallagher to let them know what Kelley had remembered.

All that had taken time. Because Tara's safety had seemed most important, they had decided to leave all their security men behind. For safety's sake they were driving a car belonging to one of the guards, as if they were part of a change in shifts. Just to be sure, Kelley was wearing her gun. Luckily Michael's house was a fortress. Once they were on his grounds, they wouldn't have to worry.

"I wish I could have gotten Felice." Kelley risked a glance at Griff. It was too dark to tell what he was thinking.

"I'm surprised she wasn't at home."

"Maybe she was there and just letting her answering machine take messages." Kelley doubted her own theory, though. Sometimes Felice screened calls, but she always picked up the phone when she realized it was her partner in crime fighting.

"Are you going to try her again at Michael's?"

"I left his number. She'll probably call us if she gets the message in time."

They fell silent again until they reached Michael's front gate. Palms swayed in the late-night desert breeze as the gate opened by an electronic command from inside the house. Michael was obviously prepared to receive them.

"He's being a good sport about this," Kelley said.

"Michael likes to be in on everything. He would have been angry if we hadn't thought of him first."

They parked and walked up the tan brick path to the house. Kelley thought about how she and Sara had pretended the bricks were yellow. They had been children in the Land of Oz on their way to the Wizard's palace.

To the child she had once been, Tom Fortney had seemed like the Wizard of Oz. He had seemed wise beyond human comprehension, a magic man who could take her image and create something wonderful from it. Now she wished it were Uncle Tom she was going to see on the porch, Uncle Tom who was going to make magic and help her create something wonderful of her life.

Griff took her arm at the steps. She couldn't tell him how she felt, but she could clasp his hand in hers. She did, giving it a warm squeeze.

Michael opened the door and ushered them inside. His cheeks were flushed by excitement. Kelley took one look at him and knew they weren't intruding. Griff was right; Michael wanted to be part of this.

"I found it," he said proudly. "And it was called *Twilight Shadows,* just like I said."

"Did you get a chance to run it?" Griff asked.

"I thought you'd want me to wait." Michael's excitement was tangible. His eyes glittered like a child's on Christmas Eve.

Kelley agreed. "I'd have to see it anyway, just to be sure the man I remember is the one we saw at Felice's wedding."

"There's a chance that even if the man you tested with is the gunman, he may not have played the role on film," Griff warned. "You didn't take the part. He may not have, either."

"We're just going to have to watch it to find out."

"Everything's set up." Michael led them through the house, through the conservatory with its jungle foliage and stone lions, tigers and bears. For a moment Kelley thought again of the times she and Sara had come this way to watch their favorite film. She wished that life could be that simple again, that the film she was about to see didn't hold life-and-death secrets.

Griff had never dropped her hand. Now he squeezed it, and she realized she wouldn't trade the uncomplicated days of her childhood for what life could hold as a grown woman. Like Dorothy from Kansas, she just had to reach out for what she wanted most. Like the Cowardly Lion, she had to find courage.

"You two sit," Michael ordered. "I'll get the film running."

She let Griff pick the chairs. "I don't care what Michael shows in this room again. This is the last time I walk through that door," he said.

She understood. Watching *One Way Ticket* had been a terrible ordeal. This wouldn't be much better. "But when this is over, we'll finally have a clue to what's been going on."

Griff wasn't as convinced as she was that anything was going to be gained, but he nodded anyway. He had been willing to come; he was willing to stay. He was still counting the minutes.

The lights went off and the room filled with sound, the screen with movement. For the moments it took to adjust, Kelley didn't realize anything was wrong. Then she drew a quick breath. Beside her, Griff stiffened. She could feel the tension in his body as he dropped her hand.

He rose to his feet, searching the darkness behind him. "Michael, what in the hell are you doing?"

Kelley was mesmerized. On the screen was Drake's death scene from *One Way Ticket*. This time she could not block out the explosion, the moment of impact. She covered her mouth with her hand and felt nausea sweep through her.

"Sit down, Griff. There's more to see." The voice was Michael's but he was covered by darkness.

Kelley clasped her gun. She stood, too. The lights snapped on, momentarily blinding her. When her vision cleared, she saw that hers was not the only gun in the room. In the back the gunman from the wedding stood beside a smiling Michael. His gun was pointed directly at Griff.

"Sammy. Sammy." Michael shook his head. "Did you think I couldn't figure out what you really do for a living?"

She pointed her gun at the gunman, but she knew it was already too late. If she pulled the trigger, Griff would die.

"Drop the gun," the man said gruffly.

"Marty, please. They're my guests," Michael said. "But then, you haven't been properly introduced. Griff, Sammy, meet Marty Maxwell. Marty and I worked together on my very first film."

Kelley knew she didn't have any choice. She couldn't be responsible for Griff's death. Her gun fell to the floor. Michael strolled over and picked it up.

"*Twilight Shadows,*" Griff said.

"Clever of you to figure it out, Griff. And clever of you to remember in the first place, Sammy. Marty thought you might. Eventually."

"It was your film?" she asked. "You were the director?"

"It was my first try. A low-budget thriller. I had visions of bringing in fifty times what the studio had spent on it. I would have, too, if Tom Fortney hadn't stepped in and used his clout to keep the film from being released. I was a young turk, and he hated me. He knew I was destined for great things. He was a has-been, an old man with nothing to contribute. It set me back years, but I rose again."

Kelley couldn't find any logic in what he was saying. The pieces fit together, but only so far. It was a jigsaw puzzle with corners and borders and nothing in the middle. "I don't understand."

"Sit down." Michael's voice lost its false note of joviality. The words were an order. "Maybe you'll see."

She had visions of using the cover of darkness to their advantage, but the lights were only dimmed enough for the images that were now on-screen to be clear. Following orders, they sat. Kelley helplessly watched footage of Felice's wedding, footage that had never been reported.

She didn't even know Michael was standing somewhere in the rows behind them until he spoke. "Cam came to me and said you wanted someone to film this wedding, Griff. I got you the best."

"Cam was in on this?"

"Cam?" He laughed. "Cam's a fake. She's not an artist. Movies are movies to Cam. She wouldn't have understood."

"What in the hell wouldn't she have understood?"

Kelley gripped Griff's arm. She knew he was furious, maybe too furious to be cautious. They needed caution. Nothing else was on their side.

"You still don't see it, do you?" Michael said no more. The film of the wedding continued, then ended abruptly. The next shots seemed to come from inside a moving vehicle. The desert scenery flew by, then a car, a white Volvo, appeared on-screen.

Kelley forced herself to sound calm. "You were behind it all, weren't you? You got everything on film."

"I especially like this shot." Michael laughed. "It's your best performance to date, Griff, Sammy."

She watched as the car went off the road and over the edge. The next scene was bullets blasting glass in Griff's sun room.

"You've lost your mind!" Griff jumped to his feet. Michael was several rows behind them. There was no way he could be reached, but that wasn't going to stop Griff from trying. Kelley launched herself at him and just managed to hold him back.

"There's more," Michael taunted.

"Why?"

"You still haven't figured it all out, have you?"

"I've figured out you've been trying to kill us and get it on film! I've figured out you're crazy!"

"Griff!" Kelley pleaded. "Please!"

"They're all remakes of scenes from my movies. That one's from *Holiday Horror*. Another one of my early films. You never saw it, did you? You never put two and two together."

Kelley held tightly to Griff. "Why? Can you tell us that, Michael?" She tried to sound as calm as Griff was furious.

"Why?" He looked at her as if he couldn't believe she didn't know. "You know why."

"No." She shook her head. Her eyes flicked to Marty, still holding the gun on them. She wondered if good luck ran in threes, as bad was supposed to. He had dropped his gun twice before. Perhaps he could be distracted into repeating his performance one more time.

"You've just been waiting to nail me, haven't you, Griff?" Michael asked.

Griff didn't answer.

Michael repeated his question a little louder, growing agitated. "You wanted me to suffer. You were so envious. Everyone is so envious. You were going to finish *Teardrop Creek,* then you were going to report me."

Griff remained silent.

"I didn't want Drake to die," Michael continued. "I didn't plan it. Oh, I knew he might. But the scene, Griff. The scene was better the way it was done. We shortened the fuse, just like Drake told you we were going to. I don't care what you said the other night about your conversation being interrupted. I know he told you. I saw him coming out of your trailer right before we shot the scene. He was upset. Stupid man. I told him not to worry. I thought he was a true artist, hungry for perfection, for truth. I thought I could trust him to do the scene the way it was made to be done! I knew I couldn't trust you! You wanted to ruin me. You're a hack, Griff. Always have been, always will be. Drake was different. He knew the line between film and reality doesn't exist. He knew the fuse should be shorter. He knew!"

Kelley wasn't sure she would ever understand completely what Michael was trying to say. He continued to ramble and pace, exhorting them about what the eye behind the camera sees, about reality, true reality. Her stomach knotted as she listened. Griff's body felt like granite against her.

She might not understand it all—insanity was always incomprehensible to the sane—but she understood enough to realize that Michael was going to have them killed when he stopped talking. She understood there was no exit out of the little theater except by the door where Marty stood.

Insanity could not be fought with logic. But insanity had its own twisted logic. She listened closely for the words that seemed to ring with meaning for Michael. When his speech began to wind down, she took a terrible gamble.

"You think we don't understand," she said, as if scolding him. "But we do. How could you think otherwise? I've been acting since I was a kid. Don't you think I hated all the precautions they made me take on set? Don't you think Griff hates having stuntmen do his job for him?"

He seemed not to hear her. "I've been accused of being too graphic, but all I've ever tried to do is film the world the way I see it!"

She nodded. "Of course."

He ran both hands through his hair until it was a wild silver mane. "Violence is everywhere. Animals eat each other to survive, don't they? Man destroys the wilderness and all its creatures to make room for himself. All I've ever tried to show is reality. My movies *are* reality!"

"They are! But you're not the only one with this vision, Michael," she lied. "Why do you think Griff never told anybody but me about his conversation with Drake? Because he understood!"

When she saw he wasn't convinced, she took a desperate chance. "You used the real footage of Drake's death at the screening the other night, didn't you?" She realized she'd hit the jackpot by the admiration in his eyes. "See? You thought nobody knew, but I did, Griff did! Sure, it was hard to watch, but reality always is, isn't it?"

Michael stared at her.

"You've had nothing to worry about. Didn't you know we'd understand?"

"She's lying." Marty spoke for the first time. "She's playing a game with you, Mike."

Michael's look of admiration turned to confusion. Kelley tried to turn it back. "You can see what's real and what isn't without his help," she said scornfully. "No one understands what's real the way you do."

"Drake's death was unfortunate," he said almost tentatively, "but it made a perfect statement. When the world sees it, everyone will know the truth."

"The world needs your vision," she said, hating the words but hating more what not saying them could mean. Kelley nudged Griff. He began to move toward the end of the row.

"You don't want us dead, Michael," she said softly, gently. "If you kill us, *Teardrop Creek* won't be finished. You need people like Griff and me in your movies. You need people like us, like Drake, people who are willing to sacrifice for reality. We have a film to do."

Her words seemed to bring Michael to attention. "*Teardrop Creek* is crap!"

Her heart skidded to her knees. "Crap?"

"You must know."

"Well, maybe I'd never thought about it just that way."

"Do you think I care if *Teardrop Creek* ever plays anywhere?"

"Even a movie like *Teardrop Creek* needs your touch," Griff said.

Kelley wondered if she would ever have a chance to tell Griff just how glad she was that he was a perceptive man. And what else would or wouldn't she have a chance to tell him? The thought made her weak with regret. She counted every second of silence that had ever been between them and wondered how many billions of chances she had missed to tell him she loved him.

"I saw how upset you were when Drake died," Michael said to Griff. "His death was a beautiful sacrifice. You should have seen that, but you didn't. And now you want to ruin me. You're nothing." He pointed to Kelley. "She's nothing!" He turned as if to give Marty orders.

"Michael, there are people who know we're here," Griff said. "They'll know who had us killed."

"Do you think I can't direct your death scene?" Michael asked coldly. "When you're found, no one will ever suspect you were killed here instead of on the way home." He stared at them, and for a moment confusion seemed to fill his eyes. "And it will be real. What they see will be real."

Kelley took a deep breath and her last gamble. "Are you filming this, too, Michael?"

His confusion seemed to clear. "Turn up the lights, Marty." When the room was bright, he pointed to recesses in the wall. "I film everything, but especially this. Especially this," he repeated.

"What will killing us here, in your screening room, accomplish? The film's going to show two unwilling murder victims, a fancy snuff film."

Michael looked outraged that she would compare his art to the rumored pornographic films in which the female star died on film in a terrible surprise ending.

"It's not going to have any value," she went on before he could protest, "since no one's behind the cameras to choose angles or range. A camera doesn't have the judgment of an artist, of the most talented artist in Hollywood." She paused. "You," she said.

"Mike, she's stalling," Marty said. He looked uncomfortable.

"Why would I stall? We're going to die anyway. But when we do, I want it to have meaning. Wouldn't it be better if you gave us a chance to escape, a chance to run? If we die that way, the film will have merit. Michael, you can film it while Marty comes after us. Your property's fenced, and Marty has a silencer. The chances are good we won't be able to escape, but that tiny possibility will make the film a real contribution."

She knew that in her desperation she had probably gone too far. The suggestion seemed too bizarre for even a crazy man to consider. But Michael was obviously considering it. He tossed her gun from hand to hand, as if he might use it himself. But more significantly, he didn't.

"I like it," he said at last. "You have class, Sammy."

"Tom Fortney never understood that," she said.

Her words seemed to cement his decision. "There's beauty in all this, isn't there? Everything is coming full circle. He directed your first role. I'll direct your last."

She nodded. Her smile felt like a death mask. "We'll need a good head start for this to have any meaning."

"You'll have a minute."

She watched him continue to toss her .38 back and forth. "I don't suppose you'd let it be a shoot-out instead of a simple chase?"

"You have my admiration, Sammy." He pocketed the gun. "Now, if you'll excuse me, it's going to take me some time to get my equipment together."

"All we've got is time," she said. She thought of the message she had left on Felice's answering machine. It was a wild chance, but it was possible that if Felice tried to reach them here and no one answered the call, Felice and Gallagher would come looking for them.

She looked at Griff. He was staring intently at her. She read everything she had never dared to see in his eyes. She couldn't speak because Marty was listening, and she knew he wanted any excuse to kill them here, where he was guaranteed victory. She could only stare back at Griff and try to tell him with her eyes what he meant to her.

Michael took his charge seriously. A full ten minutes passed before he returned with his equipment. Ironically Kelley realized that the revolution in video technology had played right into her hands. Michael's camera was lightweight but loaded with accessories. He might not have a film crew at his side, but he could be sure he was going to have a credible video when the night was finished. She just hoped she and Griff could write a new ending.

"I don't like this, Mike," Marty whined.

"What you like hardly matters," Michael said.

"Maybe we should call someone in to help."

Kelley forced a laugh. "What a film that would be. A pack of hunters after a couple of helpless deer. Now, there's a message film for you, Michael. An award winner."

"Just you," Michael told Marty. "And me filming it."

Marty looked unhappy, but it was clear he had no choice. "Start counting, then."

"Not until we're in the hallway," Griff said. "It would take most of a minute to get past you and out of this room."

Michael nodded. "Fair enough. Come on." He moved aside and gestured for them to come up the aisle. Griff took Kelley's hand and started toward them.

She considered jumping Marty and ending it here, but he was standing far enough away from the door that the seconds necessary to reach him would almost certainly result in a bullet or two pumped straight into her. Griff might get away, but she knew him too well to believe he would leave her and make a run for the door. He would die, too, playing the hero. Being a hero. Her hero.

Griff's fingers tightened around hers as they neared the door. She knew he had guessed her thoughts and wasn't going to let her go after Marty. She squeezed his hand in reassurance.

With her back to Marty and Michael now, she waited for a bullet. When nothing happened, she calculated, as she had in the minutes they had waited for Michael, their best route of escape.

She thanked her memory for the clear picture she had of the back acres of Michael's estate. She wasn't foolish enough to believe that nothing had changed in the many years since she had visited Sara here. But neither did she believe that Michael would have wanted many changes made. Part of his insanity seemed to be his effort to fit himself into Tom Fortney's life. Little had been changed inside the house. If she was lucky, the only changes outdoors would be the ones that time had wrought.

"One."

She took off with Griff beside her, running through the hallway toward the back of the house. The house was large enough, the layout complex enough, to need a blueprint to get through it the first time. She remembered each twist and turn, however. Her mental count was thirty when they reached a door leading outside.

She slammed the door behind them, counting on the seconds it would take for them to open it. She jumped to the ground from the small porch before she spoke. "Do what I tell you. There's a wooded area at the back of the property. Anywhere else you try to climb the fence, they'll see you, but you might be able to get over it there. Run. I'm going this way to distract them. I'll be safe. Run!"

She turned, but he grabbed her arm and tugged hard. "Come on and shut up."

There was no way she could loosen his grip and no time to argue. "Damn you," she said, but she was already running beside him.

"No heroics."

He dropped her hand, but it was clear that if she tried to veer off, he'd come after her. She shelved her plan and managed to keep up with him. There were only occasional softly colored spotlights after they passed the immediate yard. She cursed the darkness at the same time that she thanked God for it. It was difficult to run, but if the area had been better lighted, they would have been easy targets.

She heard the door slam somewhere in the darkness to their backs. She heard a shout. She was running too hard to curse or groan, but a voice inside her screamed as the first bullet whined past them.

She doubted Michael would want them killed immediately. He was too far away to get the film he wanted. She thought the bullet had been for effect, but there was no guarantee. As deranged as he was, second-guessing him was impossible. She ran faster, harder, taking chances on the shadowed ground that could lead to injury. But chances were all they had. She knew she must be holding Griff back. He was in superb condition. He was larger, stronger, faster than she could ever be.

"Run," she gasped. "I can't keep up with you. If you get there first, you can help me over."

He ignored her.

A hundred yards ahead of them, trees loomed at the fence line. They were thick, but the cover they would provide was minimal once Michael and Marty drew closer. Frantically she tried to think of other possible avenues of escape. Shouting for neighbors was a waste of breath. The closest houses weren't even visible from this part of Michael's property. Privacy had been a major consideration for everyone building here. No shouts, no muffled bullets would be heard by anyone, unless a neighbor was out for a midnight stroll. And the chance that their shouts would pinpoint their exact location for Marty was too great a one to take.

She ignored the pain in her lungs, ignored the jolting gait that reinjured the ankle she had twisted in the gorge behind Griff's house. She ran exactly as if her life depended on it.

Fifty yards from the fence another bullet sailed past them, followed immediately by another. She didn't dare look behind her, but she knew that Michael and Marty were close enough to be a threat. Neither of the men would be as fast as Griff or her, but there was a fence ahead, a fence that had to be climbed. How long did they have to get over the fence before a bullet stopped their progress? She was sure it would come down to a matter of seconds. She wasn't sure that the seconds would add up to a total that was in their favor.

The darkness grew denser the farther they ran. Here there were no spotlights discreetly displaying clusters of bushes or garden paths. The night was black, a wicked sorceress daring them to take the wrong step, a savior welcoming them with outstretched arms. So little had changed, her instincts more than her memory led her through the first of the trees bordering the fence. A bullet slammed into the tree at her side, splintering bark.

She tripped over a piece of irrigation equipment and fell to her knees. The seconds ticked away as Griff helped her up and she stumbled forward again. But the odds were clear now. The seconds belonged to Michael and Marty. Unless she could fool them.

"You go first," she said as they continued to make their way through the trees. "You can climb faster. There, in the corner." She pointed with a trembling hand to the thickest part of the trees.

"We'll climb together."

She wanted to sob out her frustration. They weren't going to make it. Not both of them. She wanted him to have a chance. She didn't want him to be a hero and go down with her.

"My ankle! You have to go up first to help me. I can't do it without you."

He dropped her hand as another bullet sped past them. They had no time, but he took time to consider. Then, with her plea obviously making sense to him, he raced toward the fence. He was already climbing by the time she heard crashing in the trees at the rim of the grove.

She didn't have to consider what to do next. With a few extra seconds to his credit, Griff might make it over the fence, but there was no way she could follow. She wheeled and ran along the fence, away from him, taking no precautions to be silent.

She knew her ploy had been successful when a bullet whined past her, kicking up dirt just where she would have stepped.

A sob gripped her throat, but she kept moving. Bullets were flying wildly now. Marty wasn't going to miss his chance to kill her this time. She saw both men approaching from a small clearing to her right. Silently she recited the only prayer she knew.

"Over here, you bastards!" Griff seemed to come out of nowhere. She saw Marty aim, saw Griff launch himself at him. Incredibly she saw Michael filming.

She screamed once, twice. Griff took a bullet and kept going. She tried to reach him, but he had already knocked Marty to the ground. Marty fired again, but this time the bullet went wild. She saw Michael stagger, then fall, still clutching the camera.

"Griff!" She screamed his name and ran toward him. As she watched, he seemed to crumple. Marty struggled to a sitting position and reached for the gun that Griff had managed to knock from his hand. She reached it first. Grasping the barrel, she slammed it hard against the side of Marty's head.

Chapter 18

Griff tried to stagger to his feet. Kelley put her arms around him to stop him. "You're bleeding," she said, struggling to sound calm. "You're going to have to stay down while I go for help."

"Griff."

Griff turned his head toward the sound of Michael's voice. He lay several yards from them, still clutching the camera. Kelley remembered that he had pocketed her gun. She was at his side in a moment, digging for it. He didn't seem to care.

"I'm dying," he said.

She felt no pity. "I doubt it."

He shifted the camera, and she saw his shirt was already soaked with blood. First aid seemed out of the question. The pity came then, just a flash to remind her she was human and Michael Donnelly was a pathetic madman. "Don't try to move," she said. "I'm going for help."

"No, I'm dying. Griff..."

She watched Griff lift himself and drag his body toward Michael. Tears filled her eyes.

Michael lifted his camera. His hands shook violently. "Get it on film," he said, trying to push the camera toward Griff. "Get my death . . . on film."

She felt sick. She wanted to scream out her revulsion. But as she watched, Griff pushed himself to his knees and reached for the camera. Kelley saw the expression on Michael's face change from terror to satisfaction. A protest rose in her throat, then she heard a click.

"The camera's off," Griff said. "Forever!" Then, with his last bit of strength he hurled it into the darkness.

Michael's eyes widened. He clutched at his chest and made a horrible sound deep in his throat. Then his eyes glazed and his body stiffened in one last spasm.

Kelley threw herself at Griff, who had fallen back to the ground. "Griff! Griff!" She saw a portion of his shirt darkening with blood. She ripped it open and found a silver-dollar-sized wound to one side of his chest. She ripped off her jacket and folded it to use as a compress. At best it was a temporary solution. She didn't know what to do, whether to continue applying pressure or take a chance and run back to the house to find a telephone. She knew if she did, she risked heavy blood loss and Marty regaining consciousness. But if she didn't, help might never arrive.

She shouted into the darkness, hoping with everything inside her that someone might hear. Her hands shook and a sob rose in her throat. She shouted again.

"Kelley?"

For a moment she believed she'd imagined Felice's voice. But when her name was shouted again, she knew she hadn't. "Here!" she shouted. "In the back! Call an ambulance!"

She heard the blessed sound of someone running toward her. Moments later she heard Gallagher's shout. "I can't find you!"

"Here." She waited seconds, then shouted again to keep him on track. At last he appeared through the trees. "Jesus." He took one look at Griff and stripped off his sports coat to cover him.

"I think it's only one wound," she said.

"Felice is getting an ambulance." Gallagher conducted the best examination he could in the darkness. "Are you still in danger?"

"No. I think Michael Donnelly's dead. He was behind this. The man over there—" she jerked her head toward Marty "—should come to by Christmas."

"I want you on my side in a fight."

"I didn't do enough." The sob that had been trying to escape did. "I couldn't. I tried. Griff threw himself at Marty to save me. I'd be dead if he hadn't."

Gallagher muttered a string of curses.

"He could die," she said tearfully.

"We're not going to let him."

More footsteps rattled the fallen leaves in the small grove of trees. "Kelley? Josiah?"

"Here," Gallagher said.

Felice, carrying blankets, found them. She took one look at Griff and knelt to cover him. Then she stood. "I'm going back to make sure the rescue squad finds you. I left the house open for them, but they won't know where to look."

"Can they get past the gate? How did you get past the gate?" Kelley asked Gallagher.

"I'm hard to stop."

"It's open now," Felice said. "I located the controls. They won't have to climb over it." Somewhere in the distance a siren sounded. She started back toward the house at a run.

Griff groaned, the first sound he had made since collapsing. Kelley leaned forward. "Griff! Griff! Can you hear me?" She saw his eyelids wrinkle, but they didn't open. "Help's on the way," she promised. "And we've slowed the bleeding. You're going to make it!"

She heard Gallagher move away to examine the other men. She leaned closer to Griff until her lips almost brushed his ear. "Don't you dare die," she said fiercely. "Do you hear me? Not when we're finally safe! Not when Tara and I are counting on you to live! Do you understand me? You'd better not die!" Her tears washed his cheek. "I love you, Griff. I wasn't trying to save your life because it was my job! I love you! I'd have died for you if you'd let me. But don't you do the same. Understand? Don't you dare die!"

She heard voices and more footsteps. Bright lights moved through the yard behind her. "They're here," she said, turning back to Griff. "They're here! You'll be in a hospital in minutes. Just hang on."

She didn't move away from him until a paramedic replaced her. With Gallagher's arm around her, she watched as the three men quickly evaluated the situation and attempted to stabilize Griff before moving him to the stretcher. Then she watched as they carried him away.

Sergeant Fred Pollock scowled at the No Smoking sign in the surgical waiting room. Kelley had watched him scowl at it at least a dozen times before.

"It's not going to change, Fred," she pointed out wearily. "This is a hospital. They want to make people healthy here."

He ran a hand over his unshaven face. "You want to go over this one more time?"

Kelley shook her head. "No. That's my statement. The same one I gave the Rancho Mirage cops. I've told all of you every detail I can remember. It's pretty cut-and-dried."

"Then we're done."

Gallagher entered the room. Kelley saw him exchange an intimate look with Felice. It was difficult to watch.

He turned to Kelley. "Heard anything?" he asked.

"He's still in surgery." She bit her lip.

"Want to hear what Marty had to say?"

"Did the bastard appreciate the fact that I didn't off him?"

"A fine piece of self-control," Sergeant Pollock said. "You listened when I told you not to go around shooting people."

"It was bad advice."

"Marty's a long-time loser," Gallagher said. "He's got a record dating back to high school. Petty stuff, mostly, but there were a few stints in jail. Apparently Donnelly befriended him when Marty decided to give up his life of crime and turn actor. He worked in a couple of early films of Donnelly's, then when he couldn't get any other work here, went east and ran con games from New York to Boston. Donnelly traced him recently and offered him a job, so he came back. The job was to kill Griff.''

"There were others involved," Kelley said. "Actors, too?"

"Luckily our Marty has an actor's memory and a con man's talent for self-preservation. We've got names, addresses. Most of them were extras, people who'd probably do anything if Donnelly promised them a part in his next film. And remember how remarkable it was that anyone could have gotten around Griff's security system? The guy who did it was Donnelly's gaffer.''

That made sense to Kelley. Any top-notch gaffer, the chief electrician on a film, had the skills to rewire a small city.

"I wonder if they knew this was real life?" she said. "Is there a bunch of more Michael Donnellys walking the streets of Southern California? Did they know Griff would bleed real blood if they killed him?''

Felice put her arm around Kelley. The two men looked at each other in an age-old male signal. "I'm going to go outside and have a smoke," Sergeant Pollock told Gallagher.

"I'll come with you and watch." Gallagher rose and the two men disappeared.

"Gallagher hates cigarette smoke," Kelley said.

Felice hugged her harder. "You're bearing up well, considering everything.''

"How much longer is this going to take?"

"Do you want them to just tack a few seams and let it go at that?''

"Jeez, Felice." Kelley lowered her head into her hands.

"You're in love with Griff, aren't you?"

"What does that have to do with anything?"

"I saw a copy of the morning paper when I went downstairs a little while ago. Griff's a hero again.''

"This time they know what they're talking about."

"So he really saved your life?"

"He did.''

Felice was silent for a little while, but she rubbed Kelley's shoulders. When Kelley finally raised her head, Felice spoke. "Josiah and I are married.''

Kelley looked blankly at her.

Felice nodded. "We were on the way home from our wedding when you called."

"You got married without me?"

"We couldn't have guests." She smiled a little. "We got married at the Convent of the Blessed Garden."

Kelley stared at her. The Convent of the Blessed Garden was miles away in stark desert country. Felice and Gallagher had met there, both undercover—Felice under the most cover, since she had been posing as a nun.

"Why?"

"Well, it seemed right, Kell. Josiah and I met there. And for a while, anyway, it was our home. Love's a simple thing, really. A simple wedding in a truly holy place seemed right for us." She paused. "And I couldn't bear the thought of my mother planning another social event of the season."

"She's going to throw a fit."

"I called her from the lobby a little while ago. She thanked me."

Kelley smiled, then she hugged her friend. Tears welled in her eyes, a feeling that was becoming familiar.

"Josiah and I are stubborn," Felice said. "We didn't come to this point easily. Neither of us really knew how to share. There are always so many things that separate people, learning to be together is hard."

"You're not talking about you and Josiah, are you?"

"Sure I am, but maybe I'm talking about you and Griff, too."

"I've been such an idiot."

"Have you?"

"I was so afraid of being fooled, I fooled myself."

"It's hard to trust if you're in our line of work."

"That's fine on the job and a disaster if you carry it into real life." Kelley stared at Felice. "Maybe I'm not really that different from Michael. I saw Griff on-screen and I couldn't tell the difference between the man I saw there and the man I was learning to know. The edges blurred."

"Michael Donnelly was insane. You were frightened. There's a world of difference."

"I hope so."

"So what are you going to do?"

"I'm going to tell Griff I love him. Not because he saved my life. Not because he's a real hero. Because he's a man."

"And what will he say?"

"I . . . I don't know."

"Then you still aren't sure who he is." Felice looked up and saw a man in surgical green standing in the doorway. She answered his smile. "Kell?" She nodded in his direction. "Someone wants to tell you something."

Kelley looked up.

"Mr. Bryant's going to be fine," the surgeon said. "He'll have a scar, but hell, in his line of work, it'll look normal. Give him a week here, a few weeks at home and he'll be dangling bad guys from the top of the Statue of Liberty before you know it."

Kelley felt tears roll down her cheeks. "May I see him?"

"He's in recovery. He'll be groggy, but he should be waking up. You can only stay a moment."

Kelley gripped Felice's hand.

"I'll wait outside the door for you," Felice promised.

They rose and followed the doctor through a maze of hallways. Kelley was too dazed to note more than the antiseptic smell, the sparkling clean walls decorated with expensive desert watercolors. Griff had ended up in one of the best hospitals that money could buy, a special benefit of nearly dying in the land of the rich and famous.

Felice stopped at the double doors leading into the recovery room. "I'll wait here."

Kelley panicked. "I don't know what to say!"

"There's probably a screenwriter in one of these rooms. I could have him scribble some lines."

"Just once I'd like some sympathy."

"What kind of sympathy do you need?" Felice demanded. "You're in love. That's all. It's not a disease. No one's going to cut off your arm in there. Go tell the man you love him. Say 'I love you.' It's a piece of cake!"

Kelley pushed the doors open. Griff was the only patient inside. The walk to his bedside seemed miles long, the equipment ticking and whooshing around him as sinister as Michael Donnelly's heart.

She was relieved to see he was breathing on his own. But she had seen fewer flashing lights and electrical wires in a day at Disneyland. She wondered if there was a vein in his body that wasn't connected to something.

She wound her way through the maze and glared back at the young nurse who obviously didn't think she belonged there. At Griff's bedside she inched her way toward his head with excruciating care. After all they had been through together, she didn't want to be the one to disconnect him from life support.

He looked so pale, so still. She wondered if the surgeon knew what he was talking about. Tentatively she touched his arm. He felt cool, but not cool enough to make her scream for help.

"Griff?" She cleared her throat. "Are you awake?"

His eyelids wrinkled, as they had in the dark grove of trees.

"It's Kelley," she said. "You're in the recovery room. You're going to be fine."

His eyes opened slowly but didn't focus.

She drew a deep breath. Until that moment she hadn't really been sure he was alive. "Griff." She could say no more.

His head turned slowly, as if it were relearning the movement. "Kelley?"

"Yes. Oh, Griff." She squeezed her eyelids tightly together to stop her tears. "You're going to be all right!"

"I don't feel . . . all right."

"You will! Very soon."

"Michael?"

She wished she didn't have to be the one to tell him. But she couldn't lie. "He didn't make it," she said gently.

"Something . . . snapped."

She nodded. "Yes. Maybe it was the guilt of knowing he'd killed Drake with his quest for perfection, I don't know. But you couldn't have guessed, and there was nothing you could have done."

"Were you . . . hurt?"

"No! I'm fine. You saved my life."

"That's what heroes . . . are for."

"You were a hero. And you're going to be fine. You're going to be fine!"

He rested before he spoke again. Images swirled through his mind. Voices clanged. He concentrated. "Tara?"

"She's waiting to hear. I'll call her as soon as I leave the room. They won't let me stay more than another second." Kelley scowled at the young nurse who was coming closer. She stopped a distance away, but her foot tapped an impatient rhythm in time to Griff's monitored heartbeat.

Kelley took a deep breath. There was so much to share, but this was not the place to share it and obviously not the time. Courage deserted her. She thought of all the reasons why she shouldn't tell Griff what was in her heart, reasons that outweighed Felice's advice.

"I have...have to go," she said. "But I'll be nearby. And I'll come see you as soon as they put you in a room." She patted his arm ineffectually. Tears escaped down her cheeks. "I'm so glad, so glad—"

He couldn't let her go without knowing if one voice he'd heard was real. "Did you tell me...you loved me?" His tongue passed over his lips.

"I...I..."

"I thought I heard..."

She began to cry in earnest, her secret out. "Yes! I love you."

"When did you..."

"I told you before they took you away. I love you, Griff! This isn't the time or place to tell you, but I do!"

"Everything got black. I kept...hearing your voice. I kept trying...to reach you."

"I love you!"

"I don't care if...I never make another movie."

She didn't care that he hadn't told her he loved her, too. She was elated she had finally gotten enough courage to say the words when she was sure he could hear them. "You don't have to ever make another movie!" she said. "Not ever."

"But I care...if you leave."

Something jabbed at her heart. She squeezed his arm, then bent low so he wouldn't miss her words. "I'm not leaving. Not ever."

"I love you."

"I'm so glad you do!"

"Marry me?"

"Darn right."

He smiled. Then his eyes closed.

Kelley kissed his cheek before she straightened. The young nurse was staring at her, her eyes wide. Some of the starch seemed to have dissolved from her uniform.

"Did you hear him ask me to marry him?"

The nurse nodded.

For a moment Kelley thought of all the reasons Griff might have told her he loved her. Gratitude that she had tried to sacrifice herself for him, emotion at finding he was still alive, reaction to anesthesia. Then she smiled.

"Good," she said. "When he wakes up again, remind him what he said, will you?"

The nurse's eyes widened further.

Kelley stepped away from the bed. "Because Mr. Bryant there is never going to be allowed to forget it. Not for the rest of his life!" She flashed the nurse another watery smile, then she carefully picked her way across the room and went to call Tara.

Epilogue

"You could have eloped." Felice brushed her chin-length hair over her ears and anchored it with an amethyst-studded comb. Her dress was the color of amethysts, too, sleek and simple. "You'd be all finished with the wedding by now and a happily married woman."

Kelley looked around the bedroom in Griff's house that had once been hers. It was a guest room now, the walls a pale peach, the area rug an Oriental weave of contemporary pastels. Hand-loomed tapestries decorated the walls, flowers in crockery vases decorated the furniture, much of which was hers. Even Griff's big house—their big house—could hardly hold her collection.

"If I had eloped," Kelley said, "I would have missed all the fun of watching Griff plan our wedding. And it gave him something to work on while he recovered."

"My mother says he called half a dozen times for advice."

"He likes your parents almost as much as he likes mine. The last time I passed them, all our parents were talking about buying a condo here together so they could spend more time in Palm Springs with us."

Felice rolled her eyes. "I suppose Josiah could get his old job back in Washington."

Kelley smoothed her skirt. She still wasn't sure what romantic notion had possessed her to agree to wear the wedding dress her mother had designed for the last film she had costumed. The dress was nothing like anything she'd ever worn. The tea-length oyster-colored silk with a river of lace made her feel like a lamp shade in a little girl's bedroom.

Felice examined her. "I have never seen anyone so lovely."

Kelley held out a spray of orange blossoms and lace. "Will you help with this?"

Felice pinned it carefully in place. She stepped back. "It's perfect."

"I don't look like Melanie in *Gone with the Wind?*"

"She wasn't nearly as beautiful."

Kelley grinned and cracked her knuckles. "Do you think Tara's ready?"

A tentative knock on the door answered the question. Tara stepped inside. She had chosen her own dress, a deep rose satin with handmade roses on the skirt. She smiled shyly. "What do you think?"

"I think I'm going to have to chase the boys away with a whip!"

Tara giggled. Kelley opened her arms, and Tara came into them without hesitation. "You look beautiful," she said, hugging Kelley back.

She stood with Tara in her arms and thanked whoever had been watching over them for this moment. In the months since Griff's injury, she and Tara had grown closer. With time, with love, the three of them would be a family.

"We'd better go," Felice told Tara. "We've got a trip down the aisle ahead of us."

"Down the garden path," Kelley corrected. "Don't go the wrong way. Don't drag this out."

She watched them leave, then turned to the mirror for one more look.

Another knock sounded, and her father opened the door. "Ready?"

She couldn't move.

Fletcher Samuels smiled. His grin was the original of his daughter's—she had also gotten his red hair. "Come on, girl.

You're not scared, are you? You've never been scared of anything.''

"I had a bad experience at the last wedding I attended."

He held out his arm. "The music's starting."

Kelley picked up her bouquet. She wondered if anyone would believe her if she claimed that the strong fragrance of the gardenias had made her faint.

She let him guide her through the house. It was a different place now, warm and inviting. Her things and the new things Griff and she had chosen together had turned it into a home.

The house wasn't the only thing that had changed. Griff would soon be finishing *Teardrop Creek* with a new director, but it was to be his final action-adventure film. The previous week he had signed to do a family drama, with no guns and no bad guys. In the future he planned to direct. Cam had already approached him with three screenplays that she wanted him to look over.

He was almost fully recovered, although when Kelley looked at the scar on his chest, she knew just how close she had come to losing him. She would never take him for granted.

She and Felice still ran Cristy and Samuels, but more of the work was delegated to others these days. They had hired a good staff, and there was enough business to pay them well. They had worked hard to become successful. Now there was time to spend with the people they loved.

Kelley was even thinking about taking a bit part in a film Cam had recently mentioned. She hadn't told Griff yet. She was trying to figure out how to eat crow and enjoy the taste.

They neared the doors leading out to the garden. To the right of the pool, baskets of flowers decorated the terrace. Guests lined the path down to the bower of shrubbery and small trees where they would be married. Below the trees she could see the first twinkling lights of evening.

She caught sight of her Cub Scout den. Neuf sat stoically beside the dancing eight-year-old feet, a rose satin bandanna that matched Tara's dress tied skillfully around his furry neck. She noted others, too, an about-to-give birth Cam and her husband standing with other Zephyr executives and employees, cops from the local police force, film stars, relatives, friends, Felice's parents and her own mother.

And at the end of the path, she saw the man she loved waiting for her. He stood like a pirate, arrogant and terrifying, but when he caught sight of her, he smiled. The smile nearly melted her heart.

The walk wasn't as hard as she'd feared. She reached Griff and felt him take her hand. She smiled in answer, then turned and listened to the minister. Griff's hand was warm around hers. She said her own prayer of thanks that he was alive beside her.

The ceremony was short, but when Griff kissed her, she knew their life together would be long and good.

Something whizzed ominously through the air. Griff and Kelley broke apart as shots rang out. She gasped as Griff shoved her toward the bushes and dived for Tara. She watched him grab the little girl and haul her against him.

"Firecrackers."

Kelley opened her eyes and saw Felice calmly pointing down the path where her entire Cub Scout den was under siege by angry wedding guests. "Firecrackers, Kell."

Neuf came bounding up the path and launched himself at Tara.

Griff untangled himself from the girl and dog, gathered Kelley in his arms and kissed her to the applause of an appreciative audience.

"You might say we're starting off with a bang," he said as the kiss finally ended.

Kelley reached for Tara and drew her close for a three-way hug.

Not one of them flinched when the champagne corks began to pop.

* * * * *

This is the season of giving, and Silhouette proudly offers you its sixth annual Christmas collection.

SILHOUETTE

Christmas Stories

1991

Experience the joys of a holiday romance and treasure these heartwarming stories by four award-winning Silhouette authors:

Phyllis Halldorson—"A Memorable Noel"
Peggy Webb—"I Heard the Rabbits Singing"
Naomi Horton—"Dreaming of Angels"
Heather Graham Pozzessere—"The Christmas Bride"

Discover this yuletide celebration—sit back and enjoy Silhouette's Christmas gift of love.

YOU'VE ASKED FOR IT, YOU'VE GOT IT! MAN OF THE MONTH: 1992

ONLY FROM

You just couldn't get enough of them, those sexy men from Silhouette Desire—twelve sinfully sexy, delightfully devilish heroes. Some will make you sweat, some will make you sigh . . . but every long, lean one of them will have you swooning. So here they are, men we couldn't resist bringing to you for one more year. . . .

A KNIGHT IN TARNISHED ARMOR
by Ann Major in January

THE BLACK SHEEP
by Laura Leone in February

THE CASE OF THE MESMERIZING BOSS
by Diana Palmer in March

DREAM MENDER
by Sheryl Woods in April

WHERE THERE IS LOVE
by Annette Broadrick in May

BEST MAN FOR THE JOB
by Dixie Browning in June

Don't let these men get away! *Man of the Month,* only in Silhouette Desire.

MOM92JJ-1

Angels Everywhere!

Everything's turning up angels at Silhouette. In November, Ann Williams's ANGEL ON MY SHOULDER (IM #408, $3.29) features a heroine who's absolutely heavenly—and we mean that literally! Her name is Cassandra, and once she comes down to earth, her whole picture of life—and love—undergoes a pretty radical change.

Then, in December, it's time for ANGEL FOR HIRE (D #680, $2.79) from Justine Davis. This time it's hero Michael Justice who brings a touch of out-of-this-world magic to the story. Talk about a match made in heaven . . . !

Look for both these spectacular stories wherever you buy books. But look soon—because they're going to be flying off the shelves as if they had wings!

Silhouette Special Edition ®

is pleased to announce

WEDDING DUET
by Patricia McLinn

Wedding fever! There are times when marriage must be catching. One couple decides to tie the knot, and suddenly everyone they know seems headed down the aisle. Patricia McLinn's WEDDING DUET lets you share the excitement of such a time.

December: PRELUDE TO A WEDDING (SE #712) Bette Wharton knew what she wanted—marriage, a home . . . and Paul Monroe. But was there any chance that a fun-loving free spirit like Paul would share her dreams of meeting at the altar?

January: WEDDING PARTY (SE #718) Paul and Bette's wedding was a terrific chance to renew old friendships. But walking down the aisle had bridesmaid Tris Donlin and best man Michael Dickinson rethinking what friendship really meant. . . .